Isle of the Dark

Rina Brown

Acknowledgements:

I never dreamed that one day I'd publish a book,
let alone go back years later and redesign it into a better
version.
I owe my editors the world for helping me bring to life a
story that had great potential.
Especially my Mom; who spent hours sitting with me and
helping
to create the wonderful tale that it is now.
Thanks to all who have stayed by me.
I hope you enjoy the retelling of Ranger and Isle's first
adventure.

Prologue

During the Dark Ages, Juduiverians walked the Earth. Blessed with magical properties humans could only dream of, they used their gifts to create and shift the rules of everyday life. Playing with the sea, they decided to make the moon control the tides; and helped the sun grace the surface with warmth and light. They also created many new species of creatures, recording them in their archives for man to marvel at.

During the first era, they experimented with the boundaries of their magic. Growing more vain and prideful with every accomplishment, they considered themselves far superior to their human neighbors. Until they took things too far.

During a seemingly normal day, the Juduiverians played with their bases, creating another creature to add to their growing collection. Pleased with the unique design, they made it black as night, then poured magic into it. Naming it 'Datsoe', the new predator was released onto a single continent.

They watched with curiosity when the small animal took its first steps into the real world. But the predator had its own agenda. It attacked prey as expected, but its creators were confused when the creature didn't feed. Instead, it backed away to watch the dead animal shake to life. Turning completely black, the prey morphed into a soulless, hollow shell, with no identity of its own.

The Juduiverians created a walking plague.

The creatures spiraled out of control, attacking everything in their path. A single bite was all it took to spread the deadly venom, creating distorted copies of the victims. Finally setting its sights on humanity, the Datsoe created far more intelligent versions of this unstoppable predator. The Juduiverians knew it was time to put an end to the entire race.

Studying the biology of the Datsoe, they created a purple rose embedded with toxins. Large thorns could pierce the creature's thick, dead skin to inject an incurable poison. Fragrant pollen and perfume swirled in the air, burning their lungs from the inside out. The petals were harvested for precious oils to tip weapons. Using these new tools, the Juduiverians sent out their best hunters, ending the race as quickly as it had begun.

Or so they believed. Unbeknownst to them, a single creature escaped, wiggling her way down toward the core of the Earth, falling into a deep sleep.

Embarrassed, the Juduiverians left the Datsoe out of their records. Shifting their interests, many settled down with human partners to create a new race called the Asalairi. These mortals carried many magical properties, and lived fruitful, peaceful lives. Slowly disappearing from history, Juduiverians fell into myths and legends. As the years passed, people began to believe that leading a good life would carry your spirit to the Juduiverians plains of the afterlife. If you chose a darker path, you would haunt the *Jez Juwa Amedian Jarv*, or "the lake of abysmal souls".

The world shifted into the second era. The Asalairi began to choose human mates, thinning the Juduiverian bloodline even further with children they called the Araat. Two mighty kingdoms rose on each side of the continent, but they were no longer content to lead simple lives. As the decades rolled by, tensions mounted. The South was jealous of the beautiful gems and precious metals the North could mine, coveting their colors and magnificent architecture. The North bitterly resented not being on the sea, and all of its rich resources. Rather than trade, war loomed over the lands, creating *Jez Zgb Tauca,* or "The End Of Peace".

The Asalairi, disgusted with Humans and Araat alike, withdrew from both kingdoms, disappearing into their own world. Without their peaceful ways and magic, darkness swept the lands. Armies rose, spreading violence and bloodshed.

No one appreciated these days more than Bardune. Raised in a tiny shack on the edge of the Northern kingdom, he resented everything about his life. Neighbors would shake their heads, saying the boy came out wrong. They kept their kids away from him, sensing something amiss.

Bardune hated helping his father every day with the small, pitiful farm they tended. At the tender age of 6, he began to slip away, his pale green eyes watching the soldiers train in the castle's courtyard, using a stick from the surrounding forest to emulate their swordplay. By the time he was 10, his parents could rarely find him, carrying the burdens of harvest alone. His mother grieved, knowing her boy wasn't like the other children, but she couldn't quite put her finger on why. Bardune cleverly immersed himself into the soldiers ranks, performing menial tasks and chores. When he wasn't tending the horses, he was learning to ride them. Soon, few could claim to mount faster or balance as well as the boy with the quick wit and acerbic tongue. The General, impressed with his work ethic, visited Bardune's parents, convincing them to release him to the care of the army. Reluctantly they agreed, knowing their son would never be cut out for farm life, secretly hoping training would make him happy. Maybe, they thought, he would become the son they dreamed of.

Bardune never went to see them again.

Over the years, he absorbed everything he could about the ways of war. Growing up in the world of rough men, he became greedy, self-absorbed, focusing solely on bettering himself and his circumstances. Rising quickly through the ranks, he became the youngest lieutenant in history, gaining the admiration of the King himself. His swordsmanship was envied throughout the army, even if he was disliked. Power became his obsession. He made sure no one would ever know he grew up in poverty with ignorant parents who worked the land. Today lieutenant, one day King, he thought smugly. At times, he listened to the men around him, many complaining about missing home. It made him wonder why, all he ever wanted was riches, and he was amassing more than his wage rapidly.

During his free time, Bardune loved to play games of chance. He would meander through the streets of the kingdom, looking for opportunities to make an easy coin. Because of his handsome looks and youth, he had no problem tricking not only the spectators, but those that ran the events. On his 14th birthday, he was deeply invested in a card game with prizes that included not only a stack of money, but two intricately carved daggers. The weapons glinted in the sun, taunting the teen with their beauty. Over time, Bardune had learned to cheat quite well, but his opponent was no fool, and an opportunity had not yet presented itself for him to make his move. Sitting on old wooden crates in an alley off of the marketplace, the players were distracted by loud cries from the street.

"Please! I am about to lose my farm; can anyone help me? I am willing to work hard, but my wife is ill. Please have mercy on an old man!"

The man fell to his knees sobbing. A crowd started to gather, surrounding the beggar. Taking advantage of his rival's distraction, Bardune quickly shuffled the cards.

"Hey mister, are you going to make your move or what?" Bardune demanded.

Turning away from the spectacle, his challenger adjusted himself on the crate, then tossed his card down. Smugly, Bardune threw his own down, then swept the daggers up without hesitation. Stuffing his pockets full of coins, he took a small bow.

"Gentlemen, it has been a pleasure, but I must take my leave." Walking briskly from the alley, he could feel the eyes of his victim boring into his back. Weaving his way through the crowd, Bardune beheld his father on his knees at the center, weeping into his hands. The years have not been kind to you, he thought with amusement. He never regretted leaving that wretched farm, and not even a glimmer of pity stirred in his heart. Your choices led you here old man, he thought.

Their eyes met, and a flash of recognition passed over his father's face.

Tossing a single bronze coin into the dirt, Bardune smirked. His father had, after all, created the distraction that won him the fascinating new daggers.

Gripping the etched handles tightly, he walked away without a backward glance, singing 'Happy Birthday' to himself.

Time passed. Bardune practiced obsessively with his new daggers, becoming even more skilled than he had with his sword. He had been thrilled to discover that the weapons had a secret latch that released razor sharp barbs underneath the blades. He found them far more deadly in battle, and never hesitated to use them to quickly dispatch his foes.

Bardune often bragged to others about his skills of living off the land, but the truth was, outside of fighting, he was ignorant. Because of his rank, he became spoiled with rich foods and drink. Late one night, he drunkenly claimed he knew the caves in the mountains like the back of his hand, capturing the attention of his superiors.

On the eve of his 19th birthday, the King sent for Bardune. It was decided that he was to lead a squadron of scouts to find a secret way into enemy territory through the caves. If he found such a path, he would be handsomely rewarded. Hastily gathering a team, Bardune headed into the hills. A large cave lay invitingly at the crest of the trail, drawing the soldiers in. Lighting torches, the exploration began.

It quickly became apparent to the men that Bardune had no clue what he was doing. For days they marched through the endless cave system, taking twists and turns that led them to one dead end after another. Lack of food quickly became an issue since they packed for a brief journey. Bardune kept his rations quiet, for he had packed nothing but his daggers and food with no intention of sharing. Starving, lost, and filled with despair, the men devised a plan to kill Bardune. His arrogance and stupidity led them here, they grumbled. He didn't seem hungry, making them suspicious of what lay in his pack. If anything, they could split his rations and escape. Plotting, they waited for their opportunity.

On the morning of their 10th day, the group found a

vast cavern. Torchlight revealed walls that rose higher than their city. Streams of fresh water flowed over colorful rock formations. Tucking their torches into crevices in the walls, the parched men waded into the crystal pool, drinking deeply and cleansing the filth from their bodies.

Bardune watched the group with a sneer of disdain. Holding up his own torch, he gazed at his surroundings, marveling that the cave seemed untouched by any sort of life. Gold and jewels reflected in the flickering light, embedded in the walls. His mouth watered with greed. Ignoring his companions, he climbed onto a rocky outcrop and let out a series of whoops and cries, reveling in the sound of his voice echoing across the vast canyon. He was the one, the only one, who deserved to celebrate the discovery of this beauty. Bardunes eyes flicked toward the men, still blissfully unaware of what they had discovered. Just like his rations, he had no intention of sharing the riches that lay all around them. Gripping one of his daggers, he began to scheme.

Splashes and shouts reverberated throughout the underground chamber, breaking centuries of silence. Deep in the heart of the cavern, something moved.

She woke.

Bardune turned toward his men, watching them climb out of the water. Calculating, he was unaware that they planned his death as well. A heavy silence filled the air, each man shifting uncomfortably, waiting for someone to make the first move.

A strange sound rang through the air, then Bardune's body went surprisingly limp. A hooked blade punctured his shoulder, making the dagger he held clatter to the rocks below. The other men backed away with terror when they beheld a pair of glowing red eyes reflecting the flames from

11

the torch he held. Falling to his knees, Bardune no longer cared about killing his men, the riches in the cave, or becoming king. He only wanted to live. The torch slid from his hands, engulfing the surroundings with darkness.

The graceful giant made quick work of the men that had wandered into her midst. She wanted them for their warmth, draining their energy like a snake without sun. The bodies she left behind quivered and shook, crawling back to life with a dense darkness in their bones. The same darkness that had started once so long ago. The new generation of Datsoes took off from their dark home, and what took the men days, took mere hours for the creatures to tear their way back to the sun-filled Earth.

Bodies dark as night, muscles heightened to never weaken, claws tipped like spears, and venom dripping from their teeth, they infected anything they bit. Datsoes started to take over the land once more. War no longer mattered, bringing the opposing kingdoms together to mutually defeat this new threat. The kingdoms became one, naming themselves *La Tierra Unida.*

Their new defenses became routine for all the citizens of the nation, so they reset their calendar to match the schedule they had created. With 94 days per season, they made the first day of Spring the beginning of the new year. They named the seasons: SpringLife, SummerSet, FallHeart, and WinterNox. They started their new era the year the Datsoe Plague began, titling each as (year) D.P.

Fighting against these beasts seemed daunting, until man discovered a type of purple rose. The toxins it released were deadly to their creature foes. Little did they know it was the same plant that the Juduiverians had created centuries ago. Man retreated into the Southern half of the continent, leaving the Northern kingdom to ruin. Planting a barrier of the protective flowers, the fields stretched from one side of the land to the other. A mile deep, it was impossible to cross on foot. Five walkways were carved through the foliage to maintain passage between Kingdoms. These trails were guarded by mighty gates, their architecture only rivaled by the Palace itself. Watchtowers were built to provide shelter for the many soldiers who watched over the gates day and night. Men with arrows tipped in rose oil remained ever vigilant, trying to shoot down the creatures of death before they could do more harm.

Despite the precautions, too often the devilish beasts crossed the borders. Some Datsoes evolved and formed wings, swooping over the wall, pouncing upon unsuspecting animals and people, carrying them off into the night.

SpringLife to FallHeart, the people found some safety inside of the purple haven, but when WinterNox came, it made their lives a nightmare. Although the rose wall stood, the flowers and foliage withered and died when snow came, making the kingdom more vulnerable to attacks. Without the pollen and fragrance filling the air, more Datsoes would fly over the wall, searching for victims.

Man learned to accept a simple truth - these creatures existed without souls. As prey on the outside of the walls became more scarce, Datsoes worked harder to infiltrate man's barrier. In response, five mighty warriors were appointed to stand guard at the gates at all times, becoming the ultimate Guardians of the human world. They each created elite armies, trained in the ways of defeating any Datsoe, whether it be the size of a mouse, or a dragon.

One day, the present King heard of a warrior defeating Datsoes that crossed over the rose wall. He could read the land, travel vast distances, and dispose of the beasts that wandered into the safety of people's towns. This soldier was summoned to the Palace, where he was presented with the option of becoming the sixth guardian. Accepting the role, his name soon rang throughout both lands, feared and respected, and his reputation held a flawless record of captures and victories.

At the end of FallHeart each year, a mighty celebration was held. Harvests were shared, families gathered, and a Datsoe was publicly executed. The King felt it brought hope to the people, proving that man still had power over his deadliest foe. The Sixth Guardian never failed to deliver a live beast, carrying it in a cart from the farthest reaches of the land.

"One less to deal with," many would say, cheering as the light faded from the Datsoe's eyes.

"Good riddance to all of 'em!" Others would cry, feasting and dancing into the wee hours.

Then Winter would descend, driving everyone out of the fields. Freezing winds would whip through the abandoned streets, fear keeping residents inside.

Should a Datsoe make it across the defenses, they knew they could call upon their hero, no matter what the season. His arrival heralded peace once more, for they knew he would strike down their enemy, no matter what it cost him.

For decades, he watched over the land.

FallHeart the 56th of

222 D.P

The rhythmic sound of hooves filled the air. A mighty black stallion carried its beloved rider toward the sleepy village of **Washyoun**. Lush grass stirred in the wind, reminding the traveler of waves crashing upon the shore. Mud churned under hooves as they followed the faded path, charging through rain that lashed man and beast. A hat was drawn over the horseman's gray eyes, and a handkerchief wrapped around his face in a meager attempt to provide warmth. A long trench coat trailed behind him, covering his many concealed weapons, and the only thing he carried was a long leather bag over his shoulder.

His head bobbed to the horse's movement, lost within his own mind while he rode toward his destination. Crows circled overhead, their cries breaking his concentration. Pulling on the reins, he spied the butchered remains of a cow.

"Easy," he soothed, patting the stallion's neck. Dismounting, the man made his way into the waist high, soaked grass to study the carcass.

Earlier in the week, he received a letter by messenger requesting his services. A Datsoe was terrorizing the inhabitants of **Washyoun**, so he packed up and left immediately. He would return to the main city soon, and hoped he could bring back a live Datsoe for the FallHeart celebration to herald WinterNox. Although it was a short season, frost and snow covered the fields of their protective flower, allowing Datsoe's an easier passage. Soldiers were sent to what they called "The Front" to monitor their borders. Surviving on rations, enduring the bitter cold, they tried to stop any Datsoe that crossed beyond their line of defense.

During SpringLife, many returned to their lives. But for Ranger, hunting these beasts year-round was all he knew.

The smell of the dead animal was enough to make anyone gag. He carefully made his way to the bull's side. Other than a few large scratches, there seemed to be no other sign of conflict. Ranger's boots sank into the wet terrain as he circled around, noting a giant hole on the underside of the animal. Flies swarmed the hollow shell, avoiding the rain. Obviously, the Datsoe he was searching for was large. Glancing over his shoulder, his gray gaze swept the landscape. Luckily, he had fast reflexes, for the creatures would attack anything they saw. The larger ones were easy to see coming, allowing Ranger enough time to fire an arrow full of the rose's poison. The beast would fall unconscious, allowing the Ranger to slay it easily.

The letter he received described a massive Datsoe, one capable of completely eating the slain cow in front of him. Why then, were there still remains here? Was there another creature hiding in the tall grass in which he stood? Leaving the carcass to the forces of nature, Ranger strode back to his horse, mounting swiftly. The horse trotted past the Datsoe's leftovers with a snort of unease.

The sun broke its way through the heavy cloud cover. Tilting his head, Ranger took in the small cluster of roofs and houses of **Washyoun**. It was a quaint little village, with an inn, feasting hall, and a series of houses and barns.

The old jail house looked like it had been converted to hold extra livestock during the night.

The area was quiet. Smoke from chimneys curled into the sky, blending with the mixed aromas of someone's cooking pot. Ranger's stomach growled, reminding him it was dinner time.

The town was something out of the fairy tales he heard as a child. A rainbow contrasted sharply against a cluster of gray clouds, shimmering over a group of tall trees that stretched behind the buildings. Leaves fell in a glorious splendor of reds and golds, fluttering in the breeze. The sweet smell of rain lingered while birds chirped, calling to one another. Wind nipped at Ranger's face unnoticed, he was lost in the beauty of the landscape. He had traveled long and far, but few places held the magic that he beheld now.

The buildings were in disrepair, a testimony to the fear that hung over the area. Planks stuck together with water damage and age, warping and fading to match the tree trunks around them. He grimaced slightly at the sight of the farthest barn. Part of it had been caved inwards, with fresh gouges carved into the wood. Clearly the Datsoe that had attacked the village was powerful, and by the looks of it, larger than Ranger initially imagined.

Making his way toward the inn, he was keenly aware of being watched. Glancing toward a window, his eyes met those of a child no older than five. Awe reflected on her face, and she let out an excited squeal. Rushing out the door, she yelled out to her friends, who spilled into the street, parents in tow.

"Is that...?"

"It is! It is!"

Whispers followed Ranger, making him recall the

last time he visited, but he doubted anyone would remember. It was decades ago, and he didn't recognize any of the faces in the crowd.

Dismounting with ease, he towered over the village's inhabitants. His height had always been a curiosity, and he used it to his advantage often. Silver stubble stretched across his cheeks when he smiled at the children surrounding him, peppering him with questions. None of them noticed the faded scar that ran across the length of his chin when he answered each inquiry quietly and patiently.

A small boy stood directly in front of Ranger with his arms stretched high.

"Up!" he commanded.

Swooping the ecstatic toddler into his arms, Ranger removed his hat and placed it on the boy's head. Sunlight glinted off of silver hair, streaked with chestnut from his younger years. Placing the child on his hip, his gray eyes held a ray behind them that comforted the villagers around him.

"You summoned me?" Ranger's deep voice addressed a group of elders standing behind the swarming children. Everything about his demeanor conveyed his compassion for all of them.

"Indeed sir," one of them replied. "We are afraid there are two Datsoes in our midst."

"Two?" Ranger repeated, suddenly understanding the remains he found, and why it had contrasted with the letter he received.

Gesturing toward the barn, the elder continued.

"One is as big as a house it seems, with incredible power. It's been attacking at random, taking its pick from our herds. We had to move the cattle to the far paddocks in

19

an effort to keep the monster away from our homes."

Ranger nodded, already planning his strategy. "And the other?"

Turning toward the back of the crowd, the elder encouraged a teen to step forward. "Come on, son."

Nervously the lad wrung his hands.

"He saw one of the creatures," the elder said, patting the youth on his shoulder.

"Can you describe it to me?" Ranger inquired. Studying his lean frame, he couldn't help but wonder how the boy had survived. Datsoes of any size were dangerous, and Ranger guessed this lad couldn't even lift a sword.

Reaching for the toddler on Ranger's hip, the teen handed the hat back to the guardian. Clearly, the boys were related. Gathering his courage, he recounted what he had seen.

"It was… small. Smaller than I imagined these beasts to be. After seeing the one that attacked in the paddocks, this one took me by surprise." he trailed off.

Ranger nodded, encouraging him to continue.

"I was outside the village, a few minutes up trail. I was leading a few of our cows back from the grazing fields. I heard rustling to my right, but there was no wind. I turned to see what it was, and that's when it attacked. It launched out of the grass, and bit the throat of the nearest animal. The other cows scattered, and I watched as it pulled its victim down. The creature was so lean, I am surprised it managed to pull the animal over. Crawling on all fours, a long tail trailed behind it that looked, maybe jagged? Sharp?" He said, questioning himself. "If not for the fact that it had a tail and a Datsoesque figure… it might have been a young human. It looked at me with eyes rimmed with red and black, and growled at me. At that point I lost my courage and ran back toward the village, hoping I could warn the others before it killed me."

The Ranger placed a comforting hand on the shuddering youths' shoulder, almost covering it completely. "Well, we are all glad you survived, you were very brave."

Shifting his squirming brother, the teen smiled shyly. "Thank you, Sir."

Ranger turned to the others. "Stay indoors. I will flush the Datsoes out and dispose of them."

The elders nodded, herding the crowd back into their homes. The leader met Ranger's gaze.

"Is there anything we can do?"

"Stay here, if all goes well, this will be over by sunrise."

Climbing into his saddle, Ranger flicked the reins, encouraging the stallion into a run. Plans were already forming in his mind on how to handle both creatures. If it all went according to plan, he would soon enjoy a hot meal and warm bed at the inn.

FallHeart the 56th of

222 D.P - *Nightfall*

Night swept the land. Ranger didn't mind, in fact it gave him cover while he set traps around the far paddock and into the trees. Keeping a sharp eye out, he made his way back to the stallion, grabbing his bag and sword before nudging the animal toward the village.

"You know what comes next, old friend. Stay low, stay hidden," he murmured. Ears flicking at the sound of his master's voice, the horse trotted toward the tree line, experienced enough to know what was coming. With a sigh, Ranger swung the bag over his back and fastened his sword. "Now comes the fun part," he muttered to himself.

Entering the paddock again, he set the bag down next to a giant mound of hay. Pulling out a crossbow and poison tipped arrows, he set them by his feet. Digging deeper, he pulled out a leather vest, then slid it on. Drawing a match from one of its many pockets, he lit it against his belt. Surveying the horizon, he flicked the tiny flame toward the hay, instantly igniting it. Distressed calls came from the cattle as they moved to the far side of the fence. Picking up the crossbow, Ranger slid the arrows into his custom vest, closed the bag, and set it aside.

The crackling fire was the only sound that broke the silence. Not even a breeze stirred the air to cool the sweat dripping down Ranger's brow. Movement caught his eye, making him raise the crossbow. Sliding an arrow into the track, he tensed with anticipation.

He whipped around as he heard a pained cry that scattered the herd. A slinking, black mass loomed over the fallen bull. Coiling like a giant snake, the taloned Datsoe reminded Ranger of a frilled lizard. With a hiss, it bored its beak into the side of the bull and dug in, chomping its dinner noisily.

"There you are," Ranger growled, aiming his crossbow. The arrow streaked toward the beast, hitting the creature in the side. With a roar, the mighty beast whirled around, spraying blood across the dirt from the meat hanging in its mouth. Red eyes reflected the firelight, staring at Ranger with indignation. Taking a moment to swallow, the Datsoe hissed. Ranger slid his foot back, raised the crossbow again, and fired without skipping a beat. The second arrow hit the creature in the neck, making the Datsoe shake its head before dropping to the ground to charge.

Ranger quickly rolled to the side, narrowly avoiding fangs and claws. The Datsoe twirled, looping around its opponent. The creature's eyes seemed to dance in time with the flickering flames still crackling below. It hissed with its snout open, a nightmarish grin glinting from its teeth as it looked down upon him, before diving straight for him. Ranger lept just in time, dropping his crossbow then running up the monster's coils as he pulled out his sword. There would be no capturing this one, he thought.

Balancing on the arrow still lodged in the Datsoe's neck, Ranger drove his blade into the side of the beast's skull. Powerful muscles contracted, hurling the warrior from side to side. Releasing the sword, Ranger slid down the slick scales until he landed on the ground, rolling away from the thrashing limbs. A series of disjointed shrieks filled the air, then the Datsoe fell, smashing the fence.

Panting, Ranger got to his feet and walked around the length of the Datsoe's body. Studying the filmy white eyes, he yanked his sword from its skull. Wiping black blood from the razor sharp edges, he slid the blade back into its sheath.

He let out a sigh, "One down, one to go."

Another trap snapped somewhere in the tree line, gaining his attention. A keening wail echoed from the forest, prompting Ranger to pick up his fallen bow and run toward the sound.

He traced his way through the trees, coming across one of the net traps he had set. The ropes were torn open, whatever was inside had escaped. He spun around, searching the forest and listening for any movement in the brush.

Pulling the trigger, he sent an arrow toward the sound of snapping twigs to his right. A yelp pierced the night, followed by the sound of rustling leaves. Ranger reloaded his bow, then cautiously stepped forward to follow. Brushing aside a canopy of gold and orange, he heard shallow breathing. Feeling something underfoot, he looked down and discovered a long tail. Following it up, his eyes traced over the silhouette of a fallen figure. He reached into his pocket and pulled out a match, lighting it on his belt once again, then leaned down to examine the creature.

Drawing in a sharp breath, Ranger couldn't help but notice how human it looked. It had two hands, but arms that were longer than normal. The black, lean body rippled with muscles, and he had no doubt this creature was very powerful. The witness's words from that afternoon came back to him, and he could easily see how this creature could pull a cow down on its own. The tail he stepped on extended from the base of the creature's spine and had an arrowhead shaped stinger on the end. Kneeling, Ranger picked up an arm and examined the razor-sharp claws on the tips of the Datsoe's fingers. Running his fingers over its filthy face, he exposed lengthy fangs crusted with old blood. Turning the head, pointy ears protruded out from a mop of shaggy black hair. His focus was drawn to silver scars that covered its body, most noticeably, a set that made a perfect oval on its side. He suspected that this was the original infection point. He stared at the creature for a moment, watching its chest rise and fall. It was disconcerting to think how one's life could change so suddenly. If indeed this creature had been human, it was a tragedy for him, and his family. Now mindless and soulless, doomed to be an instrument of death and destruction, it was best to be put out of his misery.

The flame reached the end of the match singeing Rangers fingers, breaking his contemplation of the Datsoe. Dropping the spent stick, he reached down and hauled the creature up by its arms. This would make a fine sacrifice to kick off the FallHeart celebration, he decided. Ranger threw the creature over his shoulder, trusting the rose's poison to keep it unconscious for hours. Making his way back toward the paddock, he whistled for his horse. The stallion immediately responded, galloping toward him until it caught the Datsoe's scent. Despite Rangers attempts, it refused to carry the unconscious body for him, leaving him no choice but to head back to *Washyoun* on foot.

The creature's head continuously hit his back as he walked, irritating Ranger. This was new to him; he had never been able to carry a Datsoe like this before. He occasionally tripped on its tail, and every now and then it would twitch, adding to his discomfort. The entire hike back, he thought about Datsoes and their transformation. He often tried to guess what the monster had been while he battled it, finding the mental game took the edge off of his fear and fury. Even after decades of slaying them, he hated the very sight of Datsoes for personal reasons. And only a fool wasn't afraid of giant, slobbering beasts with one goal: your death.

The one on his shoulder had to have been a teen boy. Did someone miss him? He wondered if he had ever met the family of this little Datsoe. They would never know that, in a way, their family member was still alive. People had been bitten before of course; it was disconcerting to say the least. The first time he came across one had been years ago, and a lesson learned the hard way. Despite Ranger's efforts to reason with it, no trace of humanity remained. Most didn't retain their human form, mutating into strange creatures.

The morning sun touched the tops of the trees. Golden rays swept the long grass that Ranger wearily trudged through. His mouth was dry, reminding him that he hadn't consumed anything since he had arrived. Finding the same trail he had traveled the day before, he reflected on his next move. He needed a cage of some sort to transport the creature to the main city. WinterNox was weeks away, so he had plenty of time to gather materials and prepare. The familiar smell of smoke from a chimney brought him out of his thoughts.

Rounding a hill, the village lay before him. Despite the early hour, people were out tending the fields, taking care of livestock, and preparing for the day. New horses were tied to the long pole outside the inn, capturing his attention. He hoped there were still rooms available, for he was hungry and weary.

Suddenly a woman let out a horrified gasp. Staring at the Datsoe draped across Ranger's shoulder, she took a step back. Whispers followed him as he continued his way toward the inn. Ranger was forced to slow his pace when a crowd formed around him.

"You carry it as if it were a bag of potatoes!" someone yelled.

Ranger turned toward the voice with a heartfelt smile.

"Cliff!"

A tall, lean blond leaned against the fence surrounded by a group of familiar faces. With a swirl of his cape, Cliff made his way toward Ranger, clasping his outstretched hand. The morning sun highlighted his golden beard and twinkling brown eyes. To the casual observer, he seemed jovial and relaxed, belying the fierce warrior he actually was. A sword similar to Ranger's hung at his side, ready for action.

"Marco! Quail! Leeon!" Ranger greeted his friends with delight. "What brings four of the Gatekeepers here?"

"We heard you were on the hunt and made bets that you were after the FallHeart sacrifice!" Marco replied. His fiery red hair contrasted sharply to Cliff's blond, and his beard was twice as long. Instead of a sword, Marco preferred the long ax that lay strapped to the back of his stocky, muscular frame. He proudly wore a helmet that resembled a Viking's headpiece, despite the teasing he took from Leeon about it.

"We brought a surprise for you," Cliff gestured toward a wooden cart sitting next to the inn. A large cage sat on top of it, constructed of thick oak.

Ranger's mouth dropped open with surprise.

"It looks like Marco was right, you did catch something."

The soft-spoken statement had Ranger turn to Quail.

Quail often took people by surprise. Many were shocked when they learned the Guardian was, in fact, a woman. Silky black hair fell over her eyes, concealing her features. Gesturing toward the Datsoe with her katana, she grimaced.

Ranger looked at his cargo, then let the creature drop unceremoniously to the ground. Cliff and Leeon kneeled next to it, examining the same scars Ranger had.

Leeon poked at the Datsoe with the tip of his bow. "What were you planning on doing with it? Toss it on your bed while you ate?"

Marco tugged on the tight, black bun Leeon sported on the top of his head. "Hush boy, Ranger always has a plan. Tell me, how did you nab this little thing? It looks like it could be agile and quick. "

"It is smaller than all the ones I have seen," Ranger contemplated the sleeping form. "I thought it was going to be impossible to spot let alone catch compared to the bigger one out in the paddocks. But it set off a trap and was nearby long enough for me to get in a shot. Pure luck really." Shaking his head, he focused on his friends once more. "Where is Kion?" he asked, noticing that the fifth and final gatekeeper was missing.

"He sent a message; he will meet us at the city Palace," Cliff stood, brushing his hands off onto his pants as he stood. "Always been a loner, Kion. Even more so than our lovely Quail." He chuckled at her piercing gaze.

"I was not expecting to see any of you until the first snow," Ranger leaned down and picked the Datsoe back up.

The villagers had crowded around the Guardians, excitedly chatting with each other at this rare spectacle. Imagine, the warriors and a Datsoe, all in their sleepy village! Tales would be told of this day for years to come. Parting, they allowed Ranger to walk toward the cart with his catch.

"The cage was designed with a larger Datsoe in mind. We never imagined you would catch this little thing here," Cliff said, scratching the back of his head.

"No! It's great! If we can keep it intact long enough, it will come in handy next SpringLife. In the meantime, it will work admirably for this," Ranger patted the back of the Datsoe hanging limply from his shoulder.

"But it is still a good catch! Same as always!" Marco boomed. People were often startled that such a large voice came from a tiny man.

"Such a gift must be in celebration of something," Ranger said, tossing the creature inside the cage. "All of you traveling here, bringing me this, I am pleased of course, but …why?"

The others began to laugh.

"Do you not remember?" Marco asked in astonishment.

Ranger was dumbfounded. What was he forgetting? He had been so busy this season. "I am honestly not sure," he said with an embarrassed smile.

"It is your 50th anniversary," Leeon answered, placing a hand on Ranger's arm.

Ranger's hand gripped the cart in shock. "No… that can't be. That would mean I'm…" he trailed off for a moment. "Sixty-eight years old." His eyes took on a reminiscent look. "Fifty years ago, I joined the border

30

defense, fighting my first year in a winter battle." He shook his head in disbelief. "Where did the time go?"

"And you are still as spry and skillful as a wolf!" Marco waved his fist.

"I don't know how you do it," Cliff laughed.

"He has got the fire of a King burning within his soul, driving him to protect those he cares about," Quail said softly, cracking her first smile.

"I still think it has to do with your parents," Cliff chuckled, shaking his finger at Ranger.

"Ug! For the last time, Cliff! There are no such things as Asalairi! There were no half children of our mystic rulers and our mortal ancestors!" Marco insisted. "No proof has ever been found!"

"Of course they exist! They are a part of every history book the Palace owns! Besides! Ranger could be living proof!" Cliff barked, gesturing to Ranger again. "What do you think Leeon?"

"No no, leave me out of it. You have been having the same argument for years," Leeon glanced at Quail, catching her eye roll.

"Gentlemen!" Ranger locked the cage. "I cannot confirm nor deny your theories. It will remain a mystery, despite your guesses."

"Alright, alright," Cliff gave in, for now. "Let's take the day to celebrate!"

"Celebrate?" Quail snapped. "There are duties that need to be tended to."

"Always so serious my friend!" Cliff laughed, wrapping an arm around her tense shoulder. "There is more to life than duty and responsibility dear Quail! We will head out tomorrow morning at dawn. How often can we honor a man that has lived to such a prime age? Especially one that is still fighting for the people he loves?"

"You are acting like a child. We are the deadliest warriors across the land, and all you can speak of is drinking ale into the night? Partying while the rest of the world is just supposed to be put on pause?" she growled, pushing his arm off.

"Well, if you do not like it, YOU don't have to join in!" Marco snapped, making Quail's jaw drop.

"Fine, be idiots, I shall remain here and watch over the sacrifice." Crossing her arms stubbornly, Quail glared at the men.

"There will be a room available for you regardless," Leeon said quietly.

Turning toward the inn, the men left Quail by the cart, leading Ranger toward a hot meal and a refreshing drink.

FallHeart the 57th of

222 D.P

Washyoun was more than honored to share a few drinks with the great protectors, considering their presence as a gift from the Queen, and the afterlife itself. Marco drew many of the villagers into song while Cliff and Leeon sat at the bar, exchanging stories of past battles. Ranger quietly sipped on a pint of ale by the fire, pleasantly relaxed. The owner of the inn had provided a complimentary feast, and his wife blushed under the praise the Guardians gave her cooking.

Quail remained outside "keeping an eye" on the Datsoe, even though they all knew the rose toxins would keep it asleep for hours yet. As the day wore on, Marco and Cliff convinced Ranger to dance with a few of the local women. Round and round he went with different ladies, until they, and he, were red in the face. Cliff and Marco blended their voices into song, encouraging everyone to join in. Flushed, Ranger sat down next to Leeon at one of the many tables scattered around the pub. They looked at each other for a moment, and shared a laugh.

"It has been a long time since I've seen them this happy," Ranger said, watching his friends clink their pints together.

"We need to do this more," Leeon declared.

"But when?" Ranger sighed. "We must uphold our duties first."

"Stories and legends surround our names," Leeon began, making Ranger turn away from the dancers. "But I think some have forgotten that legends begin with a simple man. We have emotions and fears like everyone else." he paused for a moment. "And perhaps, one of our own has forgotten as well."

Ranger knew exactly who he meant.

* * *

The stars hung brightly overhead, encouraging the crickets to perform a lively concert. The smell of ale and chicken mingled in the cool breeze sweeping over the village. Quail leaned against a tree, carving designs in a block of wood with her dagger. A snapping branch made her spin around defensively, raising the blade.

Ranger held up two glasses. "Easy, Birdie," he cooed.

Dropping her arm, she released an annoyed sigh. "Why are you here? And do not call me Birdie!" she hissed.

Ranger laughed, unphased by her prickly demeanor. "I figured that if anyone needed a drink, it was you." Holding up a glass, he waited patiently for her to take it.

She stood motionless for a moment, searching his face. In return, she received the smile she knew all too well. Hesitantly, Quail reached out and wrapped her fingers around the glass. Inhaling deeply, her expression softened. "Blackberry with aged grapes," she smiled. "You know me too well."

"Well, I should hope so," Ranger began, sitting by the tree in the grass. "How many years did we ride together before you were chosen?"

Settling beside him, she leaned against the trunk once more.

"You were only 22 when you saved a pod of warriors from that rogue flying Datsoe. The old gatekeeper from the second forest gate was so impressed, he made you the new Guardian," Ranger reminisced. "I would like to take the credit since I trained you for what, six? No, seven years before that?" he paused for a moment. He slowly leaned forward, sweeping her hair aside to reveal bright hazel eyes that sparkled in the moonlight.

"But the truth is, you more than earned it. I cannot tell you how proud I am." Taking a swig of his ale, he continued. "This is your 12th year now as a Guardian, right?"

"Listen Ranger, I didn't mean to offend you earlier. Your service should be celebrated, it's just… it almost seems like the others were looking for an excuse to act ridiculous. They think nothing is wrong with the world," she murmured, ignoring his question.

Listening to her words, Ranger remembered her temper issues as a child. Quail was always regretful after her outbursts, and worried he would abandon her.

"Tonight, I was reminded that despite our duties, we are human. And like any human, we deserve a moment to be ourselves. Our personalities can shape what happens around us, not just our titles," he explained, raising the cup to his lips again.

Studying his profile, she marveled that even after all these years, Ranger could still give the perfect advice. At times, she wished she could be young again, protected by not only his sword, but the love of a father.

"Besides," he continued, interrupting her thoughts, "I think they were looking for a reason to have real ale," he

36

laughed. "The stuff they give you on the battlefront is so bad it is too disgusting to consume most of the time."

Quail laughed aloud, raising her glass toward Ranger. Tapping it in a silent toast, his mind wandered back to the day they met. The young, frightened girl had just lost her entire family. Ranger, having no experience with children, (let alone teenagers!) taught her what he knew best, to fight. At first, it did not go well. He was used to being alone, unable to give her the communication and comfort she needed. She was angry, and bitter. Over the years he taught her self-defense, and how to channel her fury into becoming a fierce warrior. This was something he was all too familiar with. In return, she showed him how to let his guard down, be patient, and express how much he had grown to love her.

Quail's thoughts ran along a similar path, but her perspective varied a great deal. With revenge burning within her soul, she accepted her new position as guardian; and remained stern, hoping to live up to Ranger's legend. When they started traveling together, it took her a while to realize that the quiet, somber warrior had a heart of gold. Time and time again, she watched Ranger slay beasts, bury the dead, and protect the innocent. One day, she thought, she would see the Datsoe plague vanquished. Now, things were different. During the Winter months, they would get to see each other, but only in passing. Having the whole group together like this was rare, and to be treasured. She finally understood that.

Dropping her glass, Quail scrambled to her feet. "*Juwa!*" She yelled in panic, pulling her knife.

Ranger twisted around, locking eyes with the small Datsoe. Looking past the bars, he couldn't help but notice that the creature's eyes weren't the usual bright red.

Crouching in the cage, it almost appeared to be listening to their conversation. Pushing up, Ranger stepped in front of Quail defensively, making the Datsoe jump to the other side of the cage. Hissing, its ears fell flat. Huddling in a corner, the only feature they could make out were enormous burgundy pupils, staring at them unwaveringly.

"I did not even hear it get up," Quail said breathlessly. "How is this possible?"

"I do not know. Datsoes aren't cautious. Normally, the second it woke, it would have thrown itself against the bars, trying to get to us." He took a step toward the cage. "I wonder how long it has been awake?"

"I do not like it," Quail growled. "I am rarely caught off guard."

"We will put a tarp over the cage tomorrow, that way, none of us have to look at it," Ranger stated, turning away from the Datsoe's gaze. Placing a gentle hand on her shoulder, he noted black hair covered her features once more. Their peaceful interlude was over, and Quail's guard was up. "You should head off to bed. Get some sleep before we begin the journey tomorrow."

"Are you insane? What about the Datsoe? Now that it is awake…" she trailed off.

"I will watch it," he replied. "It is my responsibility after all, and I really don't want to have to dance anymore. Cliff keeps pouring me fresh drinks and sending ladies over to my table. He seems to think I am looking for romance."

Watching Ranger's eyes roll dramatically, Quail managed a smirk. With a final glare over her shoulder toward the cage, she bid Ranger a good night, heading toward the inn. Perhaps she would spend some time with the men after all, or, at the very least, have a bit of the roast chicken she kept catching whiffs of.

The inn door closed, casting Ranger into starlight once more. With a sigh, he walked to the front of the cart that held the cage. Climbing into the driver's seat, he made a mental list of things he needed to do before setting out in the morning. He could procure some fabric from the villagers to act as a curtain for the cage. He did this every season, feeling it was better for not only the creature, but any towns they may pass through. People had a tendency to get upset at the sight of a Datsoe, and, he thought, rightfully so. They would occasionally throw things at the captured beasts, screaming obscenities and making a scene. After a couple of particularly violent episodes, he decided it was best to travel as anonymously as possible.

His stallion was strong enough to pull both the cart and Datsoe, but Ranger was reluctant to use his noble steed for such a task. He would ask for two horses from the villagers, with a promise to return them next season. Losing his taste for the ale in his cup, he set it on the seat, listening to sounds of the Datsoe pacing behind him. He briefly wondered why the creature had been watching them. It unsettled Quail, and if he was honest, it's unusual behavior bothered him. Datsoes were as predictable as they were insane, adhering to a life of violence and bloodshed. Why then, was this one so different?

FallHeart the 58th of

222 D.P

The rays of dawn struck Ranger's closed eyes, filling him momentarily with denial. His muscles were tight, a testimony of his battle from before. Dragging a hand down his stubble, he instinctively took stock of his surroundings. There was a chill in the air, making him shiver. He never made it to the soft bed waiting for him in his room, exhaustion had crept over him while he had pondered the Datsoe's bizarre behavior. Stretching, he looked over his shoulder at the creature that weighed on his mind. It was asleep, curled up almost like a feline, snoring ever so slightly. Ranger took a moment to study it. He didn't realize they slept, even after all the years he had been tracking and slaying them. He supposed it made sense, but it made him feel uncomfortable. It never occurred to him that these mindless beasts could be vulnerable, needing basic necessities past spreading death and destruction.

He silently stepped off the carriage and headed toward the inn, hoping for coffee. Ducking through the door, the scent of bacon welcomed him. His friends were up, but not all of them looked ready to greet the day. Cliff's bloodshot eyes clearly indicated he had imbibed too much, and Marco's hunched shoulders made Ranger think that he was dragging as well. Quail handed him a steaming cup, which Ranger sipped at gratefully. Settling himself next to

Marco, he watched Leeon start to untie a large white tarp. Quail joined Leeon, and soon they had the material prepared to cover the cage outside. That was one less thing he had to worry about, and shot them a smile. Joining Ranger at the table, the team gratefully accepted a hot meal provided by the innkeeper's wife.

"I will be heading out with the Datsoe this morning," Ranger announced, waving a piece of bacon. "Will you be heading back to your posts soon?"

"We were thinking, in honor of your anniversary, we would escort you to the Palace. The rose fields will hold a while longer, giving us the luxury of attending the celebration. Personally, I haven't been there for many seasons," Leeon replied.

"I was there for the last celebration, it was spectacular indeed! The Datsoe sacrifice was particularly satisfying, especially since Ranger caught it right after it slaughtered an entire field of sheep." Marco sipped his tea gingerly, knowing his stomach was not yet ready for coffee. Nibbling on a piece of toast, he continued, "As I recall, you didn't stay for the slaying Ranger."

"I kill my fair share of the beasts, I don't need to watch one ceremoniously chopped to bits. While I understand, and share in the people's anger, I am not into the bloody spectacle." Ranger scooped more eggs onto his plate.

"Ranger and I have been there many times, but I may visit some shops. I need new boots." Looking down at her feet, Quail scowled at her worn soles. "I may also want to find…"

"Bah!" Cliff cut her off. "A woman speaking of shopping is like Marco testing new flavors of ale, never ending!" Ignoring Quail's look of indignation, he continued,

"When was the last time we were all there together? Indeed, I like this plan. My troops are perfectly capable of manning the gate while the weather holds. They won't need me for weeks."

"Well then, I have much to look forward to on this trip then," Ranger smiled at Quail, who still pouted over Cliff's words. "It has been a long time since we have all been able to ride together. Perhaps we can catch up on each other's lives, learn new techniques on the battlefield, and discuss any strange mutations the Datsoes may now have."

After breakfast, Ranger excused himself to his room and prepared for the journey ahead. Bathing and changing quickly, he headed down to help the others prepare the cart containing the Datsoe. Grabbing the large tarp Leeon had unraveled earlier, he climbed into the front of the cart and stood on the seat. Tossing one end over the top of the cage, Ranger waited while Cliff and Leeon started to hammer it in place. Quail and Marco hitched a pair of strong horses to the front of the carriage. A crowd formed, wanting to see the Datsoe again. Some of the villagers spat toward the cage, others hurled insults. Children were bold enough to bang on the bars, making the creature crouch and hiss. Surprisingly, it didn't try to attack anyone, but stayed in the center of the cage, cowering. The Guardians kept an eye on the situation, but let the villagers vent their anger. Many had lost someone they cared about to the deadly beasts, and needed a way to grieve.

Finally, the Guardians finished setting up the tarp and the horses, then mounted their own steeds. Ranger's stallion was tied behind Quail's horse since he was familiar with her scent. Thanking the villagers for their hospitality, Ranger climbed up onto the seat of the carriage. The crowd followed the group down the path, cheering. Reaching the border, Cliff brought his mount alongside the cage.

"Don't worry dear people!" he called with a wave. "Soon, this Datsoe shall face justice! Its head will be mounted out on a spike after a bloody execution!"

The words rang through the morning air for a few moments, followed by a wave of clapping and shouting from the town's folk.

Ranger winced. Datsoes didn't choose to be this way; slaying them was their only escape from an undead prison. Still, they had been alive once, and he couldn't help but think about the brutal way the sacrifice was slaughtered each season. He tried to make his kills clean and quick, showing mercy even to those soulless creatures.

With a final wave, Cliff reached over and dropped the final flap of the tarp over the cage, blocking the Datsoe from further view.

Under the canopy of darkness, the creature shivered with fear. Not only did it understand what the man said, it was terrified.

There had to be a way out, and he would find it.

Glancing over his shoulder, Ranger was almost relieved when he heard the Datsoe trying to escape. Shrieking with fury, it threw itself again and again at the door of its prison. Finally the creature was exhibiting normal behavior! Traveling across the plains, the horses kicked the scent of grass into the air. Sunshine highlighted fields of wildflowers, dazzling the eye with bursts of color.

Ranger's mind wandered aimlessly. They would need to head Northwest toward the swamps. Since WinterNox was still weeks away, the trail would be dry. When snow started to fall in the high country, it tended to melt quickly during the day, flooding the swamps, making travel impossible. He had taken this trail many times, and looked forward to stopping at Marco's gate first. In years past, if he had the fortune of catching the FallHeart sacrifice in the area, he had the opportunity to spend time with his friend. This led him back to his anniversary. '50 years?' he marveled. Time was flying by. No wonder his friends and colleagues questioned his ability to still fight.

Passing under a cluster of trees, Ranger enjoyed the birdsong that surrounded their little caravan. The thought slowly dawned on him that if he could hear the birds, the Datsoe was no longer howling. Curious, Ranger turned around in his seat and lifted the tarp. There had been previous occasions when the creature he was carrying knocked itself out during its struggles for freedom, but usually the Datsoe kept up a non-stop chorus of rage for days. Again, this one broke pattern, and Ranger wasn't sure what to make of it.

Huddling in the back corner with its knees pulled to its chest, the Datsoe's head tilted away from Ranger. With a shudder, the creature sniffled and wiped at its eyes.

"Was it ... crying?!"

Pulling hard on the reins, Ranger stopped the carriage. Bracing itself against the bars, the Datsoe locked eyes with Ranger. Shock roared through the Guardian as he realized the creature was not only weeping, but now seemed embarrassed to have been caught doing so. Under his astonished gaze, it used the tip of its lengthy tail to wipe away the tears, then turned away. Squeezing into a ball, the Datsoe remained silent.

"Ranger?"

The voice made him jump. Dropping the tarp, he turned to meet Cliff's inquiring gaze.

"Is everything alright?"

It took Ranger a moment to find his voice. "Of course! I just noticed that the beast had fallen silent. I was curious."

"Well, I don't know why it shut up, but I am glad it did!" Cliff grinned. Clicking to his horse, he made his way back toward the back of the line.

Lifting the edge of the white material once more, he studied the little form cowering on the cage floor. Years of ingrained hatred had him shrug and drop the material. He knew Datsoes, and they didn't have emotions. This had to be a fluke. Maybe it had a problem with its eyes, or was still suffering from the effects of the rose poison.

Making camp, the Guardians built a fire, ate, then slept in shifts. Ranger took first watch, visiting with his stallion and making sure it was well fed. Despite his efforts, his mind kept wandering back to the Datsoe's face. Did he really see it cry? *"What made this one different?"*

The days passed pleasantly. Chatting and laughing with the others, Ranger appreciated his friends' company. Despite his cheer, he kept peeking in on the Datsoe, who remained unsettlingly quiet as they made their way through the bright trees.

Sunset crested over the land when the group made their way into Marco's town. Bustling with activity despite the late hour, everyone enthusiastically greeted their gatekeeper. Making their way down the stone pathway,

46

Quail admired a statue of the first gatekeeper that looked over the bustling vendors. Children scampered in between booths, helping with various tasks assigned to them by hard working parents.

A group of soldiers stopped and saluted.

"Sir Marco! We were not expecting you so soon!" A tall blond clasped the gatekeeper's forearm in greeting.

"We are just passing through. Our horses need rest before we enter the swamps," Marco replied. "But perhaps, we could stay the night and have a small feast?" Wiggling his red bushy eyebrows, he gave Quail a mischievous grin.

Swinging down from the carriage, Ranger joined Cliff, who dismounted to greet some of the soldiers he recognized.

"We should give our horses a night's rest and stock up on better food and supplies. That might not be a bad idea." Ignoring Quail's groan, Ranger continued. "The journey through the swamps could take over a week"

"Come, be my guests for the evening! Leeon, I think you will be particularly interested in my collection of axes. I have gathered many throughout my travels, there are some real beauties!"

Climbing back into the carriage, Ranger followed Marco past a large circle containing a group of buildings that housed the soldiers and their families. Leeon, Quail and Cliff surveyed their surroundings with interest. While each gate was the same, the towns within were nothing alike. Each gatekeeper had a different idea of how things should be run. Over the years the people made their own changes, trying to keep up with possible new Datsoe threats. Crossing a stone bridge, the Guardians left the busy town behind and entered a military campground.

Activity swirled around them. Men with crossbows were perched on top of towers, others stood ready, watching the border of roses. The sound of swords clashing echoed across the courtyard from training exercises, and arrows flew into targets. One of the six mighty gates stretched above them, dazzling the eye. It was so expansive that it took a team of horses connected to a pulley system to open the heavy oak panels. Beyond these doors lay a long path, leading straight through miles of flowers, one of the few ways into the infested part of the world.

"I have to admit," Cliff began, eyebrows raised, "I did not expect all of this to be so organized."

"Ha!" Marco laughed. "If there is one thing I take seriously; it is to not ever let the monsters in." He raised his hands and gestured to the landscape. "No Datsoe has ever passed this way, and they never will!"

Ranger heard an annoyed scoff behind him. Turning, he saw Quail rubbing the velvety side of his stallion, and assumed she made the sound.

It never occurred to him that the occupant of the carriage was listening to their conversation.

Catching her eye, he shot her a smile, then turned back to Marco. He found himself wondering what changes she had made in her town since taking over as gatekeeper. None of the Guardians messed around when it came to protecting the borders. He knew each would defend it with their lives, but despite Marco's claims, he also had first hand knowledge that some Datsoes did slip through. He would have been out of a job otherwise.

A stable boy came to collect the horses, leading them toward a night of rest and a bucket of well-earned oats. Marco continued to boast about security, trying to impress his friends. He pointed out all the comforts and benefits he had set up for his men and would occasionally snap at those not working.

Ranger shook his head, laughing, Marco never changed. Grabbing a nearby soldier, he quietly explained that they had a Datsoe in the carriage, and to keep the tarp over the cage. The man's eyes grew wide, but he nodded.

Joining the group, Ranger's thoughts drifted back to the day he met Marco. He was very confident, and came across as being rather vain. At first, Ranger was mystified why a man so self-absorbed had been selected to be a guardian. Leading the charge against a group of rogue Datsoes wasn't the place for someone like that. Trying to give him a chance, Ranger watched him around the other men. Many of the younger boys had never seen a Datsoe before, let alone battled one. Marco took the time to reassure each one, gave them pep talks, making them laugh. Realizing he was a people person, Ranger appreciated how Marco used humor to connect with his troops. It had been a bloody battle, tragically many of the youths died under fang and claw. Marco would have fallen himself that day if not for Rangers quick thinking and steady sword. They had been friends ever since.

Ranger glanced back at the tarp covered cage, nervous about leaving the Datsoe. Marco's boasts were probably true, and his troops were well trained, but the creature had already proven to be unpredictable. Perhaps he should go back and see…

"Ranger!" Marco called, "where do you think you are off to? We're going back into town. I know my people will want to meet all of you."

With a shrug, Ranger dismissed the Datsoe, then

49

crooked his arm for Quail to take. Looking at him, she sniffed, snubbing his gentlemanly gesture. Leeon slid his arm through Rangers, making the group dissolve into laughter.

They spent the evening in Marco's home, which was surprisingly modest. Unlike the previous gatekeeper, he felt a larger home was an unnecessary luxury. Pulling out old maps, they debated over which trail to follow, what bodies of water to avoid, and how long the journey could take. Sounds of revelry outside captured their attention. Peeking out a window, Marco let out a boisterous chuckle. Townsfolk had closed the road outside his home to travel, filling it with tables laden with food. A whole roast boar lay as a centerpiece, with a shining red apple in its mouth.

Following Marco out the door, the Guardians began to mingle, shaking hands and greeting people. Quail tried to stay out of the spotlight, but everyone was so friendly and kind, she unwound enough to try some of the colorful dishes that filled the air with delicious aromas. Cliff reconnected with the soldiers from earlier, sharing a pint and stories. Marco opened his home, allowing young and old to wander through as he showed Leeon his prized ax collection.

Ranger found a plate thrust into his hands, and smiling, tried some of the boar. Conversation flowed around him as he wandered, admiring the tidy houses and landscaping. Passing by a group of women, the words "Little Datsoe." had him stop in his tracks. Serving beverages and gossiping, they thought they couldn't be heard.

"That is what he said!" one voice hissed.

"If the Guardians find out ..." the other one murmured, concerned.

"Oh please, it is not like they're going to kill it. He

said something about wanting to take a look at it close up before it was gone tomorrow morning," the first voice reassured.

Putting his plate on a nearby stool, Ranger headed toward the stables.

"Oui, Ranger! You alright?" Cliff called.

"Fine," Ranger answered instinctively.

Quail's head snapped up. All too familiar with his tone, she knew something was wrong.

"I forgot something in the carriage," he replied, "Be back in a few."

Two girls blocked his path, alarmed. "Is there something we can get you, sir?"

"No, ladies, that will not be necessary. A nice walk in the fresh air will do me good." Stepping around them, his long legs carried him quickly from view.

FallHeart the 63rd of

222 D.P

The tarp to the Datsoe's cage flipped up, waking the captive inside.

"Spirits above! Look at that thing! It is so small!" a soldier whispered excitedly, lifting his torch higher. The Datsoe hissed, backing away from the light.

"Go around to the other side and prod it forward a bit, I can't see it anymore."

The second soldier walked around the carriage and picked up a steel rod laid out to secure horses. Thrusting it through the oak bars, he hit the Datsoe on the calf. Spinning around, it growled. Looking at the gleaming metal in the man's hands, the creature slowly backed away toward the center of the cage. Dropping its ears, the Datsoe's eyes shifted between its tormentors, then started to snarl threateningly.

Ignoring the warning, the first soldier shoved the torch through the bars to shed more light on the creature. The flames made the Datsoe hunker onto the floor of the cage, making the men snicker. Overconfident, the second man stuck the creature on its back, leaving a satisfying welt. Leaping, the Datsoe dodged the flames and struck out in fear.

Dropping the torch, the soldier jumped back with fright as the Datsoe's claws came tearing through the bars, narrowly missing his face. He wasn't fast enough to avoid the second blow, sputtering with astonishment at the three bloody slashes on his arm. Looking up at the cages snapping occupant with anger, he reached for his knife.

"You slimy little brute!" he rasped.

"Hey, what are you doing?" the second soldier whispered frantically.

"Oh, nothing," he ran his thumb over the shining blade, "I'm just going to return the favor."

He took a step forward, enjoying the look of fear that crossed the Datsoe's face. Its eyes were locked on his knife.

"I don't think so," a stern voice made them gasp with surprise. Ranger's hand rested lightly on the hilt of his sword, and the scowl on his face compelled the men to back away from the carriage.

"Marco is a very dear friend of mine, but you and I know he has a temper. If he knew what you idiots were up to, it would not go well for you, would it?"

Both men gulped audibly. Marco was a great man; they did not want to anger him.

"Here's what you're going to do," Ranger began, "You will go to the medical center and get that patched up. Then, for as long as we are here, you will avoid this carriage and its cargo. Do I make myself clear?"

Staring at the tall guardian, the men quaked in their boots. His piercing gray eyes bored into theirs, and the younger soldier's knees actually knocked together. Facing Ranger's wrath was more frightening than the Datsoe had been.

"Yes sir!" one blurted.

"Get lost," Ranger thundered.

Stumbling, they raced toward the stone bridge and into the guards' quarters. Ranger watched them until they disappeared from view, then leaned over to pick up the forgotten torch. The grass was smoldering, so he stomped out the flickering embers. Circling the carriage, he reached out for the steel bar still protruding from the cage.

A hiss made him freeze. His hand hovered above the metal as his eyes slowly made their way up to lock with the Datsoe's. Its ears were flat and its tail flicked, reminding Ranger of a nervous cat. Clasping the rod, he swiftly pulled it out. Setting it where it belonged, he studied the Datsoe. The creature's tail lay still now, and it tilted its head, almost as if it was trying to determine whether he was friend or foe. Ranger watched its eyes fall to the knives strapped to his sides. It looked at his face, then back to the knives, before shrinking away.

Ranger watched the Datsoe turn and was momentarily startled when it jumped up onto all fours. Following its gaze through the bars, he saw Quail leaning against one of the stable posts.

"I think you scared it." Ranger laughed, walking around the cage.

"Good," she said, "now we are even."

"What are you doing out here? I thought you were enjoying the party." Moving the torch away from the cage, he studied her face.

"I could ask you the same thing." she murmured. "You were not exactly subtle when you left."

"I overheard some of the village girls talking about the Datsoe. I came out here to check on it…" Ranger trailed off with astonishment as Quail's finger jabbed him in the chest.

"You are obsessing."

"What? What do you mean I am …"

Her finger poked him again. "Don't think I haven't noticed. You have been hovering around the cage. You won't let any of us drive the carriage, you're even sleeping there Ranger!" Blowing the hair out of her eyes, she craned her neck up to search his face.

"You are holding a grudge against this creature for scaring you." he laughed.

Quail held his gaze a moment longer, unamused. With an exclamation of frustration, she turned on her heel, knowing she wouldn't get a straight answer from him.

He sighed, watching her stomp away from the carriage. He thought about what she said, realizing she was right. He had spent a lot of time thinking about this Datsoe. He couldn't wrap his head around the undeniable fact that he *had* seen the creature crying.

Facing the cage again, he found the Datsoe staring at him. Taking a deep breath, Ranger dared to step up to the cage, well within reach of its occupant. The creature didn't seem to mind his scrutiny, in fact, its ears perked up. The torch crackled, its light dancing across the bottom of the cage, revealing chew marks in the back corner. Leaning forward, Ranger wondered if he would need to patch the hole. The Datsoe shifted almost nervously, capturing the Guardians attention once again.

Sitting in the center of the cage, the Datsoe curled his lengthy tail. The towering man kept staring at him. What was he looking for? The others had been mean, even now he felt the sting on his back from the metal bar. But this one seemed different, almost, curious. What should he do? His stomach rumbled yet again; it had been days since he ate. What did it matter, he was going to die anyway. Sinking his

56

head into his chest, he glared at his captor.

If Ranger didn't know better, he would almost think this Datsoe was... smart. It seemed to glower at him, and he couldn't help but notice how unusual its eyes were. Most Datsoes had no pupils. When the venom took over, the eyes tended to become a solid black or blood red. This one had pupils with a burgundy hue, and they flashed with intelligence.

He couldn't explain it to himself. He hated Datsoes passionately for his own reasons, and he had sworn to protect his people from them. Slaying hundreds, Ranger never gave the creatures a second thought, pushing on day after day to destroy the plague. If he was known as a hero to his people, he was surely thought of as an unforgiving murderer to the Datsoes.

And yet here he was, puzzling over the very thing he despised. It made no move to attack him. Surely it was starving, yet it didn't howl or carry on. Any other Datsoe would have killed those two soldiers in a blink, but this one only defended itself against their stupidity.

The flames from the torch slowly flickered out, casting the carriage into shadow. Lowering the tarp, Ranger left the creature, lost in his own thoughts.

Little did he know, the Datsoe went back to chewing in the corner, desperate to be free.

FallHeart the 64th of

222 D.P

The edge of the tarp flipped up before dawn broke across the sky. Perking his ears, the Datsoe watched the tall man with silver hair hitch the horses to the carriage while the others made preparations to depart. What was it they called him? Ranger? Was that his name or what he did? Confusion filled him. He remained silent, even when soldiers came near the cage. Some sipped out of wooden mugs, others munched on crispy food. His stomach growled again. Hunkering into the furthest corner, he wondered what "Ranger" smelled like. He hadn't gotten close enough to tell. It would be a shame if he accidentally hurt the tall man when he escaped, he needed to be sure to avoid him when the opportunity presented itself. He didn't care much about the rest, if they got hurt, so be it. True, the tall man was the one who caught him, but he seemed different from the rest. Especially the girl, she had hate burning in her gaze every time she looked at him. With a shudder, he watched the town and its irritating occupants fade behind him. He was glad to move on, there were less prying eyes to see what he was doing.

The landscape steadily became increasingly muddy, slowing their progress. Grassy fields gave way to rougher terrain, making the carriage rattle over each dip. Insects swarmed the travelers, looking for a tasty meal.

"Forgot how much I hated this place." Marco grumbled, smacking the side of his face.

"This is the worst. I always forget how miserable the swamps are," Cliff slapped at a mosquito on his arm.

"Oh, come on guys," Ranger called over the noise of the wooden wheels slogging through the muck. "It's not that bad! If you babies cannot handle a few harmless bugs, then how can we rely on you to protect the front!" he mocked.

"Ha ha, very funny, Ranger." Marco scowled.

Ranger laughed, leaning back in his seat. The unexpected trail condition would slow their progress, but so far everything was going great. Glancing at the blue sky, he heard a snuffle behind him. Whipping around, he realized the Datsoe was inches away from the bars, apparently sniffing him.

Jumping back, its tail thrashed around the cage, knocking into the bars repeatedly.

"Well, what were you up to?" Ranger asked. Pausing, he realized he spoke out loud to the creature. Meeting the shining burgundy stare, he knew there would be no answers from the small form. Turning its back once more, the Datsoe appeared to be ignoring him. With an irritated sigh, Ranger dropped the flaps of the tarp. He wasn't even sure why he had them up all morning. It had been so quiet, he hadn't felt the need to hide it from view.

Returning his attention to the trail, he noticed Cliff had stopped. Pulling on the reins, he brought the carriage alongside his friend.

His lips parted in shock.

For miles, all he could see was the surprising, mocking, glint of water. Flooding the ground as far as they could see, the trail had been completely engulfed.

The swamps flooded in early winter, providing a draining point for snow melt off. But snowfall was supposed to be weeks away.

Ranger's mind raced as he stepped off the carriage. If the swamps were full already, that meant that winter was upon them now, and no one was prepared. He had heard whispers of WinterNox arriving early, but it had been long before his time. This could mean disaster for the kingdom. Since the weather here was mild, everyone would assume they still had time to prepare. Datsoes could start making their way over the frozen parts of the rose wall, and five out of the six Guardians were away from their posts.

"What is this BLASPHEMY?!" Marco yelled.

"The water columns should not be filled yet. Why haven't we received any message from Kion?" Leeon said, referring to the sixth guardian.

"We can go around." Quail suggested.

"We cannot go around; it would take weeks. Especially with the water this high." Cliff rubbed his temples.

"Well, we can't just go through, the horses and carriage would sink." Quail responded.

"We have to do something." Marco grumbled.

"And what would you have us do? I have not heard you make any suggestions!" Cliff snapped.

"I have not heard anything from you either!" Marco thrust his finger at Cliff.

Everyone began to squabble.

Ranger remained silent, dismissing one idea after another. "Be quiet for a moment!"

Ignoring him, they argued on.

61

Kicking water at them, he interrupted their heated words.

"Aye! What was that for?!" Marco bellowed.

"You remind me of arguing children. Marco, do you have any maps on you?"

"No. They are back at my library, but that does not matter. No trail can lead us through the swamp now."

Leeon smashed a bug on the back of his neck. "What is the closest town if we go around?"

"What if we didn't go around the swamp?" Ranger paused. "I know another way, one that hasn't been used in years."

The others leaned forward. Even the Datsoe's ears perked with curiosity.

"What is this way?" Leeon asked.

Ranger pulled a long bag off of the carriage. Flipping open the leather, he began to rummage through its contents. With a grunt of triumph, he withdrew a small, worn, piece of ancient parchment. Unfolding it, he smoothed it flat over his seat.

Surrounding Ranger, the others studied the map. The top was labeled *The Other Side*, and faded colors distinguished different regions. A purple line stretched from the middle of the page to the right top corner. One side was labeled *swamps* in tiny letters, the other showed branching streams that all lead back to one river. A stone bridge stretched over the river's width with a pale line depicting a trail that led into colored woods. *Jylioon's gate* was scribbled under a block that sat at the edge of the purple line.

"Is that my gate?" Marco pointed to the map.

"Indeed it is, "Ranger replied. "And this," he gestured to another mark on the map labeled *Herson's gate*,

62

"Is Kion's gate. There is a path that leads directly from Marco's gate to Kion's on the other side of the swamp."

"That is on the other side of the wall!" Cliff stared at Ranger with shock.

"Aye. I knew there was an old path that led from my gate through the woods, but I had no idea where it went," Marco murmured.

"Long ago, I used to walk this trail." Ranger said. "I was part of a team of skilled warriors that hunted Datsoes before they made it to the wall. We finally decided the dangers outweighed the benefits. The gates had to be opened, exposing people to possible attack. It's been decades, but I still carry the old map I made. The Palace is a little over a day's journey from Kion's gate. We can double back, warn your people, then open the mighty gate."

"Ranger, it is a good suggestion, but what are the risks of going this way? It sounds like suicide." Cliff protested.

"I agree." Quail spoke up. "There has to be a better solution."

"Do you have wings to fly over that water? Any of you?" Ranger snapped. "Right now, our main priority is getting to the Palace so her majesty can light the torches. The torches will spread along the land and let the kingdom know that WinterNox is here *now*. I traveled that trail a hundred times. Are you implying you are not up to the task? Quail recently pointed out that we are six of the deadliest people on the *planet.*"

Marco put his foot up on the lip of the carriage. "Aye! I agree! What are we? A bunch of scared kittens? No Datsoe would dare attack us!"

"We are definitely up for this," Leeon agreed.

63

"As a team, yes," Cliff clapped Ranger's shoulder.

Throwing her hands up, Quail muttered something about men under her breath, which they took as an agreement.

Climbing into the carriage, Ranger glanced at the cage. He could swear the tarp was pushed out a bit, almost as if the Datsoe had been peeking through the edges. Picking up the reins thoughtfully, he clicked his tongue, encouraging the horses to turn around. Following Quail and his stallion, Ranger guided the carriage back through the mud that still contained their footprints.

All through the night they rode, until they came upon the shining lights of Marco's town. The guards greeted Marco with confusion.

"Did the journey not go as expected, Sir?" The night guard inquired.

"WinterNox is upon us, spread the word to the men to start preparations. At sunrise, have men at the gate. We will be traveling through it to the other side." Ignoring the man's gasp of surprise, he continued. "Take our horses to the stables and unhitch the carriage. If anyone messes with the Datsoe, they will answer to me."

Ranger's eyebrows shot up. He hadn't said a word about the soldiers he caught the night before by the carriage. Perhaps Marco paid better attention than he realized.

"My friends, once more I offer my hospitality. Let us rest so we are fresh for tomorrow's adventures." Marco led the group toward the guest house.

Trailing behind, Ranger lifted the tarp of the Datsoe's cage. Peering inside, he saw the creature curled up and snoring in the opposite corner. Dropping the fabric, he followed the others, looking forward to the luxury of a bed.

64

FallHeart the 65th of

222 D.P

The sun's rays inched their way up the sides of the landscape, melting away the cold air with their warm touch. Voices called to each other, and it seemed the entire town had gathered. News that the gate was to be opened spread like wildfire, and since it had been closed for decades, many of the townsfolk had never seen the mighty doors moved. Muscular stallions, including Ranger's, were being hitched to the pulling systems that operated the doors. It had been decided that his horse would stay with Marco's soldiers, since Ranger was in the carriage anyway.

Archers stood at the tall towers, bows drawn and ready just in case a Datsoe was foolish enough to appear. The smell of roses filled the air, but the people had been informed that WinterNox was upon them. The season was always dreaded, but now that it was coming weeks early, everyone was on edge.

The crowd parted, allowing the carriage passage to the gate entrance. The Guardians trailed behind him on horseback, prepared for anything. Ranger's hand rested on the map in his lap, but he didn't need it. The Datsoe moved restlessly in the cage, making him flip up the tarp to see what the creature was up to. As soon as sunlight hit him, the Datsoe locked eyes with Ranger. A chill ran up the warriors spine. Once again he could not shake the feeling that his captive knew exactly what was happening, and was just as worried as he was.

Marco greeted everyone by name, proving once again that he cared for his people deeply. His patience for their questions was endless, doing everything he could to reassure them. Pausing by a group of soldiers, he spoke to the commander, giving him instructions. Turning his horse, he faced the expectant crowd. Silence settled across the courtyard. Raising his hand, he gestured toward the horses connected to the gate.

With a snap of his fingers, everyone sprang into action.

The horses strained, pulling thick cables that connected to giant wheels. With a groan, the gate doors began to move inch by inch. The crowd remained quiet, uncertainty written on many faces. Ranger inhaled deeply, appreciating the mossy scents that followed the progress of the doors. The forest on the other side offered many mysterious plants, many of which he had yet to learn about. Armed soldiers lined the roadway, adding an extra layer of protection.

Marco was taking no chances.

The gate opened just wide enough to allow the carriage to pass through. Studying the road before him, Ranger noted the changes time had brought to his old stomping grounds. Nature had prevailed, leaving a faint memory of the path he had traveled. He smiled a bit, reminiscing of days gone by. Because of those memories, he was also keenly aware of how dangerous the landscape was. With a flick of his wrists, the reins signaled the horses to begin their journey.

Cliff and Leeon rode side by side behind the carriage,

taking in the sight before them. Marco and Quail brought up the rear, followed by the silent crowd. With a final glance at his town, Marco signaled to close the gate behind them as he crossed the threshold into what felt like another world. Grateful for Ranger's unhurried pace, the teammates took in their surroundings.

Gazing down upon the rose fields from the tower had never quite done them justice in Quails opinion. They were not bushes, but stood as tall as trees, with blooms that rivaled the size of a dinner plate. Silky purple petals shimmered in the light, giving the flowers an almost magical quality. Pollen floated thickly through the air, creating a yellow haze that gave her the urge to sneeze even though she had no allergies. Under the fringe of her hair, she took in Marco's expression smugly. He appeared to be struck dumb. Cliff and Leeon held their silence, but she had no doubt they were equally impressed. Imagine, Ranger traveling through this dense foliage every day to fight monsters. There were so many things she still didn't know about him, and she felt she knew him better than anyone.

"Incredible."

The whispered word made Ranger smile. Leeon was a man of few words, but his quiet exclamation of admiration reflected the powerful emotions he was feeling. Everyone knew the roses protected them, but, in Ranger's opinion, unless you were among them you never fully appreciated their majesty.

A hiss snapped Ranger from his thoughts. It occurred to him he hadn't heard anything from the curious Datsoe in a while. Lifting the tarp, he saw the creature pressed against the bars directly behind his seat. Shaking uncontrollably, it gagged and wheezed, clearly affected by the pollen. Taking no pleasure in the Datsoe's discomfort, Ranger quickened their pace.

Breaking free from the pathway, Ranger pulled the carriage to a stop to study the tree line looming before them. The streaming sunlight seemed to get absorbed into twisted tree trunks, casting the next part of their journey into shadow. A cool breeze swept over them, making the riders shift uncomfortably in their saddles.

Ranger cleared his throat, breaking the heavy silence. "Stick to the trail, it is easy to get lost. Be alert, keep your weapons handy, and watch your partner's back. Datsoes come in all shapes and sizes, who knows what is lurking in there. Speed is our friend now; I would prefer to push as hard as we can."

Cliff gripped the hilt of his sword tightly, and Marco brushed his fingers nervously over his ax.

"We will be at Kion's gate before you know it," Ranger said, trying to encourage them. Flicking the reins, he encouraged the horses under the thick pine canopy.

Dense mist covered the trail, adding an element of mystery to the gloomy atmosphere. Unknowingly, Ranger's calm demeanor soothed the others. They had been in dark places before, why should this be any different?

Squeaking wheels and horse hooves reverberated off of the thick bark, bringing the comforting sounds of humanity to each rider. The Datsoe stirred in its cage, signaling to Ranger that it was feeling better now that they had passed the rose field.

The day dragged on. Unable to read what time of day it was from the filtered sunlight streaming weakly through the trees, the others relied solely on Ranger to guide them. Stopping only when necessary, they stayed as close to the trail as possible when taking care of personal necessities. The trail led them through scenic twists and turns, and they all agreed that this would have been a beautiful location if it wasn't located in the center of the darkest forest on Earth.

Finally, the day began to show signs of change. The light grew dimmer, the air cold. Ranger pulled the carriage to a stop just inside of a large clearing between the trees.

"Why are we stopping?" Quail asked.

"We don't want to travel at night. Trust me, this is the best option." Stretching his stiff muscles, Ranger hopped out of the carriage.

Without a word, Quail swung down from her saddle. Following suit, the rest began to set up a simple camp. Although they had rations, Leeon slipped into the trees in search of fresh meat. Before long, his arrow found a small deer, which he happily laid out next to the fire Cliff had built.

While the others harvested the deer and put it over the fire to cook, Ranger tended the horses. Scanning the trees, he knew the smell of cooking meat would make more than people hungry. Joining his fellow Guardians around the fire, he was grateful for a hot meal. Conversation was sparse, each of them starting to feel the long day.

"I can take first watch." Ranger said, eyeing his weary friends.

"Are you sure, mate? Don't you want to get some sleep?" Cliff asked, gesturing to Ranger's sleeping bag.

"I am wide awake. Would you care to take second watch?"

"I will," Leeon said. "I am used to short rests, come and get me when you feel the need."

Spreading out around the fire, the Guardians each tried to find their rest. Unfamiliar sounds came from the surrounding blackness, making rest a challenging feat. Ranger made his way to the carriage, climbing into its seat for an elevated view of the camp. Leaning back in his seat, he tried to determine how many nights it would take to reach Kion's gate.

Over the sound of the crackling fire, an odd growl made him jump. Standing, he gripped his sword and scanned his surroundings. A tense moment passed, then he heard it again, a low gurgling noise. A pained moan had Ranger turning toward the cage, realizing the sound came from under the tarp. Lifting the material, he peered inside.

He could only see the silhouette of the creature. It appeared to be standing on the balls of its feet with its head bowed. A low rumble had Ranger lift the tarp higher, allowing firelight to illuminate the Datsoe. Its arms were wrapped tightly around its midsection, hinting at the problem.

It was hungry.

This did not surprise Ranger, the Datsoe hadn't eaten since its capture. The scent of cooking meat should have sent it into slobbering fits, but instead, it remained silent. Previous experience had Ranger shaking his head in disbelief. He had lost track of how many Datsoes he had transported, and it was always the same. He would often toss a bit of meat in the cage, knowing that it would be the monster's last meal. Just because he hated them didn't mean he wasn't compassionate.

Why did this one suffer in silence? Instinct should have had the Datsoe snarling, attacking, and being a general nuisance. Ranger found himself reconsidering the moment he saw tears in the creature's eyes. It wasn't long after Cliff announced the creature's execution. If it did understand what they were saying, could it have heard Cliff's comment?

Another moan had Ranger drop the tarp and climb quietly from the carriage. Making his way to the fire, he picked up a skewer laden with meat and carried it back to the cage. Flipping up the tarp once more, he captured the Datsoes attention. Staring at him, Ranger could swear one of its eyebrows slid up questioningly. Raising the meat, he waved it in front of the creature. From there, Ranger saw behaviors that didn't surprise him. The little Datsoe's pupils widened, completely erasing the intelligent burgundy. Thrashing its tail, the creature gripped the bars so tightly Ranger heard its knuckles pop. Drool poured unchecked down the Datsoes chin, and the Guardian waited for it to spring.

One of the little hands reached greedily for the skewer, making Ranger jump back. This startled the Datsoe, making it step away from the bars. Intrigued, he stepped to the edge of the cage, and studied his captive. Breathing heavily, it was almost as if the Datsoe was trying to regain control. Reaching his arm through the bars, Ranger laid the meat on the wooden floor. Releasing the skewer, he waited.

Instead of immediately falling on the food, burgundy eyes jumped from the meat to Ranger's face. All signs of the impatient monster were gone, it even wiped the drool from its chin with four shaking fingers, making Ranger's jaw drop. After a moment of hesitation, it dared to take a step forward. Creeping across the cage, it leaned in to sniff his offering. *It was checking the meat.*

Dumbfounded, Ranger found his tongue. "What? It's deer meat. Are you going to be picky at a time like this? It is not poisonous." Grimacing, Ranger suddenly felt foolish. Why was he talking to it? Why should he care if the stupid little thing ate or not?

The Datsoe's ears twitched at his words, then it pounced, startling him. Huddling on the far side of the cage, tearing off huge mouthfuls, it feasted. Pausing briefly, it looked up. Ranger froze. A piece of meat dangled from the corner of the creature's mouth, and he could swear it was grinning at him. With a nod that could only be described as thanks, it went back to gobbling the first meal it had consumed in days.

His mind was a sea of confusion. He had to banish these thoughts! The Datsoe had not smiled at him anymore than it had been crying. He was projecting human emotions, imagining things. This was absurd. Dropping the tarp back into place, he resolved to stop obsessing.

"You are too kind to them," a voice said. Ranger turned to find Leeon leaning against a nearby tree.

"I can't help but pity them. Nothing deserves to live like this."

"As usual, you see things through a different lens than the rest of us." Leeon said. "Your compassion for these death bringers will be something I never understand."

Ranger hesitated. If he explained his observations, would his friend think he was going crazy? Leeon was as wise as he was quiet, and trustworthy. There would be no judgment here, he decided.

Leeon interrupted Rangers' thoughts. "You know, I am going to miss this. The adventure, comradery."

"Are you thinking of retiring? So soon?"

Leeon fiddled with an arrow, a telltale sign he was nervous. "It is hard to believe I have been a Guardian for almost twenty years. My fortieth birthday looms at the end of WinterNox, and when I think about it, that would make you..."

"Don't go there," Ranger grumbled, making his friend chuckle.

"Age is not the issue; my predecessor was in his sixties when he retired. Things have changed for me recently, and well, my wife and I are expecting."

Reading the joy on Leeons face, Ranger immediately embraced his friend. "There are no words to express how wonderful this news is." Stepping back, he leaned against the carriage. "I assume you have not told the others yet."

"I am ready to become a father. It is getting harder to leave my wife, especially now. But being a gatekeeper is a very serious undertaking. How do I select someone to take my place? I often wonder how the previous Guardians knew who would be a worthy successor," Leeon sighed. "What will they say? Every one of them is married to the job, just like you." Patting Ranger on the shoulder, he continued. "I doubt any of them feel the loneliness I did before meeting my wife, the despair that so much death brings. I've had my fill of it. I want life, joy! Don't misunderstand me, I will always answer the call to duty, but I am ready to settle down."

Recognizing that this was a topic that Leeon had wanted to discuss with him for a while, Ranger carefully considered his reply. "I've seen Guardians come and go, and honestly, this is an age-old question. How does one balance the sense of duty with the longing for happiness? You will not pass the mantle carelessly; you care for your people too much."

"It won't be this year, or even the next."

"Something to look forward to then. Whenever you are ready, I know everyone will support your decision."

Leeon let out a sigh of relief, grateful that Ranger was willing to listen to his concerns.

"Are you ready to rest? I am happy to stand guard for a while."

"Not yet, I have too much on my mind. I will come and get you when the time is right."

"Don't feed all of the meat to your monster, I plan on having some as a snack later," Leeon called over his shoulder. Making his way to his sleeping mat, he was able to finally find some peace of mind, and rest.

With a snort, Ranger climbed back onto his perch. He was happy for Leeon. It was rare for a Guardian to get married, let alone have a child. It was a solitary life, and it took a different kind of person to handle the emotional toll it could take. Leeon was a very sensitive and caring man, which was why he had been chosen. He was also a fierce warrior. Ranger had seen him perform incredible feats on the battlefield, courageously putting himself on the line to protect the people of the kingdom. Now that he was a family man, it made sense that he would want to pass the mantle on.

With Leeon retiring, a seventh generation of Guardians would begin. When he was young, he had faint memories of news that the fourth generation Guardians were retiring. Now he was friends with the sixth generation, but they were considerably younger than he. Briefly, he wondered if he should consider retirement himself. Over the years, he had developed methods that prevented him from engaging in physical confrontations with Datsoes. Preferring his wits to brawn, he was still as sharp as a warrior half his age, but he was more vulnerable now. He was 68 for Juwa's sake. He knew that it would get harder as he aged, but he wasn't quite ready to give up the life yet.

One thing this trip had shown him, he was far lonelier than he realized. Maybe he could convince the Queen to create a team that could travel with him, protecting the land. Leeon had opened his eyes, making him think that perhaps there should be more to life than work alone.

Soft snores interrupted his drifting thoughts. Peeking through the ever-wearing gap in the tarp, he noticed the little Datsoe was fast asleep. The skewer lay discarded by the bars, completely stripped of meat. Even the bones were gone, making Ranger shudder. He had stuck his hand in the cage, what had he been thinking? The Datsoe could have bitten it clean off. Was he losing his edge? Giving the creature too much credit? Smiling and crying? Shaking his head, Ranger stood to get Leeon. Exhaustion was clearly taking its toll. A Datsoe with emotions, ha!

FallHeart the 65th of

222 D.P *-Nightfall*

A bone chilling howl broke the silence.

An answering growl came from within the cage. Exhaustion forgotten; Ranger pulled the tarp up.

"Friends of yours?" he glared at the Datsoe.

Ignoring him, the Datsoe stared beyond the bars. With ears pressed flat, a growl rumbled from its chest once more.

A chorus of howls had Ranger racing to alert his friends, but they were already scrambling for weapons.

"Do we know how many there are?" Marco swung his ax repeatedly, loosening his stiff muscles.

"No idea, but my guess is the pack smelled our supper," Cliff laid a thick branch into the embers, creating a torch. He was used to wielding two blades at once but felt fire would be more effective. He would set them aflame if he had to.

"Cliff is right," Ranger hissed, "These things travel in large packs, and they are near impossible to kill. We will have to work together in order to…"

A snap from a few yards away made them all freeze. A pair of glowing eyes edged their way into the light. It was only a couple feet off the ground, making Quail sigh with relief. Normal wolves she could handle. Dismay washed over her as the eyes began to rise higher and higher until they were above Ranger's head. And if that wasn't enough, two more sets of eyes appeared, locking onto the group.

"By Juwa," Marco cursed.

Racing for a tree, Leeon climbed until he was well above the pack. Steadying himself on his perch, he reached for the first arrow and notched it.

Tension filled the air.

"Why aren't they attacking?" Cliff whispered.

Ranger was puzzled as well. If these creatures were indeed Datsoe wolves, they would be pack hunters. Firelight reflected in the creature's eyes in an almost hypnotic pattern, but still, they didn't move. Peeling his gaze away from them, he glanced over his shoulder. A fourth wolf sprung. Pushing Quail aside with every ounce of strength he possessed, Ranger ducked just as the Datsoe sailed over his head, snarling. Skidding, the wolf leapt again, but the team was ready.

With a warrior's cry, Quail met the creature head on, slashing flesh wherever she could land a blow.

Suddenly, the campsite was filled with Datsoe wolves, dividing the team with snapping teeth and razor claws. They were huge, some reaching over ten feet in length.

Leeon let arrows fly, trying to pierce thick fur. Aiming for the eyes was a challenge as the beasts whirled and leapt to parry his friends' attacks.

A snout struck Ranger in the back, knocking him to his knees. Gasping for breath, he pushed up with his sword, only to be struck again, sailing onto his back with a grunt. A large, silver paw settled onto his chest, pinning him. Looking up past the gray torso, Ranger moved his face just in time to avoid a long, steaming stream of drool. The wolf's jaws were big enough to bite his head clean off, and bloodthirsty red eyes seemed to stare right through his soul.

Driving his sword through the beast's ankle, he tried to wiggle out from under the giant padded paw. Yelping, the wolf shifted just enough for Ranger to draw a deep breath. Arrows rained down, sticking in its nostrils, ears, and jowls. Stepping back, it lost track of its prey in a haze of pain.

Rolling to his feet, Ranger drove his sword into the neck of the creature, silencing its howls. Giving Leeon a salute of gratitude, he raced toward another towering beast, hacking at its back ankles in an effort to distract it from Cliff.

"Thanks," Cliff called, swinging his own blade in a perfect arc that sliced the cheek of his adversary. Pushing his torch into the beast's face, he singed fur into a cloud of black, inky smoke.

Quail and Marco stood back-to-back, fending off their opponents with years of combat experience.

Movement caught Rangers' attention, making him turn toward a new threat. A pitch-colored pelt helped the pack leader blend into the night as it circled the fighters. Six paws moved with a strange rhythm, and the Datsoe waited for an opportunity to strike.

"Let's dance." Ranger yelled, gaining the wolf's attention.

The Wolf lurched forward, making Ranger dive sideways to avoid it. Twisting, the combatants came together again and again, dodging, striking, sending sprays of sweat and drool flying. Thrusting his sword forward, he struck the Datsoe in the nostril, slicing it from the inside out. Blood splattered the soil as it shook its head wildly. Ranger pulled back for the killing blow when he heard thundering footsteps behind him. Ducking, he narrowly escaped the jaws of a brown wolf. How many were there, he thought desperately. Glancing toward his team, he saw they were all still engaged with the giants, fighting for their lives.

With a spurt of anger, he whacked the flat of his sword solidly across the wolf's broad forehead. Grabbing a fist full of brown fur, Ranger climbed the stunned beast's leg like a ladder. The Datsoe's initial surprise gave way to instinct, bucking and thrashing in an attempt to toss the human off.

Gripping with his knees, Ranger held the hilt of his sword, pressing the tip of his blade against the beast's head. Using the Datsoe's downward momentum against it, he drove his weapon into its skull, killing it instantly. Legs buckling, it crashed to the ground. Pulling his sword out and wiping the gore from his blade on the deceased Datsoe, Ranger slid down the shoulder onto the dirt below, looking for a new challenge. Glancing back, he saw Marco's ax embedded in the throat of his attacker. Quail had also made short work of her wolf, and as they shared grins, she wiped her blade off much the way he had.

His smile faded the moment he heard a low growl behind him. The black leader stood behind him, taking in the sight of its fallen pack members. More wolves stepped up behind it, making Ranger sigh. Nothing was ever easy.

Out of arrows, Leeon had climbed down from his perch. Racing toward the carriage for more, he dove under the belly of the nearest wolf, slashing with his dagger as he went. The beast jumped aside, knocking the Guardian down with a mighty paw.

Ranger's sword sang through the air with precision, piercing the wolf's shoulder. Leeon took advantage of the distraction and stabbed the wolf again. Pulling Ranger's sword out, he wielded both weapons against the Datsoe with skill.

Grabbing his dagger, Ranger turned just in time to avoid being bit in half. Grabbing at a patch of black whiskers, he thrust his blade into the wolf's eye. Howls of agony filled the air, making the Guardians' ears ring. Silver blood poured from the socket, contrasting against its black fur. Thrusting from side to side, the pack leader tried desperately to dislodge the dagger. Crashing into trees, the wolf churned up huge chunks of soil as it whirled and yowled. Skidding across a patch of thick pine needles, it rubbed its face over and over against low lying branches. Snapped pieces of pine began to fall all around Ranger, making him jump and weave in an effort to avoid being struck. Leeon still had his sword, he needed another way to defend himself. Making his way toward the carriage, he didn't see the giant branch coming.

Pressing its eyes against the wood, the black wolf dislodged the blade with a sickening pop! The pressure cracked the wood perfectly, and as the creature shook its mighty head, it hit the branch, sending it flying toward Ranger.

When his face hit the dirt, Ranger was genuinely confused. Something heavy struck him from behind, sending searing hot pain down his leg. Spitting out grit, he tried to push up, then realized he was pinned under a giant broken tree limb. The carriage was only a couple of yards away, mocking him with the promise of more weapons.

A loud snap had him twisting his head toward the back of the cage. The tarp lay partially open, exactly as he had left it. A white wolf circled it with curiosity, until its eyes fell on Ranger. Licking its chops, it lowered down, ready to pounce on the conveniently pinned meal.

Ranger wasn't a man of faith, but a single plea ran through his mind.

"Please, do not let the others die ..."

The wolf lunged.

Wincing, Ranger tried to brace himself. Over the years his mind had taken many dark turns, wondering how he may meet his fate. Naturally, being consumed was at the top, he just hoped he was dead before being swallowed.

Seconds ticked by. Pushing up, he stared. The white wolf was trying to claw its way toward him but wasn't moving. The carriage was tilting toward the Datsoe, rocking back and forth. Snarling, the hound twisted its head to see what dared to touch it.

If he lived to be a thousand years old, Ranger would never forget this moment. Small, charcoal arms stretched through the bars. With an iron grip, the captive Datsoe held a monster six times its size. Burgundy met gray, both gazes filled with intense emotion.

The wolf turned, yanking its tail from the smaller Datsoes grip with a howl of fury. Throwing itself against the bars, it tried to reach the cages trapped occupant.

It had saved his life.

Ranger watched, frozen, as another wolf came around the other side of the cage and began to break the wood on the opposite side. He couldn't believe what he had just seen; why had the little creature stopped the beast from killing him?

"Ranger!"

Cliff knelt beside him, covered in blood and dirt. Leeon stood behind him, watching the wolves throw themselves at the cage.

"Why are they attacking it? Shouldn't they all be on the same side or something?" Leeon seemed genuinely interested in the events in front of him.

"Who cares?" Cliff snapped. "Help me."

Together they moved the heavy branch and pulled Ranger to his feet.

"You alright?" Cliff tried to steady Ranger as he swayed.

"Leg might be broken, not sure yet." Ranger couldn't peel his eyes away from the cage. "I think…" he paused with uncertainty, "I think he saved my life. On purpose." Leaning heavily on Leeon's shoulder, he pointed. "They are breaking into the cage!"

Shoving a giant paw in between the broken oak spindles, the white wolf clawed at the little Datsoe. Leaping around, it managed to avoid the attack until the second wolf took it by surprise.

Ranger winced when he heard the small Datsoe squeal in pain. Grabbing his sword from Leeon's grip, he started to hobble toward the carriage.

"What the bloody hell do you think you can do? Let them have it!" Cliff grabbed Ranger's arm, trying to hold him back.

The side of the cage collapsed under the weight of the white wolf, spilling the small Datsoe out onto the dirt. Snapping at the second wolf, the white clearly wanted to claim its prize. Licking its chops, it descended on its prey.

A single, four fingered hand shot up, punching the white muzzle. Knocking the wolf back with a surprised yip, the little Datsoe began to shake violently.

Under the guardian's astonished gaze, it began to change. Foaming at the mouth, razor sharp teeth grew, and grew. Once perky ears elongated, twisting into thick, banded horns that ended in points. A black shell slid over the creature's head, replacing the mop of shaggy black hair. A snout stretched forward, expanding until it could accommodate a mouth with teeth that just continued to grow. Simultaneously, thick muscles rippled and popped, adding mass that rivaled the wolves, who were also watching the transformation. Under its existing arms, two more burst from the torso, covered in gelatinous goo. The black shell continued to expand down its neck, across its back and over the torso, creating impenetrable armor. The tail Ranger had tripped on repeatedly was also coated in the same armor to the tip, which seemed to mimic a scorpion's razor-sharp stinger.

"And you were just feeding that thing," Leeon muttered to Ranger.

A dark roar filled the air challengingly. Answering the call, both wolves leapt. Catching the white wolf midair, the stinger sang toward the second, piercing its skull in a single blow. Sinking its teeth into the white wolf's shoulder, the Datsoes tumbled across the ground in a vicious fight to the death.

Peeling his eyes away from the fight, Ranger shook Cliff. "To the carriage! Leeon needs more arrows, and I will grab my bow as well. We may need to tranquilize that thing!"

Cliff dashed toward the carriage, only to be cut off by the one-eyed leader of the pack. Swinging his sword defensively, Cliff dodged the ebony thrashing limbs and snapping teeth.

Ranger threw his weight into Leeon to push him away.

"Hey ugly! We're not done yet!" Hobbling, he waved his arms. "Get what you need, go go!" He motioned to Leeon, who ran in the opposite direction.

Recognizing Ranger's scent, the black wolf knocked Cliff aside and lunged.

Thick armor in the shape of a peacock's fan unfurled in front of Ranger. Looking over his shoulder, the Guardian saw the Datsoe, *his* Datsoe, standing above him defensively.

The black wolf jumped back, cocking its head at the new challenger. Dead members of its pack lay strewn across the campsite. All of its rage poured into an echoing howl, before it dove at Ranger. Once again it was blocked, but the tail now whipped toward the wolf, whizzing through the air with deadly promise. Dodging the stinger, the wolf bit into the neck of its armored opponent.

The Guardians gathered by the carriage. Pulling out a wooden splint, Quail wrapped Ranger's leg with a long cotton strap. Leeon filled his quiver with arrows, notching one immediately. Marco watched the tree line for new threats, while Cliff stood with his sword ready.

The battle seemed to shake the earth itself. The Datsoes tumbled and rolled, scratched, and bit. Snarls and growls echoed off the trees, silver blood ran like streams down both combatants. Every time the wolf tried to make its way toward Ranger, he was blocked, thrown, and bruised. Flipping through the air, they crashed into the woods then down a grassy bank.

"We have to go after them." Ranger said, his gaze fixed on the place where the wolf and his Datsoe disappeared.

"What? Are you insane?!" Leeon asked.

"We cannot lose it! It was my catch." Ranger put his

hand out for the crossbow.

"Ranger, you could be killed... it's just not worth it," Cliff's distress rang in his words.

"Please. I need to do this. This is important to me, I can't explain why."

"I will go with you," Quail gripped his shoulder. In all the years they spent together, she had rarely seen Ranger so emotional. His behavior had shifted ever since the capture of the small Datsoe, and she wanted to know why.

"Don't get dead." Marco understood Ranger's complex decisions, and he also knew once Ranger set his mind to something, you couldn't talk him out of it.

"See to the horses, will you? Make sure we didn't lose any to the wolves. Once I have the Datsoe, we will need to repair the cage and immediately make preparations to leave. All of the carnage is bound to attract more predators."

Marco, Cliff, and Leeon watched the pair make their way through the trees, then they got to work.

Following the path of destruction, Quail helped Ranger down to the base of the hill. Mist shrouded a fallen figure covered with gore. Striking a match against his belt, Raner held the tiny light up.

The black wolf was dead.

"Where is the other one?" Quail clutched her sword. She did not share Ranger's curiosity. If she had her way, they would slay this creature and move on. To hell with the FallHeart sacrifice.

A trail of silver blood led away from the scene of battle, so they followed it.

Ranger's thoughts whirled. Had the Datsoe been able to transform this entire time? If so, why did it remain a captive? Why didn't it just kill them all? Why was he the only one who had noticed these oddities?

Moonlight illuminated the landscape, revealing a tiny stream that trickled over moss covered rocks. Leaning down next to it, Quail quickly splashed her arms and face, washing some of the battle away.

"Drool, yuck!"

Chuckling, Ranger looked past her to see his Datsoe, leaning heavily against a tree. Motioning to Quail, he frowned when she lifted her sword. Crouching beside her, he whispered, "Let's see what it does."

Glaring at Ranger with disbelief, Quail missed the beginning of the transformation.

Two arms fell to the ground, making Ranger shoot to his feet. Was the Datsoe... molting? The armor shell receded back to reveal charcoal skin while the tail thrashed around in the dense foliage. It shrank at the same time the creature's horns seemed to fade away into perky ears once more. Its mouth no longer contained row after row of razor teeth, but regular fangs. Falling to hands and knees, The Datsoe panted until its metamorphosis was complete, once again resembling a lean human.

Ranger didn't feel Quail's iron grip on his arm or see her gaping expression. He was too busy studying the fallen Datsoe. Even from a distance he could see it begin to shake, huddling in a pool of silver blood. It tried to get onto its feet, but its limbs failed, collapsing onto the rocks of the stream bank. It didn't move again.

Finally registering Quail, Ranger peeled her hand from his arm and started to make his way toward the fallen figure.

Long claws shot out from under his Datsoe, making Ranger freeze in place. Lifting her sword, Quail watched a long centipede start to crawl to the surface. Moonlight reflected off of the slime coating its reddish shell. Not a sound reached the horrified observers as the creature lifted the small Datsoe with pincers then rose higher and higher, until it loomed at least ten feet above them.

Ranger saw the little Datsoe lurch, suddenly aware of what was happening. It tried to struggle, wrench its way out of the monster's grip, but it was hopeless. A set of long jaws with teeth sharp as swords opened greedily, prepared to swallow its catch whole.

He stopped fighting, head falling back in defeat. Shutting his eyes, he gave up. This was just too much. Let fate have him, he was done. He had tried to… what exactly? Something about the tall man, the Ranger, yes, that was his name, made things clearer. He wanted to be better when the Ranger was around. He had been lost and lonely for so long. Too late, he thought dimly. Perhaps this was for the best.

An arrow struck the centipede in the eye, making the monster flail and squeal. Turning his head, he looked to see the Ranger take aim again. The woman was hacking at the base of the writhing beast, was he seeing things? Were they… helping him? He was falling! The monster let him go, but he had nothing to grab onto. Hitting the rocky bank once more, he whimpered in pain. Cold water washed over his toes, reviving him a bit. Pushing up on shaking arms, he blinked in awe.

The Ranger stood in front of him, blocking the monster. Arrow after arrow flew, many of them blocked by the countless arms of the centipede, but some managed to hit soft spots in its neck, causing it to roar in pain. It scuttled closer to him, extending its claws. The Ranger dove, rolling and firing simultaneously. The woman was just as magnificent. Leaping onto a boulder, she twirled through the air, dismembering the creature with every swing of her shining blade. But she hated him. Why was she doing this?

Waves of emotion long forgotten overwhelmed him.

Ranger reached into his quiver to find it empty. Trying to stand, his leg gave way long enough for the monster's claw to snag his long trench coat. With a whip of its tail, Quail went flying, hitting a pine tree and landing in a heap. Dropping the bow, Ranger pulled his arms from the sleeves, but he was too late, a second claw descended.

A figure dove in front of him, catching the monster before it made contact. Its legs buckled under the pressure, almost falling. If Ranger put out his hand, he could have touched the back of his Datsoe. There was no way to think of it other than his. If he was honest with himself, he had somehow let curiosity get the better of him and found himself attached in a strange way to this creature he was sure now had been a teen boy.

The Datsoe dug its claws into the monster's skin. Blue sparks started to fly all around the slight form, and the centipede immediately tried to retreat. Stronger, Ranger's protector pushed up, standing tall. Refusing to loosen its grip, the blue light intensified, pulsing into the little Datsoes fingertips. The wounds on its body stopped bleeding, and after a few blinks, Ranger watched them heal completely. With a vicious twist, it ripped the claw completely off, spraying steaming puss all over Ranger. The monster reared back, freeing his coat. Wiping the viscous fluid from his face with a sleeve, he saw Quail standing to his left, just as enthralled in the show as he was.

Feeling stronger, the Datsoe knew he was winning, but he couldn't take any chances. Racing on all fours, he leapt onto the monster's legs, then crawled up the long neck, to attack its face. Clawing and snarling, he hit until he couldn't maintain his grip on the flailing monster any longer. He found himself sailing through the air once more, hitting the ground with a spine-tingling CRACK.

Dripping fluid and missing limbs, the monster retreated back into its dark hole, unwilling to pursue a meal any longer.

Ranger sighed with relief. Pushing to his feet, he looked over at his small Datsoe. It had its arm pulled into its chest, clearly in pain. It was panting again with exhaustion. It raised its head to return his gaze.

Ranger couldn't mistake the smile this time. Its lips curved up into a toothy grin, its ears perked toward him. If it could laugh, Ranger assumed it would be out of astonishment over their victory. Closing its mouth, it bowed at him. Ranger found himself nodding back, missing the look of utter joy on the Datsoe's face.

Catching himself, dismay filled Ranger. This Datsoe was most certainly aware. Taking in its beaming expression, he found himself in unfamiliar territory. What in the Juwa was he supposed to do with this thing? The FallHeart sacrifice was out of the question...

A tranquilizer dart hit the Datsoe's neck. Using its good hand, it pulled it out of its skin. Looking at Ranger, an expression he could only describe as betrayal crossed its features. Eyes rolling back, it collapsed.

"Datsoe's sake man! You really are insane!" Leeon lowered his bow, making his way down the slope behind Marco.

"Are you alright?" Quail asked urgently.

"I am fine... But watch the tree line." He pointed to the spot where the monster had disappeared. "The thing that left *that*," he said, pointing to the giant claw, "Is still in there somewhere."

SMACK

"OW! What the?" Ranger held the back of his head.

"That is what you get for being *stupid.*" Quail hissed. "You are lucky we escaped with our lives chasing after that creature."

"Where is Cliff?" Ranger chose to ignore Quail. It had been worth it.

"He is with the horses and packing up camp. We figured you would want to leave immediately. The carriage is badly damaged though."

"How did you get it to change back?" Leeon eyed the unconscious Datsoe.

"I didn't. It transformed right before another Datsoe came out looking for dinner. He saved our lives..."

"Did you just say he?" Quail gaped at him.

"You can't deny what we saw, Quail."

"You talk as if it's a person! It was acting out of pure instinct, saving itself. Now that we know what it is capable of, we need to keep a closer eye on it. There are steel cuffs and chains in a compartment under the carriage. We can use them. Marco, see if you can get that thing back to the cage and begin repairs."

Marco picked up the Datsoe.

"You should have just let it go!" She glared at Ranger.

"You had a hand in saving it. Don't think I didn't notice you helping back there."

"I was trying to save your hide."

"Maybe. Or you are starting to see what I see."

"All I see right now is the fact that you are exhausted, injured, and rambling like a crazy man. It's a Datsoe Ranger, nothing more." Turning on her heel, she followed Marco up the bank toward camp.

"Did you find what you were looking for?" Leeon asked once she was out of earshot. "It's not like you to go running off like that, especially with everything that just happened."

Ranger recalled bright burgundy eyes filled with triumph and misplaced trust.

"Yes," he answered dully. "I did."

FallHeart the 66th of

222 D.P

The horses were still nervous, and no one could blame them. Giant wolves lay around the camp and beyond, filling the night with the stench of death. With a heavy heart, Ranger watched his friends fix the cage and wrap chains around his Datsoe's neck and limbs.

Dawn filtered enough light through the trees for Marco to complete the unpleasant task of harvesting wolf meat. Laying strips to dry over the top of the carriage, he salted it thoroughly.

"We should not stop again. We can take turns sleeping if need be." Cliff said.

"I agree." Quail agreed. "The less time we have to spend here, the better."

Wanting to put as much distance between themselves and camp as possible, they set off. It wasn't long before scavengers crept from the trees, making short work of the deceased.

Ranger was exhausted. After further evaluation, it was determined that his leg was not broken, but the bone definitely felt cracked. He kept the splint wrapped tight, hoping he could recover a bit before they reached the kingdom.

He kept looking over his shoulder. He had insisted on leaving the front of the tarp open so he could keep an eye on the Datsoe. It was still unconscious under a pile of chains.

He sighed, trying to focus on the road ahead.

Time passed slowly; each day felt like an eternity. They took turns dozing in their saddles and snacking on wolf meat and other rations. The only time they stopped was to let the horses rest and gather water, and then were on high alert. Ranger knew they could be attacked at any moment, whether they were moving or not, so he tried to stay awake as much as possible. Even he had his limits, finally asking Quail to take the reins. Leaning back against the bars (which she thought was insane, what if the Datsoe woke?) he allowed himself to rest.

Realizing the carriage was probably the best place to rest, they all took turns riding beside Ranger; napping, studying the map, and chewing on more wolf jerky. (None of them rested against the bars, and all agreed Ranger was far too trusting.) Conversation was sparse. Each was secretly concerned that if they made noise, they would draw unwanted attention.

The little Datsoe continued to slumber, getting more rest than all of them combined. At one point, Ranger reached inside and tugged on the chains to see if he could wake it up. But it snoozed on. By the third night, they were desperately tired of wolf meat, so Leon shot another deer. Reluctantly making camp, they cleaned it and ate. Together, they made the groggy decision to get some sleep. Ranger slipped another skewer of meat into the cage, hoping to wake his Datsoe.

Marco offered to take the first watch, but not long after everyone had gone to sleep, Ranger woke to loud snoring. Much to his irritation, Marco had fallen into a deep sleep against the base of a tree. His mouth gaped open wide enough for a bird to jump into. Rubbing his eyes, Ranger resisted the urge to give Marco a solid kick. The chains behind him rattled, capturing his attention.

He was finally awake.

Turning, Ranger gripped the bars and peered into the cage. The meat lay untouched. The Datsoe looked over at him, its eyes reflecting cold resentment. Looking down at the chains, then at him, it turned away. Wincing, it began to lick its injured arm.

A knot formed in Ranger's stomach. He could understand the creature's anger, he felt it was deserved. There was no justice here, but what could he do about it? Just because he was intelligent did not take away from the fact that he *was* a Datsoe. The others wouldn't understand. Quail had witnessed the creature's actions, but she refused to believe that this one could be different. To be honest, if he hadn't witnessed it himself, he wouldn't have believed such a story.

Climbing down from his perch, he walked around to the back of the cage and lifted the tarp. Fingering the latch, he wondered what would happen if he released it. True it had saved his life (twice!) but now it was injured, feeling betrayed. He couldn't risk it.

"You should eat, regain your strength."

Burgundy eyes flicked at the food, then back to his face. Lifting the heavy chains, the Datsoe shuffled until its back was once again facing Ranger.

"Suit yourself."

Lowering the tarp, he climbed into the carriage and grabbed his crossbow. Ranger would watch over them all night if he had to.

FallHeart the 70th of

222 D.P

Ranger was grateful the night passed uneventfully. Stretching, he stepped down from the carriage and made his way to his sleeping companions. Giving Marco an irritated kick, (not as hard as he wanted to) he told the redhead to get the others moving. Stoking the dying campfire, he ripped a piece of deer meat off a skewer for breakfast.

"It's morning." Leeon said groggily, "I thought we were supposed to head out hours ago."

"Ranger, have you been up all night?" Cliff asked. "You look awful. Wasn't Marco supposed to take watch last night?"

"I will just be tending the horses," Marco grumbled, avoiding Cliff's piercing stare.

"I couldn't sleep, so I took over for him. Everyone needs to be sharp for today's events."

Quail was quiet as she packed her gear. Studying the men, it was clear what happened. Marco fell asleep and Ranger was covering for him, she had seen it all before. Exchanging a knowing glance with Leeon, she shook her head. When would Ranger ever learn?

Chewing on his meat, Ranger raised an eyebrow when Marco tapped his shoulder.

"Ranger, listen, I'm really sorry."

"I understand," Ranger yawned. "You were tired just like the rest of us. But considering where we are, you can't let your guard down, not even for a second."

"You are right of course." Meeting Ranger's stern gray stare, he squared shoulders. "Having you here has encouraged me to be complacent, which isn't fair to anyone, especially you. I won't let it happen again."

"This is good to hear since you will be leading today." Pulling the faded map from his pocket, he handed it to Marco. "I am too tired to be effective. I know I can depend on you."

Hiding his surprise, Marco took the map. "You can." Watching Ranger walk away, he felt terrible. Yes, he was tired, but there was a man twice his age that just kept going. Making a silent vow to never let Ranger down again, he prepared to leave.

Climbing into the carriage, Ranger tipped his hat over his eyes, settling against the bars of the cage on the passenger side.

To his surprise, Cliff climbed in beside him. "Marco hates being near the Datsoe. He has opted to lead on his horse."

Lifting an eyebrow, Ranger studied him. "And you don't mind it? The Datsoe."

"I wouldn't mind killing it and have no problem explaining to the Queen why we have no sacrifice."

Meeting Ranger's steady regard, he continued. "Look, I couldn't help but notice you've been a bit preoccupied. Quail and I had a, shall we say, discussion about it earlier. She thinks you are losing your edge." Noticing Ranger's expression, he rushed to explain. "It's just that you seem to be especially attentive to the Datsoe. After years of traveling with you she is concerned."

"Do the others share her concern?"

"You are the best hunter we know. A living legend. No one doubts you."

"That wasn't my question, Cliff."

"Exhaustion can take a toll, even on you. You are only human after all." Cliff thought back to the discussion with Quail and the others. She mentioned the incident with the soldiers and how Ranger protected the Datsoe. Marco was irritated with his men naturally, but they were all taken aback by Ranger's actions. Since then, Cliff had been quietly observing, and had to admit, there was something odd going on. Perhaps the Datsoe had a new power? Was mind control possible? Naturally he was confused by the creature's behavior; it had plenty of opportunities to attack them. Even now, Ranger was within arm's length, and the thing was awake. No chains could prevent it from transforming and killing him in the blink of an eye. But it didn't. Why? Picking up the reins, Cliff set the carriage into motion. Quail may have been dramatic with her opinions, (as usual) but she was right, Ranger was different.

"I am tired, and grateful that you are willing to take over for a bit. But, have no doubt that I will do whatever necessary to save lives. That is what a Guardian does, is it not?"

"It is indeed my friend. Rest now, you've earned it." Ranger's words seemed straightforward, but Cliff found himself wondering whose life he was referring to.

Observing Cliff under the brim of his hat, Ranger thought about their conversation. Cliff had always been very black and white, naturally he would think the Datsoe should be slain. He was the last Guardian selected for the sixth generation. Cliff had apparently grown up on legends of the lone soldier that slayed Datsoes, and wanted to be just like

101

him. Their initial meeting had been awkward. Cliff was so desperate to impress Ranger that he had bragged about all of his exploits, following the Guardian around wherever he went, even the bathroom.

Reminiscing, Ranger fell into a deep sleep, rousing just before dusk. Blinking, he took in the dark branches looming overhead and sat up. Groaning, he stretched his stiff muscles until his eyes fell on Quail holding the reins. Running water could be heard in the distance and the path was covered in colorful leaves.

"It lives." With one hand wrapped around the reins, she studied the map. Marco rode next to Leeon, deep in conversation. "We were beginning to think you might not ever wake up." she turned, giving Ranger one of her mysterious smiles. "But you look a little better."

"I am surprised we have already made it this far." he said, "You've made excellent time."

"Are we halfway yet?" she asked.

"Even better." he tapped the map. "Can you hear the river? That means we are here, right before the bridge. Once we cross, it should be a straight shot to Kion's gate. Only three days or so, tops."

"What a relief!"

"I think we are all ready to get out of here."

"Too true. Plus, I have not missed your snoring."

"I do not snore!" Ranger crossed his arms indignantly.

A rare laugh escaped Quail. "Sure, if you say so." Drawing a deep breath, her next words were rushed. "I need to apologize."

"For?"

"The way I've been behaving. It has been brought to

my attention that I have been abrasive." she said quietly.

Ranger's thoughts jumped to his earlier conversation with Cliff. "Oh?"

"It's not that I don't trust you. If anything, you're the one I trust the most. It's just, I am not used to traveling with peers, my men do what I say immediately. And then, there's that thing!" Glaring over her shoulder, she continued. "I'm used to killing them, not fighting for them. I find myself confused by your actions, feeding it, wanting to follow it into the woods, for Juwa sake, saving it."

"He saved me first." The words flowed out without thought, and Ranger regretted it immediately.

"It Ranger, *IT*! I never thought I would say this, but your behavior frightens me. I've seen you kill scores of Datsoes, never once have you hesitated."

"I've never been intentionally cruel to them either. Slaying is a mercy, not a sentence."

"It will kill you without hesitation! I can't lose another father Ranger, I..." her voice broke.

Wrapping his arm around her shoulders, he rocked her. "Birdie don't fret. And for the record, I love you too."

Tipping her head, she briefly rested against his shoulder. Memories filled them both. With a discrete sniff, she pushed away. "So, what now?"

"We press on, we have a kingdom to warn. Let's see if the bridge is still intact, shall we?"

"And if it isn't?"

"We find another way."

"Because that's what Guardians do." With a brief smile, Quail handed him the reins and stepped off the carriage.

Listening, once again his opinion shifted. Heavy chains weighed him down, his arm burned and ached. But he could not, would not blame the Ranger. Much to his disappointment, the woman hadn't changed her mind.

"He saved me first." The words rang in his head over and over. The Ranger had understood his intentions! This was encouraging.

The man with the black hair spoke to him of having a child, and he was kind and understanding. The woman spoke to him like a father. Was she his daughter?

His aching arm distracted him, it hurt to think. He hadn't thought like this for ages and ages, he only survived.

The chains were so heavy. He was so scared and alone. Silently, he wept.

Ranger set the map aside. Quail was right, what if the bridge hadn't survived all this time? How would they cross? Years ago, he could have sent a hawk across, but times had changed. With flying Datsoes plaguing the skies, hawks, which were their original means of communication, had become tasty meals. Fearing extinction, the original King and Queen banned the use of the birds in hopes that the population would grow. There were exceptions to the rule, but finding one these days was difficult.

Turning the bend, a deep chasm stood before the travelers. Rain clouds loomed overhead, filling the air with low lying mist. Moisture glistened from low hanging branches that spanned over the edge like daring children. The sound of rushing water was enough to stir the Datsoe, who had moved to the edge of the cage. Gripping a bar with its good hand, it sat behind Ranger, taking in the sights. Glancing at the small hand, Ranger absentmindedly spoke.

"Well Bud, I guess we will see if we can make it across. The bridge seems to be intact."

"Ranger?"

Turning, he saw Cliff staring at him intensely.

"Welcome my friends." Ranger announced. "To Droichead na mbeithíoch, or the Bridge of Beasts. Stories say a Datsoe hides beneath it, dragging people into the depths... no one ever crosses alive," he explained with an evil grin.

"Very funny, Ranger." Quail muttered, crossing her arms.

"Yeah! Like we would believe a tale like that..." Marco gulped.

"Once, there was something waiting for us under there."

The others looked at him in shock.

"I lost some good men that day. We need to be careful. Let's cross one horse at a time. Leeon, draw your bow and be prepared." Drawing his own bow, he looked at the group "So. Who wants to go first?"

Eyeing the wooden structure, Marco took in the hanging moss, mist, and shrugged. "To Juwa with it, I will go." Drawing his ax, he lifted it up. "I claim the first mug of ale when we get to the kingdom, and you cowards are buying." Driving his heels into his horse's sides, he guided it onto the wooden planks. A loud crack had Marco close his eyes and hold his breath. Nudging his mount further, he patted the side of its neck reassuringly. Trotting across, he turned in his saddle and gave a triumphant shout. "Who is next? Last one across should have to buy for all!"

"Looks like I am buying," Ranger chuckled. "It will be better if all of you cross before we try the weight of a carriage and two horses."

One by one they guided the horses across the raging water below, grateful the bridge held strong.

"Ok Ranger, it is time," Leeon called. "I have my bow ready."

The sound of the horse's hooves and squeaking wheels echoed on the bridge. It was a tight fit, the width of the carriage almost touching each side of the thick ropes that bordered the edges. A loud crackle came from under carriage wheels, making sweat drip down Ranger's brow. Peaking over the edge of the bridge, his heart stopped.

What had he just seen? The fog was swirling in the wrong direction. Did something fly by? He edged closer to the edge of his seat, anxiously searching. Something wasn't right. He could feel it, like a sixth sense, in his bones.

"What keeps you Ranger?" Cliff called.

"Aye, hurry it up man. Now I have ale on the brain!" Marco bellowed.

Lifting the reins, Ranger felt the whole bridge begin to shake. A splintering crash reverberated behind him, frightening the horses. Lunging forward, they began to pull at a breakneck pace, rattling Ranger and the Datsoe over the jagged planks.

Swaying wildly, Ranger stood and peered over the top of the cage. Something had broken through the wood behind them, making the bridge start to fold in on itself. The wheels jammed in the buckling splinters, pulling the horses to a terrified halt. Rearing and snorting, they fought to break free.

The bone chilling sound of claws scraped below him, making Ranger spring into action. Reaching forward, he pulled out the bolt that held the horses.

"Ranger, what are you doing?!" Quail shouted.

"Come on! Get over here!" Marco yelled.

The bridge dropped, making the carriage bounce and rattle when it came to a jarring stop a few feet down. Ranger could see his little Datsoe inside, tugging on the chains, trying to escape. Stepping gingerly from the carriage, he limped to the back of the cage. Lifting the latch, he climbed in without hesitation. The bridge lurched again, twisting wildly under the weight of something heavy. Scrambling toward the Datsoe, he began to pull on the chains.

Shock roared through him. The tall Ranger was in the cage, trying to set him free. Hurry hurry! The smell of the enemy was filling his nostrils, making him panic. Ignoring the pain radiating from his arm, he laid his hand above the calloused one gripping the links, and pulled with all his might. Together they might have a chance.

Sliding from the oak, the steel pin clattered to the floorboards. Reaching around the creature's neck, Ranger hesitated, until he looked into big, pleading, burgundy eyes. With a clang, the collar followed the steel pin, freeing the Datsoe completely. Clasping the bars, he swung out of the cage, grimacing when his leg hit the side of the carriage. Grabbing the rope on the side of the bridge for support, he turned to see the creature climb out behind him.

With a final groan, the planks gave way, spilling the carriage into the void below. Gripping the rope so tightly it burned, Ranger swung wildly through the mist. Feeling movement above him, he saw the Datsoe swaying above him, holding on with one hand. Pulling up, he managed to wrap his good leg into the thick cord and look around him. Black tentacles coiled all around the bridge, squeezing and snapping everything it could wrap around. Following the tentacles down, he saw a massive figure looming in the mist below.

"Ranger!"

Cliff stood on a sturdy part of the bridge with a rope tied around his waist, trying to reach the dangling cable.

"Just hold on!" Cliff pleaded. He didn't seem to care that the Datsoe was right above Ranger.

A black tentacle streaked toward Cliff, making Ranger call out in warning.

"Look out!"

Pushing up, Cliff rolled to the side, narrowly avoiding the writhing limb. Marco and Leeon gave the rope a hard tug, saving Cliff just as the last bit of the bridge collapsed beneath his feet.

Jerked forward, Ranger couldn't see through the thick fog. He could hear the faint cries of his friends above, but couldn't discern what they were saying over the roar of the river below. Debris rained down from above, making him desperately try to sway out of the way. Suddenly, he was sent flying toward the canyon wall. Closing his eyes and bracing for impact, he wasn't prepared for the jerking stop. Looking down, he saw solid ground and let go, praying he wouldn't break his other leg. Rolling onto the lip of a cave, he came to a tumbling stop against a jagged, rocky wall. Just as he started to push up, the small Datsoe came tumbling in after him. Groaning, he rose shakily to his feet. Based on the cold rocky surface around him, Ranger hypothesized that many small caves like this must have been skewered throughout the river chasm.

Filtered light poured in from the cave entrance, but visibility was poor. Reaching for his sword, Ranger realized with dismay it wasn't there. Trapped in an unfamiliar area with a Datsoe lurking in the cave, and perhaps in the mist as well, all he had were the daggers strapped to his sides. Well, he would have to make due with what he had. Drawing out his favorite, he put his back against the rock and tried to assess his surroundings. Shuffling sounds to his right made him turn away from the cave entrance. The kneeling silhouette had Ranger raise the dagger just in case. A long shadow curling toward the slight figure prompted Ranger to call out in warning, but it was too late. Before he could react, the little Datsoe was captured and turned upside down like a Christmas goose. Lunging forward, Ranger never saw the tentacle coming, and found himself dangling next to his once captive Datsoe. Driving his blade into thick black flesh, Ranger took satisfaction in hearing a gurgling cry of pain. Thrust repeatedly into the cave wall, Ranger lost his grip on the dagger, and his senses as his head made solid contact with the rocks.

Losing consciousness, the last thing he felt was the wind rushing by as he was carried into the inky darkness of the caves below.

FallHeart the 70th of

222 D.P - Dusk

If there was a hell outside of the Lake of Abysmal Souls, this surely would have been it. Darkness was the only sight, the only sound, the only feeling.

Finally, Ranger became dimly aware of blue light illuminating the passageway. Traveling through a massive arch, he beheld a ravine that seemed to stretch for miles. The light source appeared to be bioluminescent blue mushrooms that grew in all shapes and sizes. Ranger awed toadstools stretching over fifteen feet tall, casting eerie light over openings that presumably led to every corner of the tainted land. Each stone was being meticulously carved, creating an intricate architecture of terror. Shrieks and calls marked their passage, followed by hordes of Datsoes. Pouring from holes in the walls, creatures of varying proportions and color raced alongside them, sniffing and slapping the guardian.

With his arms pressed against his sides, Ranger was unable to avoid the blows. His head was ringing from hitting the rock, his reflexes were sluggish, and his chances of survival were slim. This didn't prevent him from taking interest in his surroundings, and he quickly came to the conclusion that he was in the heart of the Datsoe's nest.

Pausing on the ceiling of a large cavern, his captor dropped him to the stone surface below. Landing with a grunt, Ranger pushed up to face a crowd of hissing Datsoes.

Long teeth and slobbering jaws snapped threateningly, but none of them moved toward him. The stench was overpowering, making him resist the urge to gag. Slowly, he rose to his feet, trying not to favor his injured leg. Looking over his shoulder, he saw his Datsoe huddling on the cave floor in between looming giants. A metal cuff still hung from his broken arm, connected to a short length of chain. Large Datsoes made a game of stomping on the end of the links, bringing a grimace to the little face every time they made contact. Burgundy eyes filled with fear found his. Clenching his fists, Ranger took a step toward them.

A sticky band wrapped around his wrist, halting his progress. Spinning around, he was unable to avoid another from capturing his free hand. Long tendrils lifted his arms, suspending him from the ceiling so only his toes swept the ground.

An eerie cackle swept over the crowd, mocking him.

Twisting his head, Ranger couldn't tell which of the monstrous beings made the sound. It was almost… human.

"Well, come on then," he spat, "What are you waiting for?!"

A hiss swept through the crowd, as if they weren't prepared for him to be so daring.

Bowing their heads, the Datsoes created a path to allow… *someone,* (yes, Ranger had guessed correctly, it was a human figure), walk through.

A long trench coat, black as the environment around them, shrouded a tall, lean form. The sound of boots echoed across the rocks, silencing the buzzing crowd. Charcoal skin covered a strong jawline free of stubble. Generous lips were parted in a gleaming white smile, revealing razor canines that curved menacingly. Twin horns protruded from a thick mane of ebony hair, spiraling inward like a crown. A glowing, blood red shine emanated from his piercing gaze while he swept Ranger from head to dangling toe.

Click. click, click, his boots carried him in a slow circle around Ranger until they were face to face. "Welcome."

His deep, husky voice was almost musical. Spreading his arms, he twirled for his audience.

"The great Lone Soldier! The only one of six Guardians not bound to watch the most forsaken places on Earth." His brutally handsome face reflected glee at Ranger's shocked expression. "You seem surprised that I know who you are."

"Well," Ranger laughed, dimming the smile on his tormentor's face, "It's nice to know I've done my part to get your attention. I hope I killed something that mattered to you."

Gripping the front of Rangers shirt, red eyes bulging with rage, the leader of Datsoes took a deep breath, then did something no one expected. He burst into peals of laughter. It took a moment for him to gain control, until finally, he gave the Guardian a shove that sent him swaying. "You have courage, I will grant you that. Here you are facing certain death and you dare mock me. I remember having that devotion to a cause once, long ago. A soldier through and through Ranger, I would admire you if I didn't know you for the fool you are."

"You seem to know me so well, who the Juwa are you?"

"You could not pronounce my name, for it is in a different tongue. I seem to remember, ages ago, I had a mortal name. What was it?" Pacing throughout the cave, he

113

thought back, then snapped his fingers. "Of course, now it is clear, how could I have forgotten?" Bowing formally, he gave Ranger a roguish smile.

"**Bardune,** at your service."

Ranger could not hide his surprise. In an effort to become a better hunter, he spent countless hours in the kingdom's library reading ancient scrolls, trying to learn the history of the Datsoe plague. Some mentioned Bardune and his amazing prowess as a soldier, his skill with a blade was unparalleled, his horsemanship unmatched. The chronicles claimed that he led a group of men into the caves to fight against the threat to humanity, dying a hero.

His mind raced. Could it be that the Datsoe attacks had been orchestrated? Clearly these mindless creatures obeyed Bardune, even now he held their bloodlust at bay. How was this possible? What was his angle? Was it all a sick and twisted game to torment the human villages? All this time he thought they were winning the war, but now Ranger realized if Bardune launched an invasion, the Kingdom would be lost. Becoming a Datsoe had clearly driven him insane.

Hearing the rattle of a chain, Bardune's attention was drawn to the group tormenting the small Datsoe. "Oh? What is this?"

"Leave him alone," Ranger snarled.

Surprise flickered in the red irises. Smirking, he stepped around Ranger's swinging body.

"Enough!" Bardune called.

Dropping the chain, Bardune's minions moved away. Reaching down, he pinched the cuff between his fingers, snapping the metal like straw. Watching it fall away from his arm, the little Datsoe looked up in confusion.

114

"Poor fellow, captured and tormented by this disgusting human. But, if I am not mistaken, you used to be one yourself. Tell me, what is your name?"

The little Datsoe's ears fell back, unsure of what to do. It couldn't speak.

"Of course, how silly of me," Bardune tapped his chin. "I forgot the transformation rearranges things like vocal cords. I must tell you; I have seen plenty of humans turn, and it is very rare to retain anything of yourself. I should know!" Turning to Ranger, he gave another beaming smile. "Only the very powerful, or dare I say it, stupid are able to hold on to a sense of themselves. Which are you then, hmm. Let's find out, shall we?"

Jabbing his clawed finger into the little Datsoe's chest, he ignored the pained cries that echoed around the cavern. A red glow, like a fire burning just below the skin's surface, followed his fingertip up the creature's chest, and into its neck.

Fighting against the tethers that bound him, Ranger couldn't help but notice that the tone of the screams changed, becoming more human with each passing moment.

Bardune whisked his hand away, leaving the little Datsoe to catch itself with its good arm, panting and moaning in agony.

Bardune crouched beside his victim and whispered, "what is your name?"

The little Datsoe slowly raised its head and swallowed "My n-name? Isle. My name is Isle."

Closing his eyes, Bardune seemed lost in thought. "It is almost poetic. Isle; just like the isle of dark in which we all reside down here." Pushing up, Bardune studied him as he clutched his neck. "Sorry for the pain, dear boy. I know from experience how unpleasant that is, I had to fix my own much the same way," Bardune tapped a faded scar that matched Isle's.

"But speaking of pain, what is this?" Bardune asked, forcefully pulling on Isle's broken arm.

Isle gasped.

"You know, I might have just the solution for this…" Bardune dropped Isle's arm and stepped back. Tilting his head back, he took a deep breath.

Ranger watched with fascinated horror as Bardune's chest began to glow. With a loud crack, his jaw stretched wider and wider to allow a glowing orb to float past his fangs. The other Datsoes shifted and drooled, whined and groaned. Clearly, this orb was extremely valuable to them.

Bardune raised his hand, and the orb gravitated towards his fingers, floating above his palm. Panting, he pushed his distended jaw back into place, then looked at the shimmering ball of energy reverently.

"I was blessed with the ultimate gift, no wonder her majesty chose me to be her *mate*. I provide her with enough energy to not only survive, but thrive. She will never have to leave the safety of our home again. It can be exhausting; her appetite is insatiable… But, I can spare one." Bardune presented his palm to Isle.

Ranger watched Isle's pupils grow in hunger, much like they had the first time Ranger had offered him meat. Hesitantly, he held his hand out, allowing the orb to melt into his fingers. A loud pop made Isle release a satisfied sigh.

Bardune watched Isle intently and did not miss the fact that he did not fall upon the orb like a slobbering beast. Even now the Datsoes around him barely maintained self-control. The Queen kept them in check, otherwise Bardune would have been torn apart ages ago. This little one was important, he decided. An intelligent ally could be used to his advantage, and much like days of old, he was not above trickery to get what he wanted, even from the Queen of Datsoes. Transformation had not dimmed his thirst for power. This nest was merely the beginning.

"Why are you helping me like this?" Isle asked nervously.

"Because you are one of us! We all face the threat of their savagery." Bardune scooped the fallen chain off of the ground. "Let me guess. This confinement, your arm, the human you stink of." Red eyes glared at Ranger accusingly. "You think you are so superior. Not to mention your quaint little custom of capturing and executing our kind."

Pausing, Bardune let the Datsoes in the room snarl in anger for a moment before continuing. "Then, as my brothers blood dries on your altar of death, you feast. And it is said we are the monsters!" Studying Ranger, he focused on the wrap covering his leg. "What do you say, kid? A limb for a limb?"

Nervously, Ranger tried to push back on his toes, reading dark intentions in Bardune's expression.

Strolling toward the dangling guardian, Bardune ran a finger across Ranger's chest. "A few days ago, you killed my favorite pack of wolves. I was quite put out when the black leader fell." Amusement filled his voice when he noticed Rangers' surprise. "I know everything that happens in these woods, and I must admit, it was impressive." His eyes flicked to Isle, "Even if you did have help."

Isle's ears tilted back, but he remained silent.

Without warning, he grabbed Rangers injured leg, and drove his fist through the splint, cracking the bone in

117

half.

An agonized scream burst from Ranger, making Bardune clap his hands with delight.

Isle's eyes filled with tears as he watched Ranger's head fall back. Clenching his jaw, the Guardian regained control, but was unable to contain his groan when Bardune grabbed the leg again.

"So heroic!" he sang. Snapping his fingers once more, he called "Release him!"

Ranger fell to the ground, hitting his chin against the rocks. Humiliation filled him as he listened to the Datsoe crowd grunt with amusement. He hated being pushed around like someone's toy. Wiping at the blood with his sleeve, Ranger sat up.

"What do you think Ranger? Is it fair that you get to kill my friends and family? You are a murderer and deserve to be punished!" Bardune pulled Ranger to his feet with one hand. Releasing him, he took a step back. "But, I am not without understanding. I remember what it was like to follow orders like a good little soldier." Tapping his chin, he turned his back to the Guardian and spoke to the bloodthirsty crowd. "What do you all think? Should we give him a chance to explain himself?"

Snorts and snarls filled the cavern.

"Oh my, I will take that as a no. But, just so you don't think that chivalry is dead, I will give you one free shot. I mean, what else have you got to lose? Come on, hit me! Humans are the true savages here."

Ranger almost took the offer. A right cross across Bardune's slimy face would have felt great. But as he watched Bardune wave to the crowd, he realized he was putting on a show. If he attacked, he would prove Bardune right. Well, this human wasn't going to humor the leader of the Datsoes.

"No."

Bardune froze, clearly confused. "Excuse me?"

Ranger managed a chuckle. "I said 'No. I won't play your little game."

"You call fighting for your life a *game?*"

"No. But you are trying to make it one. You are using me as a way to, what? Prove your point? Rally your forces for some egotistical gain before a surprise attack? Truly you are so noble."

Isle shifted. During his time with Ranger, he had heard many encouraging conversations, but he had never heard the guardian's tone get so... *dark*. He was hopelessly outnumbered. What did he hope to gain by taunting Bardune?

"You stand here and preach that we are monsters. You seem to know who I am, and what we do from day to day. Then you also know what we go through, what we suffer when your pawns come and attack *us*." Ranger wasn't trying to convince the Datsoes of his innocence, he was simply angry. "As you so *painfully* pointed out, I am a soldier doing my duty. Do you seek approval by attacking a defenseless, injured, old man? If you are going to kill me, *kill me*. But do not stand there and pretend to be some benevolent leader. They may not be able to tell, but even a human child could see you're clearly insane."

Ranger struck a nerve. Bardune flew forward and hit him across the jaw, then drove his knee into Ranger's ribs repeatedly until he heard a satisfying crack. Wrapping his claws around Ranger's neck, he effortlessly lifted him into the air. He regained his humor when Ranger tried to pry his fingers away.

"Defenseless old man huh! Who cares if I give you a sporting chance? All that matters is there will be one less of you to deal with," Bardune hissed. Squeezing slowly, he enjoyed watching Ranger gasp for breath. Only a few more seconds and then…

"Wait! You need him alive!"

Bardune turned his head toward Isle. "What?"

The crowd of Datsoes roared in protest, but a low hiss silenced them.

Slinking from the shadows, a black scaled head spiraled from the top of the cave. Giant, hypnotic eyes rested on Isle with interest. The crowd shrunk away from the enormous head as it was followed by a long, sinuous body that reflected the surrounding blue light.

"Ah, my love, you grace us with your presence." Bardune rested his free hand on the side of her face, which stood as tall as he. She dominated the room, radiating power. With a tap from her claw, he lowered Ranger and released his grip.

Choking and gasping, it took Ranger a moment to focus on the new Datsoe. Clearly, she was ancient. Her scales grew moss that glowed the same color as the mushrooms. Reminding him of tales of dragons, he wondered if this was the Queen.

"Explain yourself Isle," Bardune demanded. "You better have a very, very good reason for speaking in the presence of royalty."

Trying to avoid the Datsoe Queen's intense gaze, Isle bowed with what he hoped seemed respectful. He had heard of her of course, and her frightening power. He spent most of his remembered life trying to avoid her, and now, was face

120

to giant face with her. Could she read his mind? That multicolored, penetrating stare seemed to pierce right through him.

"He is a guardian. The others... I mean, other people... I have seen how they treat him, how they interact. If you keep him alive, maybe offer him as a hostage, the others would surrender guaranteed! Just to make sure he stays alive!"

Ranger felt his blood run cold. Would his friends do that for him? Yes, they would. He knew they would. They would fight until their final breath for him, just as he would for them.

Bardune's anger morphed into interest.

"He is lying." Ranger panted.

"Oh? I don't think he is," Bardune said. "Your pulse just got deliciously quick. Soldier to the end, I would tip my hat to you if I had one." Rubbing the top of the Queen's head, he waited for a moment. "What do you think, My Sweet?"

Staring at Ranger, the Queen saw the same potential she had seen in Bardune. Years of experience had given her an insight on what creatures would serve her best, which would retain their intelligence, and who she should use as disposable pawns. Turning her massive head, her swirling eyes met Bardunes.

Bardune grinned, "Good enough for me. Take him down to one of the pits, he shall remain there until further notice."

Ranger found himself wrapped in sticky bands once more.

Isle watched with a heavy heart as they pulled Ranger across the cave floor. An arm wrapped around his shoulders.

"Dear boy, you and I have a lot to discuss." Bardune said.

Isle tried to smile but was quickly distracted by the Queen's silent retreat to the top of the cave. Where was she going? What were they planning? Where were they taking Ranger?

Bardune cleared his throat, making Isle realize he better pay attention to what could happen to him instead.

FallHeart the 70th of

222 D.P - *Nightfall*

Ranger didn't particularly enjoy bumping along the rocky surface through the dark. Completely bound, he couldn't tell where he was going, or where he had been. The adrenaline rush had more than worn off, leaving him to feel every injury he had sustained. Finally, his Datsoe captor stopped, untied him, and threw him into a dark void. Completely unprepared, Ranger was unable to stop himself from tumbling out of control until he hit the cave floor face first.

He lay still for a minute. Then a minute more. Finally peeling his eyes open, he was met with inky darkness. The air smelled musty, but he didn't hear water trickling nearby. That was a shame, because he was really thirsty. He was so tired, and for the first time in a while, felt his age. Maybe he could rest for a bit.

Drifting in and out of consciousness, his thoughts wandered to Bardune. Surely, he was planning an attack, and WinterNox coming early was the perfect opportunity to strike. Why had Isle told Bardune to use him as a hostage, was he trying to keep him alive? Pain overwhelmed him, and he slipped into a fitful slumber.

Time passed.

Jolting awake, Ranger forgot where he was for a moment. He was freezing, laying face down on unforgiving stone. Longing for the spicy tea Quail used to make made him wonder where she was at this moment. That thought led to another, until Bardune was once again the main topic. The King of Datsoes would use him to hurt Quail and the others. He couldn't allow that.

Curling his hands into fists, he slowly pushed himself up into a sitting position. First things first, he thought. Patting his pockets, he took inventory of what he still had. Matches, a bit of twine, some dried up rose petals (why did he have those?), and a piece of wolf jerky. Not much. Flipping open the heel of his boot, he took out his trusty folded knife. The Datsoes had stripped him of his other blades, but thankfully missed this one.

Lighting a match, he squinted against the harsh light. Taking a moment to adjust, he surveyed his surroundings. He appeared to be at the bottom of a ravine of sorts, with loose soil and rocks stretching up around him. It was a little taller than his head, he knew he could easily climb out, but he needed to do something about his leg first. Holding the tiny flame up, he realized the splint Quail had wrapped around his leg was still there, just broken. Shoving the tip of the match in his mouth, he unwrapped the cotton, spilling the supporting pieces to the ground. Picking them up, he overlapped the edges, placed them against his throbbing leg, then wound the fabric the best he could. It would have to do.

Threatening to burn the tip of his nose, the match went out.

Reluctant to waste another right away, Ranger rolled onto his hands and knee in the dark, then pushed upright, resting his weight on his good foot. Hobbling, he slowly made his way forward with his hands out until he felt the edge of the pit. Taking a deep breath, he pushed his foot into the soil, and began to climb up. He made it over the edge fast enough, but the progress up the slope was agonizing between his ribs and leg. Finally, he found himself panting at the top.

Lighting another match, he saw another long tunnel. Holding the light up higher, he was dismayed to discover a large pair of black eyes, staring at him. A Datsoe guard. He hadn't thought of that. With a flick of its tail, it sent him tumbling down the decline.

Landing on the rocks below, Ranger cursed in several languages. Catching his breath, he sat up.

"Back to the drawing board," he muttered. Now what? That Datsoe guard was a problem.

Remembering the rose petals, he played with an idea. There weren't many, but maybe he could use them as a smoke screen of sorts. Peeling a bit of cotton off of his brace, he used a match to light the fabric, casting a glow around him. Dropping the petals onto a flat rock, he picked up another and began to grind them into a powder. Using his knife, he sliced a pocket off from the inside of his coat. Scooping the dust into the pouch, he cut a bit of twine and wrapped it around the opening of the pocket. Wiping the sweat from his brow, he looked around for inspiration. His knife wouldn't provide him much protection against those brutes.

The cotton burned out, making Ranger sigh with frustration. He had a limited number of matches, no weapons, and was in the heart of a nest. Admitting to himself he had low odds of survival, he gripped the pouch, squared his shoulders, and limped to the wall once again.

He was sure the Datsoe could hear him climbing. It was almost like it was toying with him, waiting until he got to the top, only to knock him back down. Well, it was in for a nasty surprise.

A series of growls and snarls made him pause, unsure of what was happening. Loud popping noises were followed by a heavy thud.

Clinging to a rock, his foot began to slide in the soft dirt beneath him. Gritting his teeth, he pushed up hesitantly.

"The Ranger," a voice whispered.

It was oddly familiar, but not one he recognized. Gripping the pouch tighter, Ranger climbed a bit higher. He had no idea if Datsoes could see in the dark, so he tried to be as stealthy as possible.

"The Ranger! Can you hear me?"

The voice was closer now, making him hesitate. His hand was on the rim of the pit. So close…

Blue light spilled from a tiny mushroom less than a foot away. Squinting, Ranger made out the outline of Isle.

Offering a hand, he waited until Ranger clasped it, then pulled him the rest of the way up. He held the mushroom in one hand, offered his tail with the other.

"We can't risk any light once we leave this chamber." Tucking the mushroom into one of Ranger's pockets, he whispered, "Follow me."

"Wait!"

"We don't have a lot of time."

"Why are you helping me?"

A beat of silence passed before Isle replied. "Because I know you would have come for me if things were reversed. Hang on to my tail and I will lead you out. Let's go."

Shock poured through Ranger. Would he? Isle hadn't crossed his mind during his plan to escape. Guilt immediately followed. Now that his suspicions were confirmed about Isle, and how much of himself he had retained, Ranger SHOULD have considered his rescue instead of being wrapped up in himself. Feeling the tail move, he stepped forward.

Blindly following Isle had its challenges. Limping slowed his progress, making it difficult to keep up. He had no idea where they were and had to place his trust completely in this small creature he had captured and intended to kill. Life was full of irony, he decided.

Bumping into Isle's back, he let out an involuntary exclamation.

An answering growl sounded ahead of them. Realizing it wasn't Isle, Ranger wasn't sure what to do. Unraveling the twine from the pouch of petal dust he had created, he waited.

Feeling Isle's hand on his, he dropped the tail he was holding. He was shoved firmly back a step, and heard a faint "Wait here."

Scratches, snarls and struggling filled the cave. Unable to stand his lack of vision, Ranger pulled the tiny mushroom out of his pocket. It didn't light much, but it was enough for him to make out two combatants. With incredible speed, Isle moved in and out of the mushroom's glow. Jumping, twirling, clawing and biting, he raced around the larger Datsoe. Twin mouths snapped at him, tentacles writhed and snapped, knocking Isle into the cave wall.

Springing forward, Ranger tossed the contents of his makeshift pouch into the enemy's face, spraying it with rose powder. With a cry, it rolled all of its tentacles inward, frantically wiping its many eyes.

Grabbing Ranger's hand, Isle pulled him out of the cavern. Even as injured as he was, the Guardian still used his wits and the tools on hand to get the job done. Isle could not help but admire that. Knowing the overwhelming odds they were up against, escape was forefront on his mind. It wouldn't be long before his handy work was discovered, and the alarm sounded. Bardune would be after them and then there would be no reprieve, no tricks he could use to get away. Years of hiding from the occupants of the nest had taught him which tunnels to take to evade notice, and he used that knowledge now. Ranger was incapable of moving as fast as Isle would like, but as long as they kept quiet, they should be ok. He knew a secret way out, they just had to reach it. His eyes darted to every dark corner of the caves, searching for stray Datsoes. Taking a sharp turn, he led Ranger into a large cavern filled with light. Giant, luminescent mushrooms grew in clusters. He rushed into the heart of a group on the edge of the wall.

Ranger marveled at the inside of the mysterious mushrooms. Each gill seemed to pulse with bright blue veins, creating the now familiar glow. Isle pulled him toward what looked like large roots, and shoved one aside, revealing a passageway. Ducking down, the little Datsoe crawled in. Sticking his head out, he motioned urgently for Ranger to follow.

Awkwardly lowering himself, Ranger crawled in after Isle, dragging his leg. For once he envied Isle's smaller stature, unable to travel through the narrow tunnel with the same ease. Tiny mushrooms lit their way, and he did his best to avoid crushing them. Drenched in sweat, he pushed on, fighting nausea and trying to ignore the pain.

Time seemed to stretch for an eternity, until finally they were able to climb their way up into a large circular cavern. Blinking at the wondrous sight, Ranger beheld a field of multi-colored mushrooms. Like a burst of fireworks, they covered the ceiling and walls. Some glowed, others twinkled, a few even had long tendrils of damp moss that swayed in the air. A waterfall tumbled over large stones, pooling into a small pond. A strange wooden structure stood in the center of the space, resembling a bird's nest.

A low moan had him peel his eyes away from the multihued display. Leaning against the wall, Isle was pulling something sharp from his abdomen. Dropping it to the ground with a clatter, he held his hand over the wound to stem the bleeding.

"Here, let me look at that."

Isle growled at him.

"Come on." Ranger urged. "I cannot help you if you do not let me…"

Black eyes glared at the guardian. Before Ranger could step back, Isle grabbed him. Wincing, Ranger looked down at the claws digging into his arm. He was reluctant to fight Isle, but he was still uncertain about the Datsoe's behavior. Trying to pull away, he realized his muscles were frozen. Sparks started to flow from Isle's fingertips, much like when he fought the giant centipede in the woods. Just like before, his wounds healed, but not without a price. Ranger's eyes rolled back, and he was unconscious before he hit the ground.

FallHeart the 71st of 222

D.P

Something was poking him in the back. Rolling onto his side, pain radiated up his leg. Jarring fully awake, Ranger sat up. Clutching his ribs, he took in his surroundings. The waterfall splashed nearby, reminding him how thirsty he was. Movement above had him look up directly into Isle's burgundy eyes. Hanging upside down, his black hair swept Ranger's forehead.

Lurching back, he realized Isle was hanging from the strange structure.

"Sorry! I didn't mean to startle you! You have been asleep for so long I was starting to worry." Swinging down, Isle crouched beside Ranger.

Gesturing to Isle's side, Ranger leaned against the wood. "That is a handy talent you have, the ability to heal yourself I mean. When did you figure out you could do that?"

"It took me a while," Isle replied, "Sometimes I can control it, sometimes I can't. I'm sorry, I didn't mean to grab you, it's more of a reflex really…"

"Hey," Ranger cut him off. "Do not even worry about it."

Isle stared at him with wonder. "You aren't angry with me?"

"Not at all. I'm ok, and it seems you are too, so all's well. Where are we? I had no idea such a place existed. It is truly beautiful."

"This is my place, I found it a while ago. Despite what Bardune would like to think, it's kill or be killed down here. He doesn't have nearly as much control as he says he does, even with the Queen's influence. I took refuge slipping into places that other Datsoes can't. I followed the sound of running water and discovered this sanctuary. That tunnel leads all the way to the surface, making it much easier to avoid all of those monsters."

The irony of Isle's words filled Ranger with amusement.

Noting his expression, Isle continued. "Hey, I do not like them anymore than you do. Vicious, gluttonous, mindless beasts..." Realizing he was rambling, he trailed off, looking at Ranger sheepishly.

Shifting, Ranger tried to stand up.

"Let me help you!" Leaping to his feet, Isle grabbed Ranger's wrist and pulled a bit too enthusiastically. Ranger started to tumble forward, unable to hold his weight on the broken leg. Swooping in, Isle used his shoulder to steady him. "Where are you trying to go?"

"To that inviting pool of water. Is it safe to drink?"

"I have been drinking out of it for a long time, it should be ok for you too."

Leaning heavily on Isle, Ranger hobbled over to the waterfall and cupped his hands. Drinking until he was satisfied, Ranger felt much better. Leaning against a tall rock, he looked down at Isle. "You know I haven't properly thanked you. I would not be alive if it were not for you, and for that I really am grateful."

"You're welcome. I couldn't let them kill you."

"Why?"

"Why what?"

"Why have you continued to save me? First with the wolves, then repeatedly down here?"

"I don't know, I can't explain it. At first, I was so angry with you for capturing me, then when I heard what the man said about me being a sacrifice, all I cared about was getting away. But you kept those soldiers from hurting me, then gave me food, it confused me. Why were you being so nice to me?"

"Guess I can't really explain that myself, I just felt like you were different."

"Putting yourself between me and the other Datsoe along the bank, even the grumpy woman helped. I couldn't..."

Ranger's bark of laughter interrupted Isle's explanation. "Quail, that's her name. I assume you know mine by now."

"Of course! You are The Ranger."

Laughter threatened again, but Ranger kept himself in check. Extending his hand, he couldn't prevent a wide smile. "Let's shake hands and introduce ourselves like civilized men. I am Ranger. No 'the', just Ranger."

Hesitantly, Isle placed his hand in Rangers. He liked the way Ranger said, 'civilized men,' almost as if he was accepting Isle. Oh, how he longed to be accepted. Then, an awful thought occurred to him.

"Are you afraid of me? I am the very thing you kill."

"I don't want to start our friendship off by lying to you Isle. At first I was, but the more I spend time with you, the better I feel." Squeezing his hand gently, Ranger looked into Isle's eyes. "You have repeatedly shown great courage, and more than that, character. I've seen hardened soldiers flee at the sight of one Datsoe, you held strong in front of many. I am in your debt."

"Oh no! No you're not! Maybe we can call it even?"

"Fair enough." Releasing Isle's hand, Ranger ignored the Datsoe's swimming tears. "Alright Isle, how long will it take us to get back to the surface? I need to get back to my friends, and frankly, I need medical treatment."

"It will take several hours, and I have to warn you, it is a steep climb. I will help you as much as I can, but it will be difficult."

"I see. Well, we should get going as soon as possible."

"Now is a bad time. Datsoe patrols are especially heavy during the night. It would be better to rest, grab a bite to eat, and go at daybreak."

"Good advice, but how can you tell if it's day or night?"

"I've been down here long enough to know," Isle said quietly.

Taking in Isle's somber expression, Ranger decided to follow his advice. "Ok, well, as far as food is concerned, I have this bit of wolf jerky." Reaching into his pocket, he pulled out a dried lump of meat.

"Uh, no offense, but I have a better idea."

Shifting his weight, Ranger winced. "Oh, do you have a secret supply of chicken soup hiding somewhere?"

"No." Looking at Ranger's leg, Isle couldn't help but be concerned. "How bad is it?"

Ranger sighed. "Not great, but I am managing. I need to repair the brace somehow, that will ease some of the pressure."

"I may be able to help with that. What do you need?"

Looking up at the wooden structure, Ranger thought for a moment. "Well, do you have some wood strips about this long?" Holding out his hands, he showed Isle the length he was hoping for.

"Let me see what I've got." Hopping up little platforms that jutted out from the center, he started rooting through his supplies.

Looking up, Ranger called "What is this thing anyway? Did you build it?"

Peaking over the edge, Isle grinned. "I did! I sleep up here. In case any Datsoe were to make its way in, I have an escape plan, see?" Reaching up, Isle clung to some of the mushrooms hanging from the ceiling. Crawling swiftly, he made his way toward another tunnel Ranger hadn't noticed before.

"Very clever."

"Down here, you always need a plan." Crawling back, Isle pulled out two planks and returned to Ranger's side.

Sitting on a boulder, Ranger unwrapped his makeshift brace. Removing the broken pieces, he revealed dark, bruised flesh. "Ouch!" he spat, "what I wouldn't give for some *Taogwonnzl.*"

"What's that?"

"Painkiller. There are many kinds, but any would be nice."

Isle looked around at the ceiling for a moment. "Hmm. I have spent a lot of time trying all of the mushrooms, one of them may help." Walking over to a patch of multicolored fungus, he carefully selected one with a purple hue. Presenting it to Ranger, he continued. "I have been in plenty of fights, over time I realized these definitely help when I was really hurt."

Taking the mushroom, Ranger briefly touched Isle's arm. "I am sorry you have had to face all of this alone. I admire your courage Isle."

Clenching his fingers, Isle wasn't sure what to say. He couldn't remember a time when he ever had someone simply be kind to him. Using a claw, he sliced open the top of the mushroom.

"Beware, it tastes pretty bad." Isle murmured.

Lifting it to his lips, Ranger took a small bite. "Ug, it reminds me of moss and uncooked garlic."

"I warned you! Just gulp it down."

Scooping water into his palm, Ranger used it to chase the awful flavor down. "How long until it takes effect?"

"Oh, pretty much right away. It is very powerful."

No sooner were the words spoken, Ranger started to feel the pain recede.

Watching the color come back to Ranger's face, Isle swished his tail. "Better?"

"Much, thank you."

"The best part is it lasts for *hours.*"

"That is terrific. Let me get myself wrapped up once more and then we can share this mighty feast." Patting his pocket with the wolf jerky he wiggled his eyebrows.

With a snort Isle shook his head. "Pass. Like I said, I have something better. You wrap yourself up and I will grab something for us."

Watching Isle walk over to the wall again, he watched him pluck more mushrooms, but this time they were green. He sincerely hoped they were better than the purple one! Immediately, he reminded himself he was lucky. Living off of the land, he had learned to take what he could get, and be grateful for it. Focusing on his task, he created a new brace, wrapped it, and pushed up from the boulder.

"These are actually pretty good," Isle handed Ranger a bright green mushroom about the size of a grapefruit. Biting into his, Isle ate the fleshy exterior then tipped it to take a drink of the fluid sloshing around the stem.

Ranger looked at his own, then with a shrug, sank his teeth into the top. He immediately regretted taking such a big bite.

"Woah! That's just like a lemon!"

"What's a lemon?" Isle asked.

"A lemon is a fruit, smaller than this," Ranger waved the mushroom. "But it's yellow instead of green... and not as glowy. But it tastes exactly the same."

"I guess there is a lot I need to learn about." Isle shuffled his feet. "I appreciate you being patient with me."

"You have a lot of wonderful things ahead of you Isle, but first let's get out of here alive." With a yawn, Ranger stretched.

"I could use some rest first," Isle admitted.

"I probably could too."

"I am going to sleep up there, do you want help climbing up?"

"I'm good here, thanks. It's close to the water, and my leg is feeling pretty good right now. I should save my energy for the journey to the surface."

"Alright."

Ranger watched Isle scurry up to the top of his structure, then heard him shuffling around. Removing his coat, he laid on it and tried to get comfortable. A wooden block came tumbling down, landing a few inches in front of him. Curious, Ranger picked it up and studied it. A flower had been whittled into the center. The craftsmanship and skill clearly indicated it had taken hours to create such an intricate design.

"Hey Isle? Where did you get this?"

Leaning over the edge of the platform, Isle looked at what Ranger was holding. "Oh, uh, I made it."

"It is wonderful, I haven't seen a flower quite like this before, where did you come up with the design?"

"Honestly," Isle whispered, "I don't know." After a moment he continued. "I have a lot more, would you like to see them?"

"I would, thank you."

Isle's head disappeared for a moment, then he hopped down with a handful of blocks in his hands. Pouring them onto the ground, he remained silent while Ranger studied each piece.

Ranger examined each piece with wonder. A royal emblem, star, tree, a human hand… had all been carved with incredible detail. The one that drew his attention the most was a ship. He could almost hear the sails catching the wind and the waves splashing against the hull.

"These are truly impressive Isle. Have you seen all of these things?"

"Not all of them. Sometimes images just pop into my head and I feel like I have to carve them, or I will go crazy. I can't really explain it but I'm glad you like them."

"I like them very much. Do you mind if I keep one?"

"Really? Of course, that would be great!"

Tucking the ship into his pocket, Ranger smiled at Isle's beaming expression. "Thank you, I will cherish it. Let's get some rest."

Scooping up the remaining blocks, Isle went back

into his bed and quickly went to sleep.

Ranger's thoughts drifted until he too found his rest.

Jolting awake, Ranger looked around disoriented. He wasn't sure why, but he was on edge. Pushing up, he looked around the glowing cave. A cry above him had him on his feet.

"Isle?"

A muffled moan had him climbing painfully up the tower with concern. Had a Datsoe climbed down from the cave Isle planned to use as an escape? Pushing himself over the edge, he saw Isle curled up in the center of what appeared to be a nest. Bits of fabric, bones, and dried grass littered the space, but the thing that drew Ranger's attention were the blocks. It seemed that hundreds lay scattered about, all carved with different pictures. How long had he been down here?

Isle jerked violently, digging his claws into the wood below him. Panting and struggling, his Datsoe began to cry.

"Hey, Isle. Isle wake up." Ranger shook Isle's shoulder. "Can you hear me? You're asleep, you need to wake up!"

Obviously, Isle was having a nightmare, but Ranger couldn't tell what about. Isle started to scream; "No. No!"

His hands flew to his side, clutching the crescent shaped silver scars. Waking with a final shout, Isle lashed out at Ranger, who caught his fist in his palm.

"Hey, it's ok, you are ok."

Focusing on Ranger's face, he could clearly read the concern in the guardian's eyes.

"You alright?" Ranger whispered.

Pulling his fist out of Ranger's hand, he unclenched

140

his fingers. Avoiding Ranger's searching gaze, he pulled his knees into his chest.

An awkward silence fell between them.

"Sorry." Isle finally muttered.

"For what? Having a nightmare? That is nothing to apologize for, everyone has them."

"The same one? Over and over?" Isle's voice cracked with emotion.

Unsure of what to say, Ranger went with instinct, placing his hand on Isle's trembling shoulder.

"I have the same dream almost every night," Isle started, "I was hoping this time would be different, that you wouldn't see…"

"Why would you not want me to see? There is nothing at this point that could surprise me. If you're embarrassed or afraid of what I might think…"

"And what if I am?" Isle's burgundy eyes welled once more, making him frantically wipe away the tears.

"Isle, you've done nothing but help me. Why would I judge you for having a bad dream?" Patting his shoulder a final time, Ranger leaned back. "Everyone has nightmares, even me."

"But you're a hero, a warrior."

Ranger chuckled. "I am still human, you know. I've seen things that would make any man's hair stand on end. It comes back sometimes when you least expect it. When it does, I don't have to worry." With a wink he added, "The benefits of living alone."

Isle's ears fell back with confusion. Ranger was alone? "But, what about the others you were traveling with?"

"They're just friends. In fact, this is the first time in

years we have all been together. Isle, if you don't want to talk about it, you don't have to. Just know that someone is here if you need to." Ranger shifted, wincing. One of those purple mushrooms would come in handy right now. Searching the cave's ceiling, he contemplated asking Isle to get one for him.

"It's a golden field."

Ranger looked back at Isle, noting one of his hands rested over his scars.

"It starts with a beautiful golden field. Nothing definite or clear, just tall yellow grass, a bright sun. I think I'm running through it. Maybe… echoes of laughter and calls. But the feeling changes. There's screams and a dark shadow. It ends every time with a shapeless black mass walking out from around some sort of wall. Bright red eyes… before it... I can't see..." Isle trailed off, the knuckles on his side white. "It has occurred to me that maybe it's not a dream or a nightmare, but rather…"

"A memory," Ranger completed his thought.

"I remember waking up on the sides of a riverbank, already a Datsoe. There's nothing of a life I had, if I ever had one. I've always been a Datsoe. This bad dream is the one thing that tells me that I may not be like… them. I know I have flaws; I've killed to survive and I'm not always in control, but I don't think I'm like them," he trailed off again, wiping his eyes. "I can't be. Is it stupid to say I feel different? I know I'm not really, but when I saw you for the first time, talking to that woman… *you* seemed different to me. You were so encouraging and so nice to everyone, even me. Out of everything I've seen and come to know, humans are killers of my kind. I've been through villages, keeping to the shadows, watching. People always try to hurt me, throw things, yell obscenities, but not you." Looking at Ranger directly, his voice grew ragged. "I've always wanted someone to see me as Isle, not a monster. I don't want to be a monster!" Expressing raw emotion, Isle turned away in shame.

Without hesitation, Ranger wrapped his arms around Isle and held him close. Isle may be a Datsoe, but he was also a lost, heartbroken young man. Adrift in his foggy existence of trying to understand what he was and how to survive, he spent years trying to figure out if he had been or could be anything more. Ranger realized that he could trust Isle, and more, he was someone worth saving.

How? He had never considered himself to be a father, even all the years he spent guiding Quail was more as a student than a child. He had no idea how old Isle had been at his death, but he seemed younger than Quail had been when he took her in. He never expected to live for as long as he had, cheating death over and over again. Each time he came within an inch of his life, there were the inevitable what ifs. What if he had gotten married? What if he had a child? What kind of father would he have been? He had no memory of his own father, so had little to draw from.

What he did know was that Isle was lonely. Personally, he had felt a hole of sorts ever since Quail left to become a guardian. There was always the chance that Isle could lose control, maybe even hurt him, but he was willing to take that risk. Hopefully he had enough power and influence across the kingdom to proceed with the plan forming in his mind. But, he would need to start with the other Guardians.

"You know." Ranger began, "I've never really had anyone either. A big part of that is my fault, I shut people out. Having all of my friends together like this has been eye-opening."

Isle pulled away, turning to look at Ranger somberly.

"I kind of get the impression that you and Bardune aren't exactly the best of friends."

Isle snorted, and with a smirk, Ranger continued. "I was wondering, maybe you would like to help an old man out, and travel with me? I could train you, teach you, we could be partners."

Isle's jaw dropped.

"It might take a while, even bring some hardships on the both of us, but together, we can figure out a long-term plan." Ranger smiled.

"Do you really mean that?" Isle asked. His heart was pounding, his mind filled with possibilities. No more darkness, scrounging for food, and best of all, no more empty days with no one to talk to.

"Of course I mean it." Ranger said, leaning back. "Would I suggest it if I didn't mean it? Besides, who better to partner with than a strong, fast, 'innocent' creature of destruction?"

Partner. Isle liked that word. It sounded almost like a promise. Ranger nudged Isle's shoulder.

"What do you think?"

"I think, yes! Most definitely yes."

"Come on, then. Let's take our first step on getting out of here." Standing, Ranger extended his hand.

Isle took it, letting Ranger pull him up.

"Will you need any of this?" Ranger asked, gesturing to the wood blocks in Isle's nest.

"I won't be needing them anymore."

Climbing down, Ranger asked Isle to gather some

mushrooms for light, food and medicine. Tucking them into various pockets, Ranger grabbed a long branch to use as a cane, and with a final glance toward their temporary oasis, they headed into the tunnels.

Isle led Ranger quietly through dark passages that got narrower as time went on. The twists and turns seemed to last for an eternity, both straining to hear the slightest sound. A couple of times Isle would hold up his hand, signaling for Ranger to hold still. Since Isle's hearing was much better, Ranger never hesitated to follow his directions.

Exhausted, Ranger wanted to ask how much further, but pride had him push himself along. Finally, Isle pointed toward a small crevice.

"We are almost there." Isle said. "But we must pass through the Devil's eye."

"Oh that's encouraging." Ranger muttered.

"It is a tight squeeze, but I will help you."

Crawling in first, Isle all but dragged Ranger through a narrow tunnel that made them both claustrophobic. Yellow light encouraged them to crawl faster, until a burst of fresh air washed over their sweaty forms.

Blades of grass tickled Rangers fingers as he pulled himself to the surface. The smell of fresh pine made him want to hug a tree, and he realized how lucky he was to be alive. Rolling onto his back, he stared up through the tree canopy at the most beautiful blue sky he had ever seen.

Isle sat beside him, searching their surroundings.

"What a fantastic day. Just look at those clouds Isle. Have you ever seen anything so wonderful?"

Glancing down, Isle couldn't miss the lines of exhaustion that marked Ranger's face. But a genuine smile greeted him.

"I hate to dim your enthusiasm, but we are still in danger. They can track our scent, so we need to keep moving."

Rolling over, Ranger pushed himself up with the help of his cane. "You are right, but these might help." Hobbling over to the base of a tree, he dug his hands into the dirt, pulling out a handful of small, gnarled, brown blobs. "This" he said, "Is garlic root." Taking a bite, he crunched noisily.

Isle pinched his nose. "Man, that stuff stinks!" he exclaimed.

"Well, the truth is, it isn't usually harvested to eat plain. But, if you think it is strong, the other Datsoes will too. Hopefully, it will mask our scent." Ranger took out his knife, and began slicing the roots, exposing a milky fluid. "Rub this on yourself."

Isle looked at the roots with disdain, then reluctantly plucked one out of Ranger's palm.

While Isle worked with the root, Ranger realized he had no idea where they were, let alone how to find his friends.

"Hey Isle."

"Hmm?"

"Can you track things? Like an animal?"

Isle hopped onto a branch, rubbing the dreaded root over his feet. Maybe that would be enough to mask his scent, and he wouldn't have to suffer the stench as much. "Well, you're looking at the best talking, tracking Datsoe this side of the death fields."

"Death fields?"

"Sure! Datsoe's can't pass over your miles of stinking flowers. I've seen them try, but they always drop dead into the foliage before they get too far. So, I dubbed it the death field."

"You can't fly, how do you keep getting across?"

"Um… the details are not important. Why'd you ask me if I can track?" Isle stuttered.

Realizing it might be a while before Isle fully trusted him, Ranger let it go. "I was wondering if you can track my friends down."

"Ranger, are you sure they're even still in the forest? I mean, they could be out by now. Or, they could be…"

"No." Ranger cut him off. "They are some of the most stubborn-headed people on the planet. They wouldn't give up that easily."

"Alright." Isle sighed. "Let me see what I can do."

FallHeart the 72nd of

222 D.P

Dusk brought a sky stained with reds, oranges, and yellows, creating a backdrop worthy of a painting. Unfortunately, the group below couldn't see any of it. The dark, dense trees and fog blocked any source of positivity. After repeated Datsoe attacks, the Guardians had lost the trail, and now found themselves traveling across the forest without direction. Their horses were gone, and all that remained of their supplies had been distributed evenly. Exhausted and filthy, they mourned a friend they believed to be lost forever.

Ranger's sword was sheathed across Quail's back. Everyone agreed she deserved to keep it since she was the closest thing to family Ranger had. When they arrived at the Palace (if they arrived) it would be taken up with the Queen to decide who should go through his office. Sporting a bandage on her arm and another across her eyebrow, her thoughts raged. Curse Ranger anyhow! Who did he think he was, dying like that? All for a stupid little soulless creature that would have killed him on the spot. Didn't he know he had a responsibility to the team? To her? Now she wouldn't have the chance to tell him all the things she had bottled up for years. That was how their relationship had been, those unspoken words forever passing between them. Did he even know she loved him? He had taken on the role of her father since the moment he found her, broken and bleeding…

As the night began to fall over the land, Quail stopped under a large tree. For whatever reason, the others voted her the new leader, much to her dismay. Looking back, she studied the grim little group.

Leeon took a swig of tepid water swirling in the bottom of his canteen. Marco sat on a rotting log, digging through his bag, no doubt for more of that disgusting jerky. Cliff pretended to scan the area, but she knew he was trying to hide that he was weeping again. Poor Cliff, he always wore his heart on his sleeve.

"I suppose another conversation needs to be had about what we should do for camp." Marco said gruffly.

Leeon and Cliff gave him a side glance.

"No more fires. We don't need everything in these woods zeroing in on us again." Cliff murmured.

"How about we get up into the tree? At least we'd be off the ground." Marco suggested.

"Ug! Again with that one," Quail snapped. "It was that genius idea that got our horses and half our supplies eaten!"

"Well, I don't hear you giving any ideas," Marco shouted. "We never should have let Ranger talk us into this! At least then we might have still had a chance."

Quail snapped. Whipping around, she had her dagger pressed to Marco's throat before any of them could blink. Tear-filled rage blinded her to the fact that the grief on his face mirrored her own. "Don't ever speak of him that way again."

"Hey!" Leeon put his hand on her shoulder. "None of us, not even Ranger, could have predicted this. We all knew the risks."

Marco let out a sigh of relief when she moved the

blade away. Aiming an accusing stare at Cliff, she snarled, "Well, maybe if you had grabbed him before he fell we wouldn't be in this mess."

"What are you accusing me of? I'd like to see you crawl across a bridge that's being blown to bits by a Datsoe, THEN YOU CAN TALK," Cliff yelled.

"If Ranger were here…" Marco began.

"If Ranger were here," Leeon cut him off, "He would be shaking his head and laughing at us. Then you know what he'd say? He'd tell us to pull our heads out of our asses."

Marco cleared his throat. "He wouldn't want us fighting amongst ourselves. Like it or not, Ranger was our peacekeeper, and was always able to find light when it was the darkest. But now that he's gone…"

"It's our turn to take a stand, to prove to ourselves what Guardians really are. Ranger was right to trust that we'd be able to handle whatever this place threw at us. If we work together," Leeon's eyes flashed, "We can make it out of here alive. This forest isn't endless. No matter which way we go we'll make it out. We all want vengeance, and to pay proper respects to Ranger's memory, but we can't do that if we're stuck here. So, let's prove to all those Datsoe bastards what we're willing to do."

"Aye! Leeon's right!" Marco said. "What are we? A bunch of cowards? Or bloodthirsty killers that hunt these creatures year 'round?"

"Bloodthirsty might be a bit much," Leeon muttered.

"Bah! You know what I mean!" Marco snapped, waving his hand. "If we all work together, then we can get outta here, just like Leeon said! Sticking his hand out, he looked at Cliff. "For Ranger."

"For Ranger," Cliff mimicked, placing his hand on

151

top of Marco's.

"For Ranger," Leeon agreed, placing his palm on top of Cliff's.

They all turned to Quail.

Her hair concealed the emotion in her eyes. Sheathing her dagger, she completed the stack with her hand. "For Ranger."

"Aye, there we go. I suppose if we can survive each other, we can survive anything," Cliff chuckled.

Leeon sighed. Even in death, it seemed Ranger still had the ability to bring them together. For the first time in days there was a sliver of much needed peace. He wondered for a moment if he should tell the others about his planned retirement but decided against it. Maybe after we get out of here, he decided, then prayed they wouldn't lose anyone else.

Little did he know Quail's thoughts ran a similar course. Climbing onto a set of boulders, she took first watch. Settling, she swung her feet over the edge and thought about their conversation. She cared for the others even though she often disagreed with them. They were a part of her team, and she dreaded the thought of losing one of them. Sure, they made her crazy, they were ridiculous and loud, but she'd give her life for them. Had it really taken Ranger's death to make her realize this? Studying the trees, she half hoped he'd come walking out of the woods saying something snarky like the old days. He always told the worst jokes! What was that one he loved so much?

A light in the distance broke her concentration. "Hey! Which one of you idiots lit a torch? I thought we agreed not to use them because they could give away our position!" Another light appeared, then another. "Leeon! Get up here! Something weird is going on."

Leeon scrambled up the rocks next to her and followed her gaze. Orbs seemed to be weaving in and out of the brush, but they were low to the ground.

"Search party?" Quail asked. "Are we closer to the trail than we thought?"

"No," Leeon said, catching a glimpse of the light source. "A new threat."

Datsoes they hadn't seen before caught their scent. Creeping through the trees, luminescent holes covering their backs cast an erie, orange light. Swarming around the Guardians, they snapped and snarled. Resembling skeletal coyotes, the furless forms licked their chops, delighted with this unexpected meal opportunity.

"Oh joy," Marco sighed, lifting his ax.

The pack attacked in unison.

"Why do there have to be so many of these stupid things?" Marco grumbled, cleaving the first attacker's skull.

"Don't know..." Cliff beheaded two at once, spraying Quail with silver blood.

She chose to use Ranger's sword, it made her feel more confident. Swinging the razor-sharp blade, she cut through several more beasts, but they kept coming.

Leeon had run out of arrows ages ago, but he was quite capable of using his bow as a weapon. Swinging the wood, he knocked a Datsoe back, making it yelp.

Slowly, the pack pushed them back until they were under a large pine tree, fighting for their lives. Exhaustion and hunger had taken a toll, and the Guardians were losing.

A long, drawn-out whistle echoed around them, drawing the pack's attention. Dark shadows stood a few yards away.

"Hey! Your boss is looking for us, not them! Come

153

and get us!"

Quail glanced at Cliff questioningly. He shrugged; it wasn't a voice he recognized.

The Datsoes reacted immediately, forgetting their prey. The Guardians watched the pack bound toward two forms running through the brush.

"Up! Up! Go!" A different voice shouted, making Quails' jaw drop. Surely, she was mistaken? Rushing after the pack, she sliced through the hindquarters of a retreating Datsoe, making it turn on her with a snarl. She dispatched it quickly.

Following her lead, the men attacked, dividing the confused Datsoes.

"NOW!"

A slight figure burst out of a tree, rolling into the group of beasts. Fangs and teeth drew blood. Death cries filled the air, until finally, the last Datsoe fell.

Panting, Quail wiped the blood from Ranger's sword.

"Birdie, I believe that belongs to me."

Walking into the moonlight, Ranger held out his hand.

Dropping the sword, Quail barely kept from tripping over it as she flew into his arms.

With a muffled "Oof!" Ranger dropped his chin onto the top of her head, ignoring the pain in his ribs as she squeezed the breath out of him.

Her words were muffled against his torn coat, but he understood her. "You were dead. There were so many things that I didn't get to tell you, and I've been so angry with you." Pulling away, she grabbed him. "Don't you ever do that again Ranger! I won't allow it! You can't, I didn't..."

"Easy now, it's ok. I'm alright."

He was anything but alright. Taking in his ragged appearance, Quail winced. He was filthy, but that was the least of it. She had never seen him this worn down.

"You are a sight for sore eyes." Cliff moved to embrace Ranger.

It was like a dam burst. Talking over one another, they surrounded Ranger, asking questions, telling him what happened, and trying to embrace him. No one noticed the slight figure leaning against a tree, shrouded in shadow.

"Geez you look terrible," Marco said.

"Yes, well, it would have been a lot worse if not for Isle..." Ranger gestured toward the tree where Isle stood. His burgundy eyes seemed to glow as he stared at them.

With a gasp, Marco raised his ax. Cliff stepped in front of Ranger defensively, raising his sword. Leeon and Quail stood silent, neither surprised by this turn of events.

"Ah, Ranger you're too kind! Although, I must admit, it might not have been the best idea to piss Bardune off the way you did," Isle said with a bow.

Placing his hand on Cliff's shoulder, Ranger stepped around him and walked to Isle's side.

"Now tell me, who's the best tracker this side of the death fields?" Isle knew he would have to tread carefully. He may have gained Ranger's trust, but his friends were of a completely different mindset.

"You definitely proved yourself, it could not have been easy to find them. I'm grateful," Ranger replied.

Isle smiled. "Of course. Besides, that one wasn't hard to find... his stench could reach the clouds," he gestured to Marco.

Marco stared, taken aback by being insulted by a

Datsoe.

"Ranger." Marco barked. "Explain please."

"Yes, how is it… why is it..." Cliff stuttered.

"It can talk?" Leeon exclaimed, "Could it the entire time?"

"I have so much to tell you, but we can't stay here. Datsoes are searching for us, and they have a leader more dangerous than anything we could have imagined. Getting to the Palace and speaking to the Queen has to be our number one priority. This is so much bigger than WinterNox arriving early."

"Surely you don't plan on marching into the castle with that thing, do you?" Quail demanded, pointing at Isle.

"I plan on doing exactly that. Isle has shown me that not only are some Datsoe's intelligent, but they are capable of much more than we ever realized. Believe me when I say we are very lucky to have him on our side." Pointing to Marco's hand, he continued. "Ease your hold on the ax, my friend. He is not our enemy."

"I have heard rumors of Datsoes having the power to control minds. You have been drawn to this creature since the start, Ranger." Cliff glared at Isle. "What if this is some trick? How do we know it can be trusted?"

"Do I seem irrational to you? He speaks, you see it for yourself. I am alive, because of him! Even now, he doesn't attack. What more do you need?" Ranger argued.

"It is a Datsoe, Ranger! If they are as intelligent as you say, maybe this is some elaborate scheme," Cliff replied.

"If I may," Quail broke the tense silence. Walking to Isle, she stared into his eyes.

Shifting uncomfortably, he held her gaze.

"I have been watching Ranger since the beginning

too. You didn't see them on the riverbank, helping each other, protecting each other, but I did. I wouldn't have believed it if I hadn't seen it with my own eyes. I can't explain this creature's behavior any more than you, but I know Ranger. If he says," she hesitated, almost choking on the next word, "*Isle* can be trusted, I am willing to give it a chance."

Isle's ears tilted toward Quail, and he offered her a hesitant smile.

Leaning closer, a breath separated their faces. "Understand this, I will continue to watch. If I think, even for a second, you intend to do him, or any of these men harm, I will kill you without hesitation. Any questions, *Isle*?"

"Quail…" Ranger began.

Ears dropping back, Isle gulped. "It's ok Ranger, really. No Ma'am, I understand."

With a grunt, Quail stepped back, unsure how she felt about being called 'Ma'am' by a Datsoe.

Pressing his lips together, Leeon did his best to hide his amusement. Leave it to Ranger to return from the dead and ask them to trust a beast of destruction. Much like Quail, he had every intention of watching the situation carefully. He didn't buy into mind control the way Cliff did, but he had to admit this was odd.

"Right." Isle said suddenly, "Now that I'm not about to become a kabob, let's focus on leaving, shall we?"

Marco snorted, then tried to cover his laughter with a cough. Datsoe's making a joke, what was next?

"Well, I have no clue where we are, and couldn't even begin to try to make sense of which way to go. Do you think you could lead us out of here, Isle?" Ranger asked.

Scanning the Guardians' faces, Isle chose to ignore

157

their scowls and focused on Ranger instead. "No problem. I know these woods pretty well. The tricky part will be avoiding Bardune's scouts. I also know of a river nearby, it may help to uh, wash away some of your scent." Glancing at Marco meaningfully, he missed Ranger's broad smile.

"What's a Bardune?" Marco asked.

FallHeart the 72nd of

222 D.P - *Nightfall*

True to his word, Isle led them to a raging river. Filling their canteens with water, everyone took the time to bathe and refresh themselves. Despite Ranger's confidence in Isle, someone was always close by, watching the pair. Sharing the tart mushrooms with his friends, Ranger made sure they were divided evenly, along with the rest of the wolf jerky.

Casting a glance at the darkened sky, Isle suggested they begin their journey. Over the next few hours, they hiked in awkward silence. Ranger placed himself between Isle and his friends, hoping that his presence would shield the Datsoe from the hostility emanating from the group. He had given each of his friends a piece of the garlic root, explaining the benefits and encouraging them to mask their scent.

Coming to a clearing, Isle suggested they wait while he slipped away. Returning with a small deer, they created a temporary camp. Isle dug a pit deep into the ground, and they lit a very small fire to cook the meat. They exchanged stories while they ate.

Bardune was the main topic.

"The history books must have it all wrong," Cliff grumbled.

"Indeed. I don't think he went to stop the plague, but rather, had a hand in creating it," Ranger replied.

"If that's the case, why hasn't he made his presence

known? Clearly, he is a narcissistic lunatic," Leeon said.

Turning to Isle, Quail tried to maintain a neutral expression as she watched him eat an entire deer leg, right down to the hoof. Clearing her throat, she captured his attention. "What do you know of Bardune? When does he plan to attack? Why hasn't he yet?"

Wiping grease from his hand self-consciously, Isle hesitated. "We didn't exactly travel in the same circles. I knew who he was, so I spent most of my time trying to avoid him."

"He is the reason Isle is able to speak now. Who knows what else he is capable of," Ranger mused.

"That light thing he did was really bizarre. It healed me in an instant. I can see why he holds such power over the others. If the Datsoe Queen is depending on him as an energy source, no wonder they obey him." Isle looked at Ranger. "After they took you away, he wanted to talk, press me for information, see what I knew. The Datsoe Queen wasn't part of that. I wouldn't be surprised if he has plans that don't include her."

"What did you tell him?" Marco demanded. Realizing that Isle had been in his city made him nervous. He had seen things no other Datsoe had been privy to.

Isle shrugged. "I told him I was unconscious most of the time. My injuries gave credence to that, so he seemed to believe me. I tried to tell him enough to satisfy his curiosity, but I'm guessing he looked at me as another useless pawn. I wasn't with him for very long, then I came to find you, Ranger."

"You were very brave Isle," Ranger praised. "After he gave you the ability to speak, and healed your arm, you saw through him and his intentions. I am proud of you."

Beaming with delight, Isle missed Quail's dark expression. Looking at the sky, he stood. "You should all get some sleep. We will want to move out at dawn and travel as quickly as we can. I am guessing Bardune will send out as many scouts as possible."

"Wouldn't it be safer to find a place to hide?" Leeon asked nervously. "If the woods will be filled with Datsoes…"

"The trick is to do the unexpected. Trust me, I have been avoiding those idiots for years. They will be searching for a concentration of your scents, a fire, and will be out hunting for food themselves. This is the best way. Rest. I will watch over you, and let you know when it is time to go."

"I know I could use some sleep, thank you Isle. Quail, would you be willing to wrap my brace again? I haven't done a very good job of it." Pushing up, Ranger hobbled over to a tall rock and leaned against it.

Pulling fresh material from her pack, Quail joined him. Kneeling, she began unwrapping the old splint.

"Ranger, this looks much worse than before."

"That's because it is. Bardune, shall we say, wanted to make a point. It is completely broken."

"By Juwa Ranger! After all that has happened, being in the nest with all those monsters, how can you say you trust Isle? Have you lost your mind?" Jerking angrily on the material, she made Ranger wince. "It's not that I'm not appreciative of what he's done for you. What he's doing for us… but you can't just expect us to follow him so easily. Surely you can understand."

"No, I get it, but you said yourself he is different. He has saved my life so many times these past few days… but it is more than that. He is a scared kid doing the best he can with what he's been given."

"Datsoe, Ranger. Not a kid. Don't fool yourself."

"I guess we'll just have to agree to disagree Quail. He needs someone, and maybe, so do I. I am thinking about speaking to the Queen about making him my travel companion, adopting him."

"Adopting him?" Thunderstruck, Quail stared at Ranger.

"I can't be out here forever, Quail. Like it or not, I'm not as young as I pretend to be. He is fast, powerful, and makes a worthy ally. But it's more than that. I genuinely like him. He's a good person. Eventually, I am going to have to retire. Imagine what an amazing warrior he can become. He could be instrumental in defeating the Datsoes permanently!"

"I don't know how to respond to this. I know you have a special relationship with the Queen, but even she won't agree to this foolishness." Standing, she gathered her materials. "I've done the best I can with your leg. You need professional medical attention. Rest will probably do you good, I will also watch over you, and *it*."

"Him Quail, him."

"Agree to disagree, Ranger," she spat.

With a sigh, Ranger watched Quail stomp away. She always did have a temper and hated Datsoes with good reason. Getting her to see things his way would take time, but he knew she would come around. At least she agreed to let Isle lead them out of the forest, which was a start.

Surprisingly, the group had no problem sleeping in the middle of the day. Each was convinced they would never allow themselves to drop their guard with the Datsoe, but exhaustion won over caution.

163

One by one Isle watched them slide into slumber, until even Quail's head drooped. He had overheard every word of her conversation with Ranger and couldn't contain his excitement. Ranger was considering adopting him? Even Quail's reaction couldn't dim his happiness. He had no memory of a family before. All he knew was darkness. Learning to fight like a guardian! How amazing would that be? Having a travel companion, someone to talk to, someone who actually saw him! Daydreaming about his future, Isle watched the sun cross the sky.

Finally, he hopped down from his perch, and slipped across the camp to Ranger. Shaking him awake, he waited until the Guardian was alert, then made his way to the deer to harvest the remaining meat. Ears twitching, he listened to the conversations swirling around him. No one spoke to him, instead they all avoided him as much as possible, even when he tried to give them the rest of the deer. Finally, Ranger took it, dividing it up so each could carry some.

Packing their gear quickly, they doused the smoldering fire, and let Isle take the lead. Ranger fell in step beside him, so Isle shortened his stride to accommodate his new friend's limp. Despite their pace, a noticeable gap formed between the pair and the group behind them.

"Your friends don't like me, do they?" Isle asked. "I guess I wouldn't like me either."

"I know it is difficult, but try to understand, Isle. We have been trained to hate you; it makes us better warriors. Many of us have suffered losses, like Quail. Her family was slaughtered by Datsoes." Noting Isle's expression, he rushed to reassure him. "Obviously she realizes you had nothing to do with that."

"Does she?"

164

"Unfortunately, they see what you are, not who you are. They haven't had a chance to appreciate what kind of person you are, but they will. Just give me time to convince them."

"Ranger, I don't want you to jeopardize your friendships because of me. If they don't like what I am, then so be it. I already have you."

"Isle…"

"I appreciate you trying to get them to like me, but truth is, Ranger, I don't even know if I want them to."

"Really? Why?"

"I want to live in your world, and I thought that being accepted by the other Guardians would be a good start; but now I realize how difficult the idea is. I can smell their fear, anger, and I guess, that bothers me. If I make one wrong move, that's it! I know what I am, so my feelings need to be set aside. The best gift I could ask for is having you in my life, but they may have a problem with that. They are probably wondering why you would choose to travel with me, instead of Quail or Leeon or…" Isle looked at Ranger questioningly.

"I have a bit of a problem letting people in. It's more of a reflex I suppose. I had problems in my youth that I'd rather not go into." Ranger trailed off for a moment, lost in thought. "I believe I mentioned that having everyone together like this has changed my mindset. Only a fool wouldn't see how special you are, Isle, and I am honored to be your friend."

"Special? Ha, I don't think so, but thank you all the same."

"It's true! Not only were you able to retain much of who you are, but you can transform into that… thing. You

165

are pretty powerful."

"I suppose so, but I can't remember any of it."

"Wait, you are not in control when you transform? You can't remember anything at all?" Ranger was astonished. Had Isle been protecting him from the wolves without even realizing it?

"Just little things. Images, sounds, smells. Unfortunately, the pain is the thing I remember the most."

"Tough to forget that. I know from experience. When I was younger, I dislocated my shoulder, then a couple of years later, I did it again. I vividly remember where I was, who I was with... just like I will always remember Bardune breaking my leg." Gesturing to a wound on Isle's shoulder, Ranger continued. "Speaking of battle wounds, what's that?"

Isle shrugged. "It happened during the battle with the Datsoe pack. It's nothing really."

"Maybe, but it gives me an idea. You want control over your Datsoe side right? Practicing how to use your powers would be beneficial. Let's try your healing ability." Ranger held out his arm invitingly.

Isle's jaw dropped. "Ranger, I am not going to use you as a power source if that's what you're implying. It's bad enough I latched onto you in the cave. I'm not going to do it on purpose. No way!"

"That's my point. You drained me the first time, but you weren't in control. You are right now, so this could be a valuable learning experience."

"But, what if I go too far? Datsoe's are gluttons, you know that. If I can't let go..."

"Isle, I trust you."

Isle's eyes welled up. *Trust*. That wasn't something

166

a Datsoe gave, let alone earned. Well, Ranger may be willing to, but the rest of them… glancing back at the group, he shook his head. "If they see me touch you, they won't like it. Maybe we should experiment with my powers later. Besides, you are already exhausted. It would be great if I could transfer some of my power to you."

"That would be handy alright. Well, it is something to keep in mind, for both of us. The more you use your abilities, the easier it will become."

Unbeknownst to both of them, Leeon was hanging on every word. Assuming distance afforded them privacy, Ranger and Isle unwittingly gave him an inside peek into their developing friendship. He wasn't sure of what to make of the whole thing. Ranger had been right, Isle was more like a person than a monster. Leeon felt a new appreciation toward Isle, and his accurate perception of how everyone felt about him. But what to do with him? Would Ranger really just stroll through the kingdom with a talking Datsoe? Quail mentioned seeing Isle save Rangers life in the woods, and he witnessed the battle with the wolves. If Bardune was hunting Isle, then it was their responsibility to help him. Being a Guardian meant saving all lives, not just who they felt should be protected. Squaring his shoulders, he picked up the pace to join them.

Isle couldn't have been more surprised when Leeon fell in step beside him. Reading his body language, he realized there was an openness that hadn't been there before. Giving Leeon a shy smile, he was pleased when it was returned.

"Tell me Isle, how did you avoid Bardune for so long? It sounds like he is aware of everything that happens in the Datsoe world."

"It hasn't been easy, Leeon. That's why I have spent more and more time on the other side of the wall. Believe it or not, I felt safer there."

Fascinated by the prospect of speaking with a Datsoe, and an intelligent one at that, he peppered Isle with questions.

Pleased with this development, Ranger drifted back to walk beside Quail, allowing Leeon time with Isle.

Quail watched Leeon talk to the Datsoe with dismay. What was it with that creature anyway? Every now and then, it would turn around to find Ranger, almost as if it was reassuring itself that he was still there. How many times, she wondered, had she done the same thing? She thought for a moment about Ranger as a person rather than a warrior; and how he was so willing to be kind to others.

He had accepted her into his life immediately.

She wasn't the only one thinking about the day they met. Isle reminded Ranger of Quail in a lot of ways. There were obvious differences, but they were both emotionally vulnerable. He remembered a day so hot, his valiant stallion didn't want to leave the cool river bank.

There had been reports of a winged Datsoe tearing up the countryside. Picking off cattle, destroying homes, Ranger received a plea from the villagers for help. Traveling in the heart of SummerSet, he tried to stick as close to the river as possible. Rounding a rocky bend, he came across scattered debris. Following the trail, he found himself in front of a small, wooden home. Evidence of battle drew his eyes to a man's body. Dismounting, he checked for signs of life. I'm too late, he thought grimly. Searching the area carefully, he came across what he assumed was the dead man's wife. Removing his hat, Ranger said a few words to mark her passing. He didn't know it, but that was the first time Quail saw him from her hiding place. Tucked under her parent's bed, she could see him through the broken door.

His hair was longer then, and the chestnut brown seemed to glow in the afternoon sun. Making his way through the wreckage, he saw signs of someone younger that lived there. Clothing hung on the line that would not have fit the woman laying in a crumpled heap outside the main door. A rag doll sat on a nearby fencepost, filling Ranger with a sense of urgency. Where was she? Had the Datsoe slain her as well? Stepping onto the splintered porch, He carefully made his way into the cabin.

Broken dishes, shattered chairs. The remains of what appeared to have been a happy home surrounded him. Blood-stained curtains swayed in the hot breeze through cracked windows. To this day he wasn't sure what gave her presence away, she remained as silent as a ghost. Lowering onto his hands and knees, he found her in the farthest corner, curled into a ball. Matted black hair covered her face, caked with grime.

"I'm Ranger. I'm here to help you."

Whimpering, she refused to take his extended hand. He couldn't tell how old she was, but he recognized the devastation in her eyes. It was something he could identify with all too well.

More than a day passed before she was willing to crawl out. Digging graves for her parents, he waited. Tending his horse, he waited. He spoke continuously, knowing she could hear him through the broken walls. Going about his business, he figured hunger would eventually draw her out. Building a campfire, he made dinner, dozed fitfully under the stars, made breakfast, and waited. Finally, he sat on the porch, and explained to her that he had to be on his way to hunt the Datsoe that had ruined her life. She was welcome to join him, he was sure a nice family would be able to take her in.

Barefoot and bloody, she stood behind him in a ruined gown.

"I want to help you kill it. My parents are gone, my home is empty, I have nothing left."

Slowly turning, he looked up at her determined face. "Well, that's not exactly true, now you have me." Getting to his feet, he held out his hand.

Ignoring it, she threw herself into his arms, and began to sob.

Memories running along the same path as Ranger's, Quail glanced toward the tall man limping beside her. She was able to draw comfort from his embrace and calm demeanor, despite the devastation of seeing her parents slaughtered. Was that the moment he took on the role of her father? Amusement filled Quail. It had been painfully obvious he had no idea how to take care of children, let alone one in her condition. Exhausted, she allowed Ranger to lead her to the river to bathe. Leaving her there, he went back into the house to find fresh clothes for her to wear. Thinking practically, he grabbed pants and a long-sleeved shirt. Returning to the river, he found her sitting in a patch of weeds alongside the banks, staring blankly into the distance. Leaving the garments on a nearby boulder, he encouraged her to get cleaned up, then waited for her by the house. They were her father's clothes, and far too large for her, but she made them work. Ranger bandaged her wounds, then worked on healing her broken heart.

Following the Datsoe's trail, day after day, she didn't utter another word. Ranger spoke more than he had in years, explaining the signs he was looking for, describing Datsoe behavior, and told her how he planned on defeating it.

Finally, he pressed her to speak. "I understand how you feel, and your thirst for revenge, but I would like to at least know your name."

She didn't answer him.

Undaunted, Ranger continued to talk. He told her things he hadn't shared in years. Tales of battle, loss, and adventure. Sometimes he thought he would catch a glimmer of emotion, but it was gone as quickly as it appeared.

Returning to camp with a couple of rabbits, Ranger was dismayed to find she had cut off all of her hair with his knife. Refusing to eat yet again, she finally pushed him enough to lose his temper. Concern for her well-being had him suggest that he leave her in the next town at a place for children like her. Clearly, he told her, this wasn't working out.

"Quail," she blurted. "My name is Quail. Please don't leave me. I will eat. See? Eating!" Grabbing a handful of meat, she shoved it into her mouth and chewed.

Noting the stubborn set of her jaw, he realized she probably would follow him no matter where he left her. Her parents had instilled in her the will to see things through, and despite her cold attitude, she was a kind girl. Violence tended to change a person's perspective, there was a chance this event would cloud her life forever. Relenting, he allowed her to stay.

Continuing their journey, he allowed her to explore ahead, explaining the signs of Datsoe to look for. She felt safe with him, and often found herself looking back to make sure he was behind her.

Finally, they found its trail. Knowing they were close, Ranger told Quail to stay with his horse. It knew when to run, where to hide, and would guide her to safety should the battle loom to close. Slipping into the trees, he began to set up his traps, and map out his strategy, assuming she would obey. She didn't. Following him quietly, she observed his every move, memorized his ways. In the end, they slayed it together.

She could admit now that she had been an enormous pain in his butt. Rebellious and stubborn, she put Ranger through a lot the following years. Through it all, he trained her, fed her, and kept her safe.

Quail felt something roll down her cheek, drawing her from her memories. Quickly wiping her face, she glanced at Ranger to make sure he hadn't witnessed her emotional display. He was watching Leeon and Isle, and it occurred to her that he was looking at Isle the same way he had looked at her when she lay huddled under the bed so many years ago. For the first time it occurred to her that maybe, just maybe, Isle was a victim, not the monster after all. She shook her head with denial. Ranger was supposed to be *her* father. True, he had a lot of love to give, but now he was choosing this thing to travel with. Why hadn't he asked her to come back?

Maybe, she thought, because he sensed things had changed. She wasn't a frightened child anymore, but a woman full grown with a hard-earned career. Would she give up being a Guardian to travel with Ranger again? Be on the road constantly, leave the town and people she had grown to love? No. She had come too far for that.

Could she set aside her hatred of Datsoes enough to

accept this one? Quell her jealousy and allow this talking abomination to replace her in Ranger's heart? Would he replace her? She had always been difficult, and Isle seemed to be winning the team over with his open nature and kind words. Maybe they would end up liking him more than her. For the first time in years, self-doubt plagued her. He was the enemy, wasn't he?

Leeon laughed at something Isle said, making Ranger smile.

No, she wasn't sure he was the enemy at all.

FallHeart the 73rd of

222 D.P

The day dragged on.

Sticking close to Isle, Marco held his ax with a white knuckled grip. "Why is it so quiet? Do they really sleep all day?"

"No, but they don't like the sun that much. It really depends on their transformation. Some lose their sight, others become sensitive to heat. At night, the air cools, scents become richer, the energy changes. Datsoes can be social, and hunting is becoming more of a challenge now that prey has become more scarce. Working together, especially with Bardune's guidance, provides more meal opportunities." Isle shrugged. "Unfortunately, he has a hard time controlling them once they begin to feed. A madness takes control, overcoming any reason."

Marco shuddered. "Why do you think night is better for us to travel? If they are out hunting, it makes us more of a target."

"Quite the opposite, trust me," Isle said, but it was clear he was distracted. Even though they had made excellent time, it was odd that they hadn't come across any Datsoes. Surely, they weren't that lucky. Cliff and Marco were right on his heels, and he supposed he couldn't blame them. He had spent many nights slipping through the trees in fear, the forest was extremely dangerous. Pushing on, he led them toward the darkest part of the tree line. Black branches tangled together to form an ominous wall, barring their way. "We're here," he announced.

Cliff swallowed. If plants could look mean, he swore these would frighten even Datsoes away. The foliage looked as though it was waiting for something to enter so it could swallow it whole.

"Isle, where are we? I don't recognize any of this." Ranger asked quietly.

"On the other side of this brush lies your trail," Isle replied. "From here, you should be able to reach the gate in no time."

"Kion's gate?" For the first time in hours, Marco lowered his ax.

"I don't know his name, but he has fire colored hair." Isle shrugged.

Ranger chuckled. "That sounds like him. How do we get through this?" Gesturing toward the dense hedge, he waited for Isle to show him a secret way through.

"You'll have to cut your way. Usually I just climb over, but I don't think you will be able to without taking too much time and energy. I'm sure your sword and ax will do the trick gentlemen."

Ranger and Marco set to work, slicing their way through branches until they found themselves in a clearing on the other side. Ranger smiled, finally recognizing where they were. Isle was right, this was near the end of the trail. All they had to do was make it to the rose wall, then the gate.

The other Guardians poured onto the path, delighted to be out of the woods. Laughing, Leeon clapped Cliff on the back, and Isle appreciated the small smile that Quail shared with Marco. Raindrops pattered on the dead leaves at their feet, but it didn't dampen their spirits.

"Well done," Ranger said quietly.

"Thank you." Isle beamed at Ranger, thrilled to have done something they all seemed to appreciate.

Inhaling deeply, Ranger enjoyed the scent of lush pine. "One thing I'll give this place," Ranger looked down at his little companion, "It's peaceful. Take the Datsoes out and maybe you could settle here."

"Nah. Once you've been here long enough, it's not really that special. As a matter of fact, the silence can be maddening…" Isle trailed off, staring off into the distance. "I suppose my opinion might be biased, but I've never had a single good thing happen here."

"I have," Ranger said.

"You have?"

"You bet. I never thought I would thank Bardune for anything, but he did give you the ability to speak. Coming into this forest gave me a wonderful gift, and that is you Isle." Ranger patted him on the shoulder, then slid his sword into its sheath, missing Isle's expression.

"By Juwa, is he crying?" Quail exclaimed, staring at Isle in shock.

Mortified, Isle turned away and wiped his eyes.

Having captured everyone's attention, Quail took a step toward Isle, trying to see his face.

"I'm not a cold-hearted creature of death you know," Isle muttered. Standing up straight, he turned to them, trying not to care about the varying emotions each Guardian displayed. "I know it's pathetic, but you've changed my life. I'm not naive enough to think you'll accept me the way Ranger has, but I hope that maybe one day, you won't hate me."

"We don't hate you Isle," Leeon replied. "In fact, you

177

have opened my eyes to things I never dreamt possible." Exchanging a look with Ranger, he continued. "When I speak to the Queen, I will give you my support."

Cliff shuffled his feet. "Look, er, Isle, I..."

"Guys, this isn't going to turn into one of those awkward moments where you all feel you have to say things you don't mean, is it?" Isle scoffed.

"You certainly won't get that from me," Quail sniffed. "Let's get to the gate. If Kion even lets you through, it will be a miracle. One step at a time, Little Monster."

"Quail!" Leeon admonished. "He has brought us to the gate in good faith, there is no need for you to call him names or be unkind."

"He is little, and a monster. What more can I say? Just because he speaks doesn't take away the fact that he could kill us all in the blink of an eye. You are a fool to think otherwise Leeon."

"Quail…" Ranger began.

"She's right." The quietly spoken words had them all look at Isle with surprise. "I could kill you all with ease, even without my ability to transform. But the fact that I choose not to is how I cling to my humanity. I don't remember my previous life, my family, the taste of freshly baked bread on a chilly morning. Being a Datsoe fills you with an indescribable rage that bubbles constantly in your mind. I feel like I am always starving, even after a meal. You have no idea what it is like to eat until you almost burst and still feel the need to feed. I'm ashamed to admit that I felt the Datsoe Queen's sway, and for a moment, was tempted by her offer to join them. It was unspoken, a look, but it was there. I interest her. I am different, like Bardune, and she knows it. Years of loneliness takes a toll, and if I hadn't met

178

you all, I may have accepted her invitation. Ranger has changed things for me."

"Ranger changes lives without even realizing it lad," Marco said. He was moved by Isle's passionate speech, and looking at his friends, he could see they were too. Except Quail of course, her expression remained as stony as ever.

"I can't imagine what it has been like for you Isle, but I am willing to give getting to know you a try." Cliff extended his hand, and after a moment, Isle took it.

"Come, we may be out of the woods, but we aren't out of danger. Let's get to the gate, and go from there," Ranger suggested. Smiling at Isle, he leaned on the Datsoe's shoulder, and began limping toward the rose wall. Pain shot up his leg, making him aware that it was time for more mushrooms, but he was reluctant to take it in front of his friends. Once they got to the gate, and he got medical treatment, he was sure he would be alright.

The rain began to beat down in earnest, soaking them. It washed away their layered dirt and muck, as if trying to prepare them for the return home. Ranger glanced down at Isle and chuckled. Sticking his tongue out and licking the air, Isle tried to drink the rainwater. This childlike behavior was something he hoped to see more often. Isle clearly missed out on some of the joys of growing up, and if his description of being a Datsoe was accurate, he had been living in his own version of hell.

Suddenly, Isle's head snapped around. His ears tipped back, and a low growl reached Ranger's ears.

"Isle?" Ranger asked urgently.

"They're here!" Pushing Ranger toward Cliff, Isle ran to Quail, and together they looked down the trail. A flash of lightning illuminated a form swooping from above,

making her pull her sword. Three more charged through the mud toward them, snapping razor sharp teeth.

"To the roses!" Marco bellowed. "They dare not follow us in the field!"

Looking up at Quail, Isle snarled "Run! He won't go without you."

Hesitating, she looked back. Cliff had his arm under Ranger's shoulder, supporting him. Leeon stood on the other side, waiting.

"If you run now, you'll all make it. Go, go!" Isle made his way toward a tall, gnarled tree, leaving Quail to stare after him.

"Come on!" Cliff shouted, all but dragging Ranger toward the roses.

Leeon exchanged an unsure look with Marco, reluctant to turn his back on danger.

The flying Datsoe's head resembled a bird. Snapping its talons together, an eerie screech mixed with the sound of rain, sending chills up Marco's spine. Cliff was calling to him, but he couldn't make out what was being said. Looking past Quail's frozen form, he saw Isle climb a massive tree. What was he doing? Marveling at Isle's speed, Marco watched the events unfold.

Isle climbed the tree, trying to time his attack. The flying Datsoe would be the worst to face, so he would try to kill it first. He hadn't had time to assess their enemies on the ground, but he would take them all out if it meant saving Ranger and the others. Bracing himself, he pushed off of the branch he was balancing on.

Quail's jaw dropped. Isle arched through the air, diving through the rain with deadly accuracy. Landing on the back of the flying Datsoe, he yanked its head, changing its direction. With an outraged squawk, it twirled, trying to shake him off. Well, if that Little Monster could take one on, so could she. By Juwa, she was a Guardian, not some sniveling coward that was going to run away at the first sign of trouble! She had survived the forest this long, and she intended to get the team to the gate safely. Setting her sights on the closest Datsoe, she charged.

Looking over his shoulder, Ranger watched the battle. Isle rode the winged Datsoe, pummeling its head and eyes with repeated blows. Quail slashed at a scaled Datsoe. "She is taking them on alone!" Ranger gasped. "We have to help her!"

Lifting his ax, Marco's war cry echoed off the trees, taking another Datsoe off guard. Two heads moved in opposite directions on the muscular, canine body covered in spots. Grabbing the muzzle of one in his fist, Marco hit the other with the flat of his blade, making the creature yelp.

The third Datsoe barrelled past Leeon into Cliff and Ranger, knocking them to the ground. Staring into its burning eyes, Ranger immediately drove his blade up into the creature's chest. Squealing, it shook its toothy snout. The red in its eyes slowly faded away, then collapsed on top of him, making him grunt.

Rolling the dead Datsoe off of Ranger, Cliff held out his hand. "You ok?"

"That thing stank, blech."

Taking Cliff's hand, he allowed the blond man to pull him up. Hearing another screech, they both looked up to see Isle holding a handful of feathers as the flying Datsoe spiraled straight toward Quail and the creature she battled. Reaching around its beak, Isle pulled sharply, breaking the Datsoes neck with a crack. Leaping, he grabbed Quail

181

around the waist, sending them both tumbling across the path just as the dead creature impacted with the Datsoe on the ground, impaling it.

"Three down," Leeon cheered. "Let's get to the roses!"

Looking over at Marco, Ranger saw a corpse quivering under the guardian's blood-stained ax. "Take that you disgusting, double headed brute." With a sniff, he started to make his way toward Quail, who landed in a leafy bush after skidding several feet. Isle had landed on his feet and stood ready to take on a new challenge. Looking around, he flashed a fang filled grin at Marco, pleased with their victory. Lifting his weapon in salute, he acknowledged Isle's accomplishment. Stumbling, the Guardian looked down to see what he had tripped over.

A jagged hand reached for his foot once more, dripping mud from its boney fingertips. With an exclamation of horror, Marco hopped over the hand, only to be grabbed by another, then another. Swinging his ax frantically, he made contact with a long, twitching snout. Dirt sprayed from its mouth followed by a low humming sound.

Pushing to her feet, Quail sidestepped more gnarled hands popping out of the ground, followed by velvety ears. "Are they rabbits? Gah, they are everywhere!"

Retreating to Ranger's side, the group watched a throng of Datsoes pour from the earth. Hunched down on all fours, their back legs extended, they had the ability to jump great distances. Filth sprayed in every direction as each one popped out of the ground.

Whirling, Isle spoke with urgency. "They are disoriented right now, traveling through the earth blinds them. Once they fix on us, they will be unstoppable. I have seen them in action, they can strip flesh from their victims' bones in seconds. You have to run; this is a battle you cannot win!"

A strange moan came from one of the rabbit creatures, followed by a stream of mud pouring from its mouth. Hunching, it wiped its mouth, then raised its head. Beady eyes surveyed the surroundings, trying to get a fix on them.

"You'll get no argument from me Lad, they just keep sprouting up, like horrible mushrooms!" Marco shuddered.

Once Again, Cliff and Leeon flanked Ranger, taking his arms over their shoulders. "Let us be off then," Cliff agreed.

Something in Isle's expression captured Ranger's attention. "Isle what is it? Come on, we need to go."

"Isle?" Leeon patted the small Datsoes arm. "Lead the way, will you?"

"I can't. They will keep chasing us. None of you will make it out alive. But, if they follow something else ..."

"*Jez Juwa Amedian Jarv*, Isle. Don't even think of it! We have to go!" Ranger insisted.

"No Ranger listen! Just... listen." Isle's burgundy eyes were filled with emotion. "They're looking for both of us. If... I don't know... if they think we're splitting off into a different direction then maybe it can buy you some time. Look at them, Ranger," Isle said nodding to the Guardians. "They can't fight all those Datsoes, heck you can't either. I'm fast and can fend them off."

"Isle no! What were we just talking about? We're all making it out of here! A change, a fresh start, remember?" Ranger pleaded.

"Ranger, I would have never made it in your world,

you know that. I don't want to ruin your life because of my selfish desires. If all goes well, maybe I'll see you again someday. We can all kick Bardune's hide a few times. That would be great."

"You've got guts, Little Monster, I will give you that." Pulling out a curved dagger, Quail offered it to Isle. "You may need this."

Shaking his head, Isle chuckled. "I appreciate it, Quail, but I have my own blades."

More moans and spraying mud sounded behind Isle, followed by distorted bleats and grunts.

Black overtook Isle's bright eyes. "You have all given me more consideration than I could have ever asked for, I am truly grateful." With a final look at Ranger's grief-stricken face, he squared his shoulders. "Get to the gate!" Turning, he ignored Ranger's protest. Racing toward the Datsoes, he let rage consume him.

Realizing how much he had come to care for his little uncanny Datsoe, Ranger reached out for Isle, but he was already gone.

They could all hear Isle call out, hurling insults at the now alert mud bunnies. Thunder rumbled overhead ominously.

"We can't just leave him," Ranger took a stumbling step toward the pack of creatures.

"He's giving us a chance! We need to take it!" Cliff tugged Ranger back.

The words echoed in his ears and rain poured over his face. Isle was right, this was their opportunity to escape. Pained to his core, he let Leeon and Cliff pull him toward the roses. Slipping in the soaked earth, his thoughts were not on the path ahead. *"I'll get them out. Then I'm coming back.*

184

I have to. Just hang on Isle."

With every step he wanted to turn around, but he knew he couldn't. Not without putting his team in further danger. His eyes shut for a brief moment, allowing his team to guide him. A ray of light hit his eyelids, capturing his attention.

Sunlight filtered through the leaves of the rose wall just a few yards ahead. Irony filled Ranger as the sounds of battle raged behind him. He thought he could hear Isle's mighty roar echoing over the sound of their footsteps running toward safety. Had he turned into his beast form? Rounding the final bend, Kion's gate seemed to glow in the distance, and the promise of safety mocked Ranger's heavy heart.

But, they weren't out of danger yet.

Habit had Ranger look over his shoulder, looking for danger, and hoping that maybe, just maybe, Isle was behind them. A running figure made him gasp. It wasn't Isle. But it was a Datsoe. One he recognized.

The monstrous form that had carried him down into the caves was tearing its way down the path, undaunted by the rain or impending rose wall.

"You have got to be *kidding!*" Ranger groaned.

Following his gaze, Cliff skidded to a top, making Leeon turn as well.

"Go! Get Kion's archers! This thing shall not pass the gateway!" Ranger ordered, eyes fixed on the advancing adversary.

"But what about…" Quail protested.

"Oh for Juwa sake, go! I won't be able to hold it off forever!" Ranger shouted. "Bring back reinforcements."

"Let's go girl! Kion will know what to do!" Marco

urged.

"I will not leave your side," Leeon braced for attack.

"You'll be needing this then." Marco handed Leeon his ax, knowing his bow was useless without arrows. "I will be fetching it soon."

With a grin, Leeon accepted the weapon, knowing how much it meant to Marco. "I will take good care of it."

"That you will. Come on girl, let us do our part."

"Our part seems a lot like retreating," Quail grumbled, following Marco down the path. "And quit calling me girl!"

With a snort Cliff drew his sword, and the three warriors stood side by side, bracing for the Datsoe's attack.

Ranger felt the ground beneath him shake as the monster approached. Leaning on his good leg, he searched for a vulnerable spot on the giant. Cliff and Leeon flanked the Datsoe, making it turn its head back and forth in an attempt to see what they were doing. Focusing on Ranger, its eyes dilated.

Bardune told it to fetch the silver haired one, and here he stood. Ignoring the other humans, it stomped toward its prize. Maybe Bardune would give light as a reward...

Just as the Datsoe was upon him, Ranger dove to the side, avoiding its outstretched claws. With a bellow, it whirled toward Cliff, spraying blood from the wound he had inflicted with his sword. Leeon attacked from the other side with Marco's ax, making the creature lunge back in pain. Ranger rolled underneath the beast, drawing his sword up and cutting into its stomach. It released a pained shriek and lifted onto its hind legs. Datsoe blood poured onto Ranger's head, and he frantically wiped his eyes. Pushing up, he didn't notice the creature's lizard-like tail swinging toward him.

Pushing Ranger aside, Leeon took the brunt of the impact, sailing through the air and landing in a rose bush. Gingerly, he made his way around the giant thorns protruding from the thick stems. Grabbing Marco's fallen ax, he raced back to join the battle.

If he lived ten lifetimes, Cliff would never grow tired of telling the tale of what happened next. Ranger dove over the Datsoe's whipping tail, somersaulted, then sprang up and stabbed the giant Datsoe in the snout. Rearing back, the creature swiped at the blade, trying to dislodge it. Ranger held on, rising into the air while simultaneously grabbing his dagger. Using the creature's momentum, he rammed the smaller blade into the side of its head with all his might. Losing his grip, he yanked the sword from the Datsoe's thick hide and slid down its body, landing on his foot. Losing his balance, he fell on his rear with a spectacular splash in the mud. Torn between awe and amusement, Cliff rushed forward.

Thrashing wildly, the muscular tail hit Ranger's shoulder, dislocating it, again. How many times had it been injured like this, he faintly wondered. Through blurring vision, he saw Cliff and Leeon attack the mighty creature who seemed unphased by Ranger's dagger sticking out of its temple. What would it take to kill this thing?

Trying to rise, Ranger narrowly missed being struck by an arrow. Then another. Still more rained down on the Datsoe, making Cliff and Leeon retreat for cover.

"Hey, watch where you're shooting!" Cliff yelled indignantly, outraged that the rescue party was focused more on taking the Datsoe out than helping him.

The Datsoe tried to retreat under the sudden bombardment. Its roars of pain and anger echoed across the landscape as it blindly swiped at this new threat.

Ranger saw rows of armored archers come into view. He let his head fall back into the mud, knowing that they would finish the Datsoe off. His whole body throbbed.

"Ranger!" Quail knelt by his side, taking his hand.

"Easy, it's popped out again. How many times has it now, you think?"

Ranger was going into shock, but Quail had no trouble understanding his disoriented question. "Fourteen, unless you've dislocated it recently. Now let's get you up."

Pulling Ranger into a sitting position, she cradled him.

"We need to set it back into place. Are you ready?"

Weakly, Ranger nodded. He knew that once the joint was set, the pain would become bearable.

"On the count of three." she whispered, ignoring the soldiers walking by. "One." She took a deep breath. "Two."

Ranger tried to brace himself.

"*Three.*"

With all her strength, she pushed her hand into his shoulder. She felt it pop into place, and he released a sigh of relief.

With a nod, Ranger pulled away. "Thank you." Looking around, he saw that the Datsoe lay quiet. Cliff was talking animatedly with Marco, who held his beloved ax once more. Leeon stood in a circle of soldiers, gesturing toward the dead creature as he spoke.

Thoughts of Isle had Ranger trying to rise. He had to go back, maybe he could still...

"Aye *Javbozl,* you have seen enough battle. Get him back within the walls, my men shall take it from here." A deep, commanding voice accompanied a large hand that held

Ranger in place. Ranger recognized the word for *soldier,* and looked up.

"Well, it took you and your men long enough to get out here, Kion." Ranger tried to smile at the ebony face looming over him. Instead of returning the smile, Kion's golden eyes studied his friend with concern. With a snap of his fingers, several guards rushed forward with a woven mat. Gently lifting Ranger in his muscular arms, the Gatekeeper laid him on it, then ordered them to go to the medical wing.

"Well, it doesn't help that my men were taken off guard by people on the forbidden side of the gate," he rumbled. Taking in the other guardian's ragged appearance, he raised a red eyebrow. "I look forward to hearing what brought all of you to my door."

"Kion." Ranger grabbed his wrist. "WinterNox is upon us. That's why we went through the woods. The swamps are full, the air cold. And Bardune! We must get a message to the Palace."

"I will send horsemen to the nearest villages. We'll be ready at the front when the first snow comes." Kion reassured him.

"This is no longer about the front." Ranger said.

Taking in Quail's grave expression, Kion looked back at Ranger. "Well, we can discuss everything once you feel better. My men will finish up here and I will escort you inside."

Turning away, Quail began, "I would like to ask Cliff…"

"Now woman, I have no time to coddle you! Your injuries clearly indicate you need medical attention as well."

Her eyes narrowed. "You have no authority over us."

Taking a deep breath, Kion started to growl at her,

but something about her face stopped him. Every time they met, Quail was proud, arrogant, and intelligent. She wore her strength like a suit of armor, and he reluctantly admired her for her quick wit and sharp tongue. The arrogance was still in place, but he could tell she was exhausted. They all were. Biting back his anger, he changed tactics.

"Perhaps you would be willing to accompany Ranger. He trusts you, and I am sure he will be a challenging patient. My healers will have a hard time convincing him of what needs to be done."

Hazel eyes snapping with temper, Quail wordlessly left, stomping to Rangers side.

Pressing his generous lips together, Kion fought a threatening smile. Quail had always amused him, just as her temper challenged him. He found himself pushing her just so he could watch her anger explode. It was very satisfying indeed.

Surprised that Quail gave in so easily, Cliff watched her march beside the soldiers that carried Ranger away. Quail might have had her disagreement with the others, but when it came to Kion; many of them wondered if she would try to stab him. He always seemed to say the wrong thing, making her rage at him. A feud had started between them years ago, and now they couldn't stand to work, speak, or even look at each other without fighting. Maybe, Cliff thought, she was going soft.

FallHeart the 73rd of

222 D.P - Dusk

Passing through the gate, the weary Guardians were a sight to behold. Whispers followed them all the way to the medical shelter nestled in a group of trees below the watchtower. Based on his brief exchange with Ranger, Kion doubled the amount of soldiers on the wall. Knowing Ranger wasn't one to panic, he suspected they were all in grave danger.

The soldiers carried Ranger through the wide wooden door, then laid his mat on the nearest bed. Despite the age of the room, everything was pristine. The scent of antiseptic floated through the air, medical instruments gleamed, and rolls of bandages were stacked on tables throughout the space.

Pushing himself up, Ranger tried to pull the bag off of his shoulders. Rushing to help him, Cliff loosened the straps and placed the leather pouch in Ranger's lap. Lifting the mud-stained flap, he began searching through the contents. His fingers jumped from item to item until he grabbed the top of a mushroom, then pulled it out, letting the bag slide to the floor.

The others stared at the unfamiliar fungi, but no one questioned him. Breaking off a piece he popped it in his mouth, shuddering with revulsion. Swallowing, Ranger hoped it would take effect quickly.

A hand caught him by the wrist, preventing him from

taking another bite.

Kion looked at Ranger sternly. "Where did you find this plant?"

"From a cave in the forest, it is a very effective painkiller," Ranger replied.

"It is also very addictive. You should avoid taking it anymore my friend." Gesturing toward a kindly faced doctor, Kion continued. "My healers will assist you with your care. You all need treatment, good food, and rest."

Collapsing on a nearby cot, Marco smiled at a young nurse. "I willingly place myself in your capable hands, Lass. Do you happen to have any ale about?"

Rolling her eyes, Quail led Leeon to another doctor. "I doubt anyone would recommend ale in a hospital, Marco, don't be ridiculous. Have a seat Leeon, you have a nasty gash on your shoulder, your aim may never be true with a bow again."

Kion watched Quail boss the other Guardians around, but behind her abrasive words, he could tell she cared deeply for each of them. Why hadn't he noticed that before? Radiating exhaustion, he knew she would resist any suggestion to submit to care herself. Well, he would have to do something about that.

"Stop fussing woman, does your tongue ever stop?" Picking up a roll of bandages, he tossed them at her. "Patch yourself up, then see to their meals."

With a gasp, Quail threw the bandages back at him. "I am not a serving wench! I am a guardian, warrior, and gatekeeper! I have every right to the same care as they do!"

Glaring down at her, Kion roared, "Then sit on a bed if you must! Doctor, tend to her wounds, since she insists on the same treatment."

Coughing to cover his amusement, Ranger admired Kion's clever tactics. Quail glared at the tall redhead but allowed her wounds to be stitched and bandaged. Another nurse wrapped his leg while the older doctor examined his cuts, and he chafed at the time it was taking. Now that the mushroom had taken effect, he was anxious to go find Isle. Noticing his discomfort, the doctor assumed he was in pain.

"Your bone is broken. We have created a special brace for situations such as these for soldiers. It is metal, and runs the length of your leg, and holds your weight so you can move about. I suggest plenty of rest, staying off of it as much as possible, and time to heal."

"I have no time, Doctor, I must head back into the woods as soon as possible."

"Ranger! That is insane! We just got here," Cliff protested.

"I have to. Isle is waiting for me."

"Who is Isle?" Kion asked.

An uncomfortable silence settled over the group. Finally, Leeon said, "A new friend. He saved our lives in the forest."

"Surely the lad is lost to us by now," Marco muttered.

"No, I don't believe that."

Everyone looked at Quail with surprise. "Isle is resourceful, he has proved that on many occasions. A survivor through and through. It wouldn't surprise me if he has made a deal with Bardune."

"How can you say that? He saved your life!" Ranger exclaimed angrily. "Honestly your attitude disappoints me, Quail. He risked everything for us. You got one thing right, he is clever. He will know how to hide until I find him."

His tone brought a rush of tears to Quail's eyes.

194

"Ranger, you are in no condition to go out there! Or have you forgotten the dance with death you had a couple hours ago?"

Swinging his legs off the bed, Ranger stood. "I will not keep the boy waiting. He doesn't deserve your disdain, he has more than earned your trust."

"He is a Datsoe Ranger! I will never trust him, ever! You are an old fool!" As soon as the words were out, Quail regretted them. But it was too late. "You are not going to go out there again." she hissed.

"I'd like to see you try to stop me," he snapped back, "You do remember that I *literally* taught you everything you know."

"If I may," Kion interrupted.

"What!?" Ranger and Quail yelled simultaneously.

"Am I understanding correctly that the new friend you made, Isle, is a Datsoe, and Ranger feels he must rescue him from other Datsoes?" Kion exchanged a concerned glance with the Doctor behind Ranger.

"I know how it sounds." Leeon replied, "But yes, Isle is an intelligent, talking Datsoe."

"Have you all taken leave of your senses?" Kion bellowed.

"Apparently this *old fool* has," Ranger said, glaring at Quail.

"Look Kion, it sounds insane I know, but Ranger speaks the truth. He made friends with a Datsoe, and believes he was once a human. He speaks, I have conversed with him." Cliff shrugged.

"He isn't the only one who can talk. Bardune is the leader of Datsoes. He is the one who did this." Gesturing to his leg, Ranger continued. "I was his, shall we say, guest for

195

a while. There is a network of caves deep in the forest that provides shelter to an army of Datsoes. More than you can even imagine. He is controlling them, and I believe he is organizing them to attack. We must prepare for war. Isle could be instrumental in helping us win."

"Fine, if you insist on going back, let me come with you," Quail said.

"Absolutely not! You have made your opinion clear. I will not endanger Isle with your unreasonable prejudice!"

"Prejudice?" Quail gasped. "Until now you and I were of the same opinion! Datsoe's are monsters and should be slain."

"My friends, you are all weary. Perhaps after you rest, this conversation can be continued," Leeon reasoned.

"There is nothing more to discuss. I am going alone," Ranger said.

"Perhaps one of us could go with you. You are injured after all…" Marco began.

"Don't you get it? I can't lose anyone else!" Ranger roared.

"Ranger, who have you lost?" Cliff asked. "I know Isle was extraordinary, but surely you haven't gotten that attached to him already? You barely know him."

"No one! It's nothing, forget I mentioned it." Embarrassed by his emotional display, Ranger turned away.

Gesturing for the doctors and nurses to leave, Kion sank into a nearby chair. Who knew that having all of the Guardians together would be so… dramatic! Watching Quail push off of the bed, he wondered what her next move would be.

"Ranger, please," she whispered. Placing her hand on his arm, she met his gaze. "I spoke out of turn, accept my

196

apology, I beg of you. You are not old or a fool. If you think Isle is worth going after, then we shall all go, together."

"Aye, together!" Marco agreed.

"No, you were right, Quail, but not the way you think. I'm so set in my ways that everyday I'm afraid I'm going to lose…" hesitating, he paused. "I don't know where to start, how to make you understand."

"Well." Leeon said, "you can always start at the beginning."

Taking Quail's hand in his own, he gave her fingers a gentle squeeze. Searching the expressions of the faces around him, Ranger decided he could trust them. "Well. I guess for any of this to make sense I need to let you in on a little secret. Cliff has been right the whole time. *I am an Asalairi descendant.*"

Marco's mouth dropped open.

"Ha, I knew it!" Cliff exclaimed.

Looking at Ranger, Kion had to admit it made sense. His height, strength, agility, and most importantly, his age, all lent credence to his claim. The Asalairi were rumored to have very long life spans. Reflecting on all he knew, he realized he wasn't even certain how old Ranger was.

Gloating, Cliff leaned over and hit Marco on the shoulder.

"Alright, so you guessed correctly. Kion, where can a man get a cup of ale around here? I sense a story coming on, and I need to prepare myself." Marco smoothed his shirt over his stomach, "And a bite to eat wouldn't hurt my feelings either."

Standing, Kion opened the door. "Come my friends, let us hear what Ranger has to say in the dining hall. Marco, you shall have your ale, I have a feeling we all may need some."

FallHeart the 73rd of

222 D.P - *Nightfall*

Pushing his empty plate away, Ranger let out a sigh of contentment. The dining hall was quiet, allowing the Guardians to speak freely. An occasional servant would pass by to fill up goblets or replenish platters that lay in the center of the table. Initially, conversation was sparse, each gatekeeper concentrating on the fine meal Kion provided them. Sipping ale from a wooden mug, Ranger relaxed enough to begin his tale.

"My great-grandfather was an Asalairi, and one of the few that came to the old kingdoms. Affected by man's war, some decided to offer assistance to the North. My great-grandfather, Ashton Mighthem, had always been a restless soul, so it was no surprise when he was one of the first to volunteer to join the cause. Curiosity had him meander through human towns, learning their ways and culture. Staying in a camp for a time, he came to know the townspeople, who accepted him because of his humor and wit. In need of new weapons, he began to visit the local blacksmith, who had a lovely daughter. He heard rumors about her odd behavior and desire to be alone. A girl her age shouldn't be learning to read or studying other cultures, she should be preparing to become a wife and mother, some whispered.

Sneering at tradition, and fascinated by his Asalairi

heritage, she struck up a conversation with Ashton. Unswayed by the townsfolk's opinion of her, he answered her questions, shared his knowledge, and enjoyed spending time with the beautiful maiden. As you may have already guessed, they fell in love.

Their affair was brief, as tensions began to spark between the other Asalairi and men. Reluctantly, he joined his kinsmen, withdrawing from our lands. No one really knows why she didn't join him, perhaps he knew she wouldn't have been welcomed by his people. Heartbroken, she kept her pregnancy from him, choosing to raise her son alone.

My Grandfather, Luther, looked more like an Asalairi than a human, but he was raised with love and taught our customs. Then the Datsoes took over. He witnessed the creation of the flower wall, and the kingdoms unite. The first set of Guardians were selected to watch over the gates, and, seeing what the Datsoes were capable of, he decided to become a soldier. After many decades of service, he met a young lady. After a few years living together, they welcomed a daughter, who turned out to be my mother, Emily."

Nodding to a servant girl as she filled his cup, Ranger waited for her to finish and depart before continuing.

"It seems that your Asalairi traits have remained strong, despite them blending with humans," Cliff commented.

Releasing a loud belch, Marco waived his mug around. "Yes! Imagine how powerful Ranger could have been if they didn't keep falling for normal women."

"It's not like there were any Asalairi around for them to marry, and I am sure the ladies they chose were lovely,"

Leeon argued.

"Bah! Human women could never be good enough! Thinning the blood line was their contribution. Why, when I think about all of the wonderful attributes the Asalairi had, a regular female would never…"

"A regular female?" Quail interrupted. "By Juwa Marco, you had better choose your next words carefully!"

Meeting Quail's outraged gaze, Marco mumbled "Never mind," then drank deeply from his cup. Ale ran down his beard, making her grimace.

"Perhaps Ranger would like to tell us more about his mother," Leeon prompted, hoping to prevent any further argument. "How did she meet your father? Was he a soldier like you?"

"He was," Ranger replied. "She became a nurse, and her skill as a healer became well known. As a result, she found herself in a makeshift hospital just outside the rose wall, desperately trying to save lives. The conflict between man and Datsoe was brutal, and sadly she lost more men than she cared to admit. When a young warrior arrived, followed by tales of heroism on the battlefield, she vowed to save him. Caring for him around the clock, she found him to be just as courageous when it came to his extensive injuries. Never uttering a word of complaint, he followed all of her instructions during his rehabilitation. Their time together was brief and filled with blood and sorrow. Many of his friends fell victim to the Datsoes, and he found himself leaning on her sunny disposition. Finally, he was sent home, and Emily thought that would be the last time she would see him. She had grown fond of the quiet man with grief filled eyes.

WinterNox passed, and Emily went back to her life

in WolfCreek. The men in her town tried to court her, for she was very beautiful, but it was too late. Emily's heart was already lost to the reserved soldier she had saved.

FallHeart faded, and she volunteered once more, hoping to see her hero. Surrounded by the wounded, Emily fought to save lives, searching each face in vain for the man she loved. Perhaps, she thought, he found someone and settled down.

On a particularly cold day in WinterNox, the door burst open, allowing a wave of bitter wind to swirl throughout the small hospital. There he stood, making her breath catch in her throat. Frantically, she flew to him, searching for injuries. Capturing her hands in his own, he professed his love, and asked her to marry him. That man was Winston Swordsman, my father."

With a discreet sniffle, Marco took another swig from his cup.

"That is a moving tale," Cliff said, "Wouldn't you agree Marco?" With a mischievous smile, he handed Quail a napkin. "Here, he may need this, he is crying, the big softie."

"I am not!" Marco bellowed. "I got ale in my eye, and it stings. I don't cry over sappy romantic tales, bah!"

Grinning, Ranger continued. "Winston and Emily married and moved into a comfortable home. She stopped volunteering at the battlefront, and opened a small clinic, offering her medical expertise to the townsfolk. Wiston trained new soldiers and returned each year to the wall to defend those he loved against the Datsoes. Eventually, they had a son."

Raising his cup Kion toasted Ranger. "And a fine son he is!"

"Aye! Our thanks to Emily and Winston for bringing such a mighty soldier into the world!" Marco agreed.

"I wasn't always strong," Ranger replied. "If not for my mother's excellent skill as a healer, I would not be sitting here now. Apparently, the mixed bloodlines made me sickly as a baby, and it took every bit of her knowledge to save me. Together, my parents nursed me back to health, and we were as happy as any family could be.

But like all stories, there are unexpected twists and turns in life. My father died in an accident on the front when I was very young. I have no memory of him, all I know is from the tales my mother would tell me. She was so strong and hid her grief from the world.

Everyone spoke of the Datsoes naturally, and I grew up listening to horror stories of ruined towns and shattered lives. Having lost my own father, I lived in constant fear of attack. I picked at my food and slept fitfully, making my mother crazy with worry. In order to help calm my nerves, she would sing a melody while putting me to bed." Ranger paused, listening to the faded tune in his mind.

"Finally, she told me a story that her father, Luther, had been bitten by a Datsoe. Miraculously, he did not fall victim to the infection. Asalairi have natural magics and immunities in their blood, she assured me, so he was able to walk away with nothing but a set of gray scars. His friends started calling him 'Miracle man'. She explained that our blood was also Asalairi, so our bodies would fight off the poison. This filled my head with the idea that we were immune. She warned me that we could still be killed by a Datsoe, but my attitude changed, knowing that I couldn't become one. Unfortunately, truth and lies often go hand in hand. I learned this the hard way."

Ranger focused on the table and swallowed hard.

Confused by his sudden silence, Marco picked up a chicken leg and took a large bite. "Go on Ranger, what happened next?", wiping his mouth with the back of his hand, he missed Quail's look of disgust.

"On the eve of my twelfth birthday, my mother and I were tending the garden. I was rushing through my tasks, anxious to get to the cake she had made me. No one could bake quite like she could. I was feeling smug because I knew she had hidden away some gifts to help celebrate my special day. I was coming up with ideas to get her to give me a present early."

Twirling his mug, Ranger's next words were so quiet, the group had to strain to hear him. "Screams erupted from our neighbor's yard, startling us. Leaping to her feet, my mother saw a pack of Datsoes ripping their way through the walls of the house next to us. Taking my hand, she pulled me out of the yard, racing toward one of the safe houses our town had set up in case of an attack. My hands were gritty with soil from the garden, and as we ran, I kept thinking I would get her dirty."

Staring at his open palm, Ranger paused, reluctant to relive what happened next. "Mother was funny about dirt, she was always cleaning and lecturing me about staying tidy. I suppose as a healer, she wanted to prevent illness."

"My mother is the same," Cliff replied, trying to fill the awkward silence. "I swear no sooner has she scrubbed the floor; she is declaring it needs washing again."

"My wife does that as well. Perhaps it is something that women do." Leeon swiftly looked at Quail, gauging her reaction, but she was focused on Ranger.

With a sad smile, Ranger nodded. "Perhaps."

"What happened next?" Kion asked.

"We were separated. I remember hearing her calling for me, but there were so many people running and screaming, and it seemed that Datsoes were everywhere. I knew where the shelters were, so I made my way toward them. Men rushed to fight the creatures, grabbing any weapon they could find. Running past an alleyway, I saw something I wasn't expecting. There was an older warrior who had retired in our village some years ago; and I found him with a sword in his hand, standing between a Datsoe and a couple of kids. I was scared naturally, but all of the stories my mother told me about my father filled my head. He was a hero; I could be too. Besides, I knew I couldn't be turned, so I picked up a rock and hurled it at the creature, trying to capture its attention. Hitting it square in the eye, I got it to focus on me alright. With a roar, it bounded after me, foaming at the mouth with rage. Picking up a discarded pitchfork, I braced myself for battle."

"A pitchfork?" Quail exclaimed. "How big was the Datsoe?"

"Large enough to knock me clean off my feet and throw me into a brick wall," Ranger replied. "Pushing myself up, I saw my mother standing over the fallen creature. She killed it with the same pitchfork I held moments before. She never looked more amazing I thought, fierce, covered in the monster's blood, victorious. Unbeknownst to me, it had bitten her during battle. Rushing to her outstretched arms, we made our way to the shelter along with the other survivors of the attack. Wrapping her wound, she offered as much medical assistance as she could until she succumbed. At first, I didn't understand what was happening. Since she was the healer of the town, everyone looked to her for guidance, but now she was the one in trouble. I kept reassuring myself that she would be fine. Luther fought off the infection, so could she.

Three long days passed. My mother told me it had taken Luther a week to fight off the infection, so I tried to be patient, but something didn't feel right. I never left her side, watching her sleep fitfully on a tiny cot. At dawn on the fourth morning, I was dozing when she began to scream. Thrashing wildly, she knocked me from my chair. From the floor I beheld a sight I will never forget. Her bones popped and changed; her face stretched under her clasping hands. Crashing into the wall behind her, she knocked a hole through the wooden planks, allowing the early morning rays to wash over her.

Pushing to my feet, I stared at her with shock. She had turned after all; into something no one could have expected. Much like a mythical creature from the books I had on my shelves, black fur covered her now feline form. Silver covered her feet like socks, and a large tuft at the end of her silky tail glinted with the same color. An exclamation of dismay escaped me, I couldn't believe what was happening. She told me, she *promised* that we were immune. It never occurred to me that I was in danger. Despite her new Datsoe form, she was still my mother. Looking into her black eyes, I stood, trusting, like a lamb to the slaughter."

Looking at his friends' shocked expressions, Ranger ran his fingers over a faded scar on his chin. "Remember the soldier I mentioned earlier, the one from the alley?"

"The defender of children," Kion replied.

"Yes, that's the one." Ranger chuckled, catching them by surprise. Sombering, he continued. "He saved me, just as I had saved him a few nights before. Bursting into the room with a torch and his trusty sword, he startled her. She leapt through the hole in the wall, and I never saw her again."

"Oh Ranger, I am so sorry." Laying her hand over his, Quail's eyes shimmered with unshed tears.

"Truly a sad tale my friend," Cliff sighed.

"It was long ago, but sometimes it seems like it happened yesterday," Ranger murmured.

Logs collapsed in the fireplace with a crack, making Marco jump. Ale sloshed over the rim of his cup, which he wiped at with his sleeve while he watched Kion get up and add more fuel to the flames.

"Your story is tragic, and I understand why you are more forgiving toward Datsoes, considering your mother is one." Brushing his hands together, Kion picked up a pitcher and refilled Marco's cup.

"Oh, I am not so forgiving, believe me," Ranger retorted. His tone was dark, indicating his tale wasn't finished.

"After my mother's disappearance, the townsfolk of WolfCreek tried to be kind, some even offered me a place to stay. I don't remember much of the next few weeks, but I know I was rude, angry, in denial really. I couldn't accept the thought that she had lied. Convincing myself that she would beat the infection and return, I refused to go home, wandering the town aimlessly. Eventually everyone gave up on me. Starving, broken, and alone at 12 years old is a dark path to take. Madness surely would have claimed me.

Walking through the streets late one night, I was surprised when the old soldier melted from the shadows and confronted me.

"Why are you wasting away like this boy?" he demanded. "What do you think you are doing?"

"I am waiting for Mother. I can't open my birthday gifts until she comes back."

Resting his hand on my shoulder, his face softened. "She isn't coming back. You must move on."

"I can't! She is all I have. They took her from me, cursed Datsoes!"

"Do you intend to kill each and every one of them for what they did?" he asked.

I shook my head. "Some of them are like mother. They didn't choose to be like that.'

"Well then, what if you needed to defend against them? You showed promise in the alley, helping those who were trapped within their own fear. Do you think you could prevent others from turning as she did?"

"She's coming back! She will win this fight!" I screamed, overcome with grief.

"No lad, she won't, ever. You have to let her go."

"Lashing out, I punched him square in the jaw. Horrified by what I had done, it was like a dam burst, and I was finally able to grieve. He gathered me into his arms and remained quiet while I cried.

Kion, when you said he was a defender of children, you were not far off. He took me in without hesitation, integrated me back into the town and made me whole. It was a process, and took time, but he made me the man I am today."

"He sounds incredible," Leeon said. "He had no children of his own?"

"No, but he ended up with more than he bargained for." Ranger smiled. "He occupied my time and youthful energy with rigorous workout routines. There were daily sessions on how to use a sword, bow, daggers, axes, shields, bare hands... until soon I became good at every weapon. I think he suspected I was different. I never mentioned my Asalairi heritage, but he must have guessed. Especially after Mark and Raja arrived."

"Who were they? Orphans like yourself?" Cliff leaned back in his chair, as spellbound as the rest with Ranger's tale.

"No, they were the same kids I kept the Datsoe from killing in the alley the night my mother was bitten. They were already friends, and of course everyone in town knew what had happened. When I would grab supplies or run errands, they would try to talk to me. Mark was a jokester, but the prospect of learning to fight interested him, and he knew the soldier was training me. Raja was as open and friendly as I was closed and quiet. Eventually, we became inseparable. Before he knew it, my mentor took on the task of training three future Datsoe hunters. He never seemed to mind that Raja was a girl, and in fact, encouraged her."

Meeting Quail's inquisitive gaze, Ranger continued. "Women weren't considered capable of being warriors the way they are now."

"Did Raja change the way men thought? Do I have her to thank for how things are now? Imagine! Women being kept away from danger, like we aren't as useful on the battlefield as you!" Spearing a piece of meat, Quail popped it in her mouth and rolled her eyes.

"She was an incredible fighter, and definitely changed the minds of those in our town. To know her, was to love her," Ranger said quietly.

"Oh ho! Could it be, Ranger in love?" Marco teased.

"I was very much in love with her, I had been for years. The day I turned 18, I asked her to marry me."

Quail gasped. "Marry you?"

"Indeed. Mark and I were heading to the rose wall to join the WinterNox battle, and I selfishly wanted her with me. We often joked that she could disguise herself as a man and join us in the war. She was twice as good as most of the men out there."

"Did she accept your proposal?" Cliff asked.

"She did. Our mentor threw us a huge party to celebrate our engagement. The entire town came out to congratulate us. There was food, wine, dance…" Ranger trailed off, leaving his friends wondering what happened next.

"And?" Marco demanded. "Did she show those boys on the field what a true warrior could do?"

"No, she never got the chance," Ranger swallowed. "The sound of the town's revelry combined with the scents of cooking meat attracted a group of Datsoes. Plunging from the sky, they attacked indiscriminately. Mark, Raja and I fought fiercely, defending the town to the best of our ability. That was the day I got this," he tapped the scar on his chin. "How could I have walked away with just this?!"

Exchanging a worried look with Kion, Quail reached for Ranger's hand. "Raja didn't make it?"

"No," Ranger replied bitterly. "I watched helplessly as she was carried into the night by a Datsoe. The last thing I saw was her plunging her sword into the creature's neck as they flew out of sight. Mark… I found the upper half of his body when the battle was over. We had a funeral for him the day after, his mother led the prayers to the Juduiverians, asking for his soul to join them. That wasn't the only funeral we had that day. There were empty graves marked for those that were carried away, including Raja. I searched for her, hoping in vain that she was able to escape, but…"

"Life can be cruel," Kion said.

"Yes," Ranger replied, "But I learned to be cruel right back. After the funerals I left my mentor a letter and joined the battlefront. My opinion had changed you see, I wanted death for all Datsoes, no matter who or what they had been before. I let rage consume me. Through the bitter cold, long days, and grueling attacks, I made a name for myself. By the time I was 21, my name had spread to almost every corner of the kingdom. I had single handedly killed more Datsoes than any warrior twice my age.

Summoned to the royal Palace, the King and Queen wanted to meet the mystery man slaying every monster he could in their land. Her royal highness was only the Princess at the time, just 15 if I recall correctly."

"So young!" Cliff exclaimed.

"Young, but wise. She ultimately convinced her parents to make me a guardian." Ranger winced. "At the time, I wasn't exactly grateful. I wanted nothing of the fame the position offered, I just wanted to kill Datsoes. But, with the position, came certain perks. I was assigned my own team of soldiers, and we traveled the trail you all joined me on with Isle. For years we defended the gates outside of the rose wall. Eventually, we realized it was becoming too dangerous, and the team went our separate ways. Once again, I roamed the land, until I came upon a farm where I found a girl, hiding under her parents' old bed."

The others turned and looked at Quail.

"That was a turning point for me. I was completely shut off from the world, cold, unfeeling. Who knew a snarky teen could change so much?" Ranger laughed. "Because of you, I was able to make new friends, and I hope you know how much I care for you all. Just as you have taught me to feel again, Isle has shown me that not all Datsoes are evil. I think I had it right to begin with, just like my mother, some should live."

"You have come a long way, Ranger," Kion said. "Why are you sharing all of this with us now?"

"Because I need you to understand why I must go back for Isle. I have lost so much, and I have grown to care for him much as I do Quail. He needs me, and perhaps, I need him as well."

"If he survived, surely Bardune has him now," Leeon said.

"Bardune is now a threat we all face. If your suspicions are correct Ranger, he could be planning to attack our lands at any time!" Cliff pushed back his chair and began to pace.

"Aye… but what if we are ready for him? Kion has already raised the alarm about WinterNox arriving early. If he was planning on using this as a way to take us by surprise, that has already failed," Marco replied.

"He has an army that could attack us at any gate. I honestly don't know how many Datsoes he has at his disposal," Ranger leaned forward. "You need to plan a defense across the kingdom, for land and air."

"We need you to help us organize it, Ranger. Once the kingdom is prepared, we will form a rescue group to find Isle. Is this agreeable to you?" Kion stared at the elder Guardian sternly. "The lives of many rests in our hands."

Staring at his friends, Ranger sighed. "Alright then, let's come up with a strategy to stop Bardune. If I am wrong, and he isn't planning an attack, at least we know that the people will be well protected. But I have a feeling something

213

is about to happen.

Ranger had no idea how right he was.

FallHeart the 73rd of

222 D.P - *Midnight*

Deep in the Earth, iridescent mushrooms cast an eerie glow over a grisly scene. The smell of blood floated thickly in the air, creating a frenzy amongst the cave's occupants. Only the muscular Datsoe at the entrance prevented chaos, until Bardune's boots could be heard echoing throughout the chamber toward them. Many of the hungry beasts melted away into the darkness, anxious to avoid the unpredictable behavior he often displayed. None of them had a desire to die today, and lingering could lead to that eventuality.

"You can stop there."

Turning, a small Datsoe with talons tilted its head toward Bardune. Bloodlust had it hesitate. It had been feasting on strip after strip of the captive's skin, licking up silver blood after each delicious morsel.

"I told you not to go too far!" Bardune snarled, kicking the creature back with distaste. "He is not good to me if he is dead, you gluttonous fool!"

Talons clicking, the Datsoe looked longingly at his victim, drooling. There was something unique about this one, and he wanted more.

Shivering, Isle watched the brief power struggle. Finally, his tormentor took its leave, plotting ways to feast once more.

"Well, that looks unpleasant," Bardune stood tall

over Isle's kneeling form. "Are you ready to tell me what I want to know?"

"I will tell you what I know," Isle panted. Bardune's victorious smile faded at his next words. "I can tell you with great certainty, that your breath is much worse than his was, and his mouth was full of my flesh."

A sharp crack reverberated throughout the cavern. Bardune's palm stung from the force of the blow across Isle's cheek, and still the little runt refused to talk. "Now now, boy. Is that any way to talk to your King?"

"You are no King of mine," Isle replied. One more blow like that and he should be able to turn, prayed he could. If he could just tilt his palm enough to draw energy from his captor, he could heal himself.

To Isle's dismay, Bardune began to laugh. "Ah boy, you're a tough one to crack, I'll give you that," he chuckled, "Imagine my surprise when I learned that you were the one that helped Ranger escape. Why would you turn on your family like that?"

"Family?" Isle sneered, "You have no concept of the word."

"Why, you wound me to the core! I had parents, soldiers I trained with that could have been considered brothers. True, I betrayed them all to better my circumstances, but who wouldn't? And see where I ended up? As a King! But my problem, and yours too, is I want more than just life inside of this dank cave. I want to rule on high, in the Capitol. I hear the Queen, though a bit aged, is quite lovely. Imagine me by her side, guiding the kingdom to a greatness the people have never known!" Bardune's eyes grew dreamy and distant.

"You have a serious superiority complex," Isle

217

muttered.

"Why shouldn't I? I have power over these wretched creatures, and in turn, will rule over mankind. If the Queen isn't as enamored with me as my current mate, I will simply kill her and rule on my own. I am reluctant to do so, I have learned that behind every powerful leader there is a female to hold him up when he is blue, but hey, one works with what they have!"

"You are completely out of your mind."

"Am I? You are *Buddies* with *the* most well-known Datsoe trapper alive. Everyone has heard the stories of your Ranger's amazing ability to kill our kind. I hate to point out the obvious, but you are, in fact, a Datsoe. I heard a rumor that you were to be his sacrifice at that barbaric feast, is that true?"

Isle winced. "Things changed."

"Things changed!" Bardune exclaimed. "And you say I'm crazy? Think about it Isle, you are different, and he was smart enough to realize it. He used you to escape. He isn't your friend." Kneeling, Bardune took Isle's chin in his hand, forcing him to meet his eyes. "I hate to break it to you kid, but he *never* cared for you. First chance he got he let you go. If he really cared for you, he would have fought beside you, and you would have escaped with him through where, the gate? Did they crack open one of the mighty barriers to allow those wretched Guardians in? Or are they still out there, hiding from me? I have to know!"

"He was injured!" Isle protested. "He didn't want to let me go!'

"Ah, but he did, and so did his friends. They weren't hurt, were they? But, they were all too happy to let a youth die for them. They never cared for you."

218

"That isn't true!"

Squeezing Isle's chin, Bardune hissed "But it is! I haven't heard one word of his return. He used you to help him and his murderous team escape."

Isle pulled away from Bardune, who released his grip. "No, no you're lying. Ranger isn't like that."

"Isn't he? It takes a cold and calculating man to be as powerful as Ranger is." Pushing to his feet, Bardune slowly circled Isle. "Imagine, all the years of service he has given to his kingdom, all of your brothers and sisters he has slaughtered. As a soldier once myself, I can tell you I never would have become friends with the enemy, I would have killed them. They left you to your fate Isle, all alone. Where did they go?"

"If you are so powerful, you shouldn't have to ask me," Isle retorted.

"They must have escaped through the gate; it is the only thing that makes sense. Otherwise, you would still be with them, acting like a pathetic little lap dog." Looking down at Isle, Bardune changed tactics. "When I first turned, I lost myself. It can be an unsettling experience, laying there in the dark, wondering if you are in the Lake of Abysmal Souls. And the hunger, by Juwa the hunger! It consumed me, stripped me down to a slobbering mindless beast. Do you know how I found my way back? Our Queen. She cares for each of her children, shows them how to survive. We all are family down here." Crouching in front of Isle once more, Bardune smiled. "We are brothers Isle. Our connection goes way deeper than anything you can imagine. Remember the light I shared with you before? It healed you, restored you. Tell me what I want to know, and the light can be yours again. Take your place at my side, let's rule the humans together!"

Taking in Bardune's earnest expression, Isle couldn't contain his snicker. "How stupid do you think I am? You've had me tortured for hours, and call me your brother? Please. You may be right, and Ranger never was my friend, but he treated me way better than you ever have. I wonder what your Queen would think of your little plan of taking over their castle? Does she know you want a new mate? Hmmm, things to consider!"

Lashing out with rage, Bardune struck Isle.

"You are a powerful leader?" Spitting out blood, Isle continued. "You can't even hit as hard as Quail, and she's a tiny little human. Maybe this place needs a new King."

Raising his hand again, Bardune hesitated. There was something in Isle's eyes that he couldn't quite put his finger on. Almost as if he wanted Bardune to strike him. Why? Tilting his head, he studied his captive. "Perhaps I have underestimated you."

Sitting on the rocky ground, Bardune crossed his legs and leaned against the cave wall. "You know, I have to admit, it is kind of refreshing carrying on an actual conversation with someone. For years now it has been grunt, snarl, and roar. Gets old." Closing his eyes for a moment, Bardune chuckled. "Can I tell you a secret? I'm building an army. It hasn't been easy, let me assure you. When I first arrived it was just me, and the Queen naturally. Our kind had been all but wiped out. The soldiers I traveled with had been turned, and did their part to create more Datsoes, but they were quickly killed off. Once I discovered I could turn any creature I wanted into my servant, I had a grand time. Meandering through the forest, I infected everything from wolves to chipmunks. It was fascinating! Some animals retained their original forms, others completely changed. I still haven't figured out why, but I digress.

Soon, the woods were teeming with my creations, and then their creations! But that presented me with a problem. No one can take over a kingdom with a band of rabid squirrels. And everyone was, well, eating each other! I had inadvertently created a mess. Luckily, the Queen was able to get everyone under control. It has taken decades, but I have come to realize that running around biting everything is not the answer. I need an army that has a brain, like you and I, Isle. That is why I have been breeding with the Queen."

Catching Isle's look of disgust, Bardune's amusement rang throughout the cavern. "It isn't as bad as you think, once you get the hang of it. Just imagine, an army of intelligent offspring that I can control. It hasn't worked yet, but as the saying goes, practice makes perfect!"

"Why do you need an army? Can't you just be happy ruling over what you already have?"

"That is an interesting question, Isle. I applaud you. Even when I was a human, I wanted more. My parents were poor and pathetic. It took me quite a while to remember my human life. Tell me, do you have any recollection of yours yet?"

Isle shook his head, fascinated with what Bardune was telling him, despite the circumstances. The King of Datsoes was sitting on the ground, sharing secrets as though they were old friends.

"Yes, well, it doesn't always come back, and usually takes a trigger. For me, it was these." Pointing to his daggers, Bardune continued. "I won them in a game. Truth be told, I cheated. I found them in the cave where I first met the

Queen, years after I had been turned. I honestly don't remember why I had gone back there, curiosity perhaps, but there they were, and memories filled me. But, to answer your original question, no, I am not happy. I am tired of the stink down here. It is wretched, you have to admit. All of the decay, excrement, mold…" Bardune trailed off with a shudder. "I've always wanted to live in the Palace, sleep on soft beds with fine linens. Just imagine Isle, how the wine would taste! Roasted chicken and chocolate. Have you had chocolate before?"

"I am not sure what that is," Isle replied hesitantly.

"I had it once. It was incredible! We could have all the chocolate we could eat. If all goes according to my plan, we could bathe in it!" With a sigh of contentment, Bardune smiled. Focusing on Isle once more, he leaned forward. "If we are to fulfill these beautiful dreams, I need your help."

"How can I help you? You hold all the power."

"That isn't true! You can tell me if the Guardians made it through the gate. What are their weaknesses? You see Isle, in order for my plan to succeed, Ranger must die."

"What? Why!?"

"Because he has been in my way for too long. For decades I have been carefully planning, searching, trying to gather information. Do you know how irritating it is when you send a spy over the wall, and it gets killed? At first it was easy. I sent a few Datsoes over, avoided the gates, and everything was fine. But then, he came along. It was almost as if he was single handedly defeating every one of my scouts. So, I sent more, then more. Very few came back, and those that did returned with tales of an intelligent warrior that could not be defeated. Not only does he have to die, I will take great satisfaction in doing it myself."

"But you said he is smart, maybe you could talk to him, create peace between us."

"Peace? Who wants that?" Aghast, Bardune stared at Isle. "My plan is already in motion. With WinterNox arriving early, I will catch the humans off guard, cutting through that stupid rose wall like butter. Mmm, remember butter? Potatoes swimming in it, golden and dripping..."

"But Ranger already knows WinterNox is early!" Isle blurted desperately.

"What's this? He already knows? How?" Bardune demanded.

Isle's eyes shifted. "That isn't important. What matters is now your plan won't work. No butter for you! It would be better if you met with the Guardians, ended the war..."

Leaping to his feet, Bardune paced. "This won't do! This won't do at all! I have been planning for ages, things are already set into motion! I felt the shift in the air months ago and knew my time had come!" Looking down at Isle, he paused. "Did you sense it? It was almost like the snow was whispering to me, letting me in on a little secret."

Isle shook his head. "I had no idea."

"Interesting. The Queen was oblivious as well. It was all so perfect! The roses would die early, taking everyone by surprise. The men would be unprepared, the extra forces would not have a chance to arrive! My forces could sail through any gate I choose." Stomping his boot clad foot, he snarled, "I must attack now. If they already know snow is coming, then they are surely bringing that stupid army toward the gates even as we speak. If I kill the Guardians before they get the chance to prepare, I can still turn this to my advantage."

"No!"

Smiling, Bardune bowed. "This has been lovely; you have been most accommodating. Thank you, Isle. I simply could not have done it without you. Won't Ranger be surprised when I tell him how helpful you were? That will be the last thing he ever hears, how you betrayed him."

"But, no, I didn't!" Panting, Isle pushed himself up.

"Didn't you? Now I know what they know, WinterNox is early, Ranger is too injured to fight, that they are all holed up in one place. Without the leaders, those gates will fall under my forces. I owe it all to you," Bardune sang. "Perhaps I will let you live long enough to watch me kill Ranger, then I will eat chocolate…"

Isle's eyes turned black. "You will not TOUCH HIM!"

Isle finally got his wish. He felt the familiar burn of extra arms bursting from his torso and welcomed the thick shell racing across his skin.

"Oh my, this is an interesting development." Bardune leaned forward, anxious to see what happened next. He had never seen a Datsoe transform into something new before. Isle's teeth grew, his claws extended, then… nothing. Frozen, Isle's breath was labored. Turning, Bardune saw the Datsoe Queen behind him. Her eyes held Isle's, preventing his transformation. The black dragon-like head seemed to shimmer a midnight blue. Her jaws parted, revealing the row of menacing fangs that had started the Datsoe plague so long ago.

Irritated, Bardune wiped a smear of silver blood from his jacket. "I was curious to see where that was going," he grumbled.

Slowly, she turned toward Bardune. Her blood red

eyes blinked once, making him swallow.

"Of course, you made the right decision. Who knows what he would have been capable of. Well, I suppose you know. Hmm. I will need to take this into account. You had better let him rest my love. I will not be needing him any more today, but who knows, he may be useful later." Bardune would have been all too happy to let Isle die at that moment, especially if it meant keeping the little runt from squealing his plans to the Queen. But, he also knew Isle would make excellent bait.

"I won't let you do this."

The Queen and Bardune turned to Isle with surprise.

"I believe your hold is slipping my dear," Bardune murmured.

Coiling her long neck around Isle's still form, the Queen locked eyes with him once more.

"You were saying?" Bardune mocked.

Isle desperately tried to divert his eyes away from the Queen's gaze. He could almost hear her voice in his mind, calling.

"Isle, Isle, be with me, join me, let us become one," she whispered.

"Can you hear her? Such a sweet voice, so seductive, so powerful." Bardune ran his hands along her mighty jaw, drawing a purr of pleasure from her. "No one can resist her sway. You know, I have just come up with a clever idea! She can convince you to transform into whatever, and YOU can kill Ranger. Oh, it is just too delicious! Unless he kills you first!"

"Never!" Isle ground out.

Drawing her head back, the Queen looked at Bardune with confusion.

"I will give you one thing kid; you may be just as stubborn as I am. If it turns out you are right, and he does care about you, I will simply kill you both." Pulling out one of his daggers, Bardune struck Isle on the head with the hilt, knocking him unconscious.

Loosening her grip, the Queen allowed Isle's limp body to fall to the ground.

"Come along my sweet, I believe it is time for your energy fix." Bardune said. "After you are fed, I think I may take a quick journey. Won't be gone long!"

Side by side, they strolled through the tunnel into a giant cavern, filled with hungry Datsoes.

"Soon my brothers, we will feed!" Bardune raised his fist, pleased with the loud response from the surrounding occupants. Glancing at the Queen, he considered his options. She was useful in many ways, despite her lack of humanity. Maybe he could have both Queens by his side. "You know my dear, I wonder what you would think of chocolate? We would need quite a bit for you to get a real taste of it, but I have a feeling such a thing is no longer out of our reach..."

Bardune's laughter washed over Isle's prostrate form.

Clicking its talons, the flesh eating Datsoe crept from the darkness, anxious to dine again. Surely Bardune wouldn't notice if a bit more was missing. Looking furtively around, it made its way carefully to Isle's feet. Yes, it would start there.

Licking its lips, it let out an outraged squeal when the cave's guard picked it up. Opening its jaws wide, it swallowed the flesh eater whole, then let out a satisfied belch.

FallHeart the 75th of

222 D.P

The door to the soldiers' quarters burst open, sending a ray of offensive light over Berk's face. Groaning, he threw his hand over his eyes and rolled over on his cot.

Striding into the room, Kion captured the attention of the men who were off duty. "I need some volunteers."

Huddling further under his covers, Berk grimaced. Volunteer for Kion? That left him out. He already had to work his butt off day and night to watch that boring rose wall, he wasn't going to sacrifice any of his free time to do more. Especially for a snooty Guardian who never gave him the time of day.

One of the men from the cot beside him spoke up.

"I will help you Sir, what can I do?"

Berk rolled his eyes behind closed lids. It was Jenson, he was sure of it. The boy was disgustingly helpful. Yes sir, no sir, it made him want to throw up. In fact, with the hangover he had, Berk might just do that.

"Ranger has concerns about an impending attack. Come Jenson, I have much to explain. You there, Berk, come along as well," Kion ordered.

"I didn't volunteer sir," Berk mumbled.

"Consider yourself drafted," Kion snapped.

With a disgusted sigh, Berk rolled up and met Kion's fierce gaze with bloodshot eyes. "Sir, I…"

"Now soldier!"

Whirling, Kion left the room without a backward glance.

Turning toward Jenson, Berk snarled, "Why do you have to be so irritating?"

"Leave the boy be, Berk. Get your lazy, drunk arse out of bed and see what Kion needs."

Glaring at his commanding officer, Berk did as he was told.

Following Jenson into the great hall, Berk, for once, found himself tongue tied. Every Guardian of the realm sat before him.

"Gentlemen, here is what I need you to do," Kion began.

Looking around, Berk quickly tuned Kion out. Glancing at Jenson, he could tell the little idiot was lapping up every word the gatekeeper said. Gatekeeper, guardian, bah. He could fight any of these morons under the table they sat at. Focusing on the one on the end, he realized that must be Ranger. He had heard tales of his heroism, but really, the guy just looked old and tired. Wait, was that a pitcher of ale sitting in front of Ranger? Licking his lips, he shifted, trying to figure out a way to get his hands on it. The flask in his pocket was getting low, he needed a way to refill it. Movement captured his attention, and he found the woman staring at him intensely. Well, naturally she would, he was known to be considered handsome. Very few ladies could resist his charms. Smiling at her, he moved his pelvis suggestively in her direction.

"Is this really the best you could come up with, Kion?" Quail demanded. Staring at the soldiers before her, she supposed the youth seemed eager enough, but the man behind him stank of urine and old wine. After what he clearly thought was a charming invitation to share her bed, she felt compelled to voice her objection. It took everything in her power not to throw her dagger at him.

"These men are off duty and have volunteered to assist us Quail," Cliff objected. "Try to be patient."

Ah, so that was Quail, Berk thought. Wiggling his eyebrows at her, he wondered if she would be willing to step into one of the back rooms with him, with the jug of ale of course.

"Thank you for your time gentlemen, you are dismissed." Kion watched Jenson, knowing the lad would be an asset to their plan. He had heard about Berk from his commanding officer. Perhaps this was what he needed to pull his head out of his flask and onto the battlefield.

Feeling Jenson nudge him, Berk snapped out of his fantasy of Quail in a bathtub filled with whiskey and followed the youth into the kitchens for rations. One of the kitchen's servants handed him a heavy basket filled with several days' worth of food. Flipping up the lid, he was pleased to see a small flask tucked into the corner. It would take him little time to convince Jenson to give him the other flask he was sure was in his supplies. The basket was heavy, shifting his thoughts toward ways of getting Jenson to carry both.

Glancing over his shoulder, Berk caught a final glimpse of the Guardians pouring over lists and sketches by the fire. What could be so important that they were here? Shrugging, he made his way behind Jenson to the armory. After a word with the head blacksmith, Jenson handed Berk several daggers and a sword.

Strapping his own weapons on, Jenson made his way

toward the door, grabbing a large coat as he went.

Stumbling after him, Berk called out, "Where in the Juwa are we going?"

*   *   *

Kion's town was swarming with activity. Carpenters and blacksmiths worked tirelessly, creating parts for traps of Ranger's design. Soldiers followed his blueprints, assembling the trap and setting them outside the gate, along the rose path, and in the forest. Stacks of arrows lined the wall, just in case a flying Datsoe approached. Children raced through the streets, gathering materials and running errands. Groups of women gathered to prepare meals, feeding the hungry workers. Everyone participated, no hand lay idle.

Ranger was delighted to discover that Kion had a Falconry. He had no idea that there were so many hawks left, let alone trained. He asked Kion if he would be willing to send one to the Capitol to deliver a personal message, to which the gatekeeper graciously agreed. Penning a lengthy missive, Ranger went into more detail than he had in years and hoped that Queen Francine would receive it in time.

Pushed beyond his limits, Ranger ignored Kion's warnings and consumed the mushrooms he had carried from the cave. Not only did they help take the edge off of his pain, they took his mind off of Isle. Was he still alive? Wounded? Quickly running out, he thought of ways to ask Kion where he had discovered the fungus, and if there were any more around the town. Based on the guardian's earlier disapproval, he set the question aside and tried to keep busy.

Satisfied with the preparations in Kion's town, the

other Guardians made arrangements for departure. Each of them chafed to get back to their gate and set up defenses of their own. Bardune could attack anywhere, and they wanted to be ready, just in case. They thought Ranger's traps were impressive. Some were hidden amongst the grass and leaves; others lay at the bottom of massive holes in the ground, covered with branches. At their request, he made sketches of his designs for each of them to take home. Planning on going their separate ways at morning light, they spent a quiet evening together, discussing strategies. It was decided that they would start communicating via hawk, Kion agreeing it was the most efficient way to stay in touch.

Marco promised that he would send Ranger's mighty stallion to him upon his return home. Quail expressed her reluctance to leave Ranger, especially while he was injured, but he assured her he would take care. She didn't believe him, and advised Kion at length on different things he could do to keep Ranger out of trouble. Growing weary of her lecture, Kion snapped at her, leading to another argument.

It seemed, Cliff thought, that their temporary truce had ended. Sitting next to Leeon by the fire, he tried not to laugh.

Eventually, the Guardians made their way to their rooms to rest before the upcoming journey.

*   *   *

Shifting his position in the crook of the branch he balanced on, Jenson rolled his eyes. If he had to listen to Berk brag about anything else, he was sure he would shove the man out of the tree they were using to keep watch.

It hadn't taken Jenson very long to realize Berk

didn't hear a word Kion had told them, and even less time to realize his fellow watchman was drunk as a skunk. He had given up hours before asking Berk to be quiet. They were supposed to be searching for Datsoe spies, or worse, an impending attack. But all Berk wanted to do was eat fried chicken, tossing the bones onto the ground and gulping down the contents of his flask. How, Jenson wondered, was he going to make it a week with this imbecile? They were barely past their first night and he was ready to scream.

Dawn's light cast a rosy glow over the horizon, drawing his gaze. He had never been outside of the gate before and was in awe of the roses. He wished he was a bit closer to the safety they provided, but took comfort in the fact that archers stood at the ready the moment he sounded the alarm. All he had to do was slide out of the tree and get to the path. The pine in which they sat stretched well above the wall, providing him an excellent view of the meadow beyond.

"Are you going to eat your chicken?" Berk reached a greedy hand toward Jenson's basket.

"Yes, I am," Jenson snapped. Berk had already stolen his flask, not that he cared too much, he wasn't a drinker. But he drew the line at his food. It needed to last him for as long as possible. Kion may pull them back early, but he wasn't taking any chances.

"But mine wasn't that good," Berk whined. "I just know that young serving girl gave you the best pieces. I saw the way she looked at you." With a sniff, he continued. "Clearly she has taken a shine to you, but not the way Quail likes me."

Here we go again, Jenson thought. Catching movement in the distance, he leaned forward.

"I've got to piss." Berk announced, grabbing a branch.

Ignoring him, Jenson squinted. What was that? A hawk from the Falconry? Looking below the flying figure, he thought he saw shadows shifting at the edge of the meadow, but it was so far, he couldn't be sure...

Shimmying down the tree, Berk stumbled toward a nearby bush and started to relieve himself.

Rising, Jenson gasped. A huge Datsoe, no, two, were pushing what looked to be a wooden platform into the meadow. And that was no hawk! Desperately sliding down the bark, Jenson yelled, "Berk, Datsoes! We must sound the alarm!" Tripping over his own flying feet, he righted himself and raced through the trees toward the rose wall. Grabbing the horn swaying wildly from his belt, he blew into it with all his might.

Turning, Berk watched Jenson flee, forgetting he was still mid-stream. Hearing the sound of fluid hitting his boot, he looked down and let out a curse. That idiot made him pee on himself! Finishing up, he pondered if Jenson was leaving, perhaps he could have his chicken after all. Hearing the sound of the horn, the first prickle of danger captured his attention. Jenson was already halfway down the rose path, making enough noise to raise the dead. What was it the boy had said? They were going to sound the alarm if Datsoes were coming. Realization crashed down on Berk, finally setting his feet into motion. Looking back, he saw flying Datsoes approaching fast, winging their way toward him. He counted at least a dozen before he focused on the path, pumping his arms for all they were worth. Arrows landed all around him, making the creatures above him shriek with rage every time they were struck.

234

Making it to the gate, Jenson saw the archers above send wave after wave of arrows at the Datsoes, who seemed unaffected by the roses' golden pollen. Berk had burst from the trees, and was now weaving drunkenly down the path, screaming. Shaking his head, Jenson drew his sword and took a few steps toward his fellow soldier.

Looking up, he saw what appeared to be a giant lamb flapping wings of curling wool. The odd shaped Datsoe was bleating loudly, dripping drool all over Berk, making him yell even louder. Stumbling, he landed face first, skidding along the path. With a frustrated baa, the Datsoe turned, braving the roses to reach its tasty treat. Hooves shaped like pincers reached down and grabbed Berk by the seat of his pants, raising him off the ground. Flailing wildly, he cried "Help, help!" Praying, he rose higher. Looking over his shoulder, he whimpered when the wooly Datsoe tried to take a bite out of his shoulder. "Please, I will stop drinking, be a better soldier, show up to practice on time, and will never tell another lie! Just let me live!"

By Juwa, Jenson thought, he was about to become a Berk bite! Leaping onto a giant rose vine, he shook with all his might, sending plumes of pollen into the air. Sneezing violently, the flying lamb started convulsing, dropping Berk into a heap onto the path. Running to his side, Jenson pulled him to his feet, and dragged him toward the gate. Blubbering, Berk clung to him, rambling on and on about how he would be a better man.

One of Ranger's traps went off, crushing another Datsoe that had charged up the path toward them. Pushing Berk through the gate, it slammed shut behind them. A medic grabbed Berk, guiding him toward the hospital. Jenson looked up at the wall in time to see Kion shout orders at the men. Taking the stairs two at a time, Jenson grabbed up a bow. Feeling a hand on his shoulder, he looked back to see Kion regarding him.

"The first wave of Datsoes are dead, we were able to take them by surprise." Looking over the roses, Kion grimaced. "Did you see anything other than the flyers?"

"I did, sir. It looks like they are setting something up in the field beyond. I didn't have enough time to see what they were doing." Jenson looked down, filled with shame.

"You are the hero of the hour. The Queen will hear of your courage."

Lifting his head with surprise, Jenson said, "Sir?"

"Your warning gave us the advantage we needed. And don't think I didn't see you save Berk."

"He was uh, struggling a bit."

"I see." Kion stared at Jenson, then shrugged. "I will deal with him later. For now, we must turn our attention to beyond the wall. War is upon us."

FallHeart the 76th of

222 D.P

Fear overshadowed the army. Seasoned soldiers had never seen anything like this. Datsoes swarmed the path that led to the gate. Running, slithering, and flying, they bellowed, snarled, and clawed. Those that were new to the front quivered in terror.

Flapping over the wall, the same lamb Datsoe that had grabbed Berk earlier bleated hungrily, surveying the tasty men below. Selecting a target, it dove on woolly wings.

Ranger burst from the wall, landing on its back. Gripping tightly with his thighs, he rode the Datsoe while he forced it downward, applying pressure to its wings. Bucking and bellowing, it frantically tried to unseat him. Piercing its skull with his blade, Ranger rolled off of the thrashing creature as soon as they hit the ground and immediately got to his feet. Leaning heavily on his good leg, he was grateful for the brace provided by the doctor. He ached, but it was manageable.

The men watched this spectacle in awe, then let out a cheer. Holding up his blood-stained sword, Ranger waited until they were silent.

His deep voice rang across the courtyard. "Friends, today the world of man faces a force never before seen. The Datsoe leader, Bardune, used to be one of us. He has betrayed his people for power."

Angry murmurs swept through the crowd.

"I have spent my life defeating these creatures of death, and I have no intention of stopping now. I am going to march out there and show Bardune what real men are capable of. Who is with me?"

"I am!" one man called.

His voice was joined by a chorus of others, until Ranger held up his sword once again.

"I'm going outside the gate and facing the Datsoes head on. Will any of you join me?"

"You know I am with you," Quail replied.

"Count me in!" Marco yelled.

Other men raised their hands courageously, and soon, Ranger had a formidable force ready to fight outside the safety of the gate.

Leeon led a group of men onto the wall to join the archers already engaged in battle.

Young soldiers followed Cliff, setting more traps, and killing every Datsoe they saw.

Watching the other Guardians take charge of the hoard of men, Kion was grateful they hadn't had a single casualty... yet. Running up a flight of stairs, he joined the fray.

Catapults had been set up in between the rows of archers, hurling boulders with deadly accuracy. Scores of Datsoe bodies lay on the path outside the gate, but more just crawled over the corpses. Others stopped to feed, losing sight of their original purpose. Everything Bardune told them was quickly forgotten, and a frenzy began.

Arrows rained down, creating cover while Ranger led his soldiers out of the gate. The noise was stifling, giving him the urge to cover his ears. Some of the men behind him hesitated, taking in the scene. Datsoes were gorging themselves on their fallen comrades, others fought each other. A flying creature that may have been a fox landed in front of them, struck by a flying rock from a catapult.

"Maybe we don't even have to do anything," a soldier behind Ranger said, "They are too busy taking each other out."

"This is only the beginning," Ranger replied. "Bardune must have known this could happen. All of our focus is here, but I'm told a soldier named Jenson saw something happening in the meadow beyond. We need to make sure this isn't a distraction."

Traveling down the edge of the path, Ranger led his team toward the forest, killing any Datsoe they came across. Quail and Marco brought up the rear, making sure the new soldiers knew what to do. Pollen created a thick haze, making visibility difficult. Every time a Datsoe fell from the sky, it crashed into the roses, sending fresh plumes of the yellow dust skyward.

An eerie silence surrounded them. New Datsoes were reluctant to enter, finding it difficult to breathe. The soldiers on the wall couldn't see the ground, so they stopped firing and prepared for another attack.

Finally making their way to the trees, Ranger took a deep breath. Looking back, he saw the men were covered with pollen. Good, he thought, that could be used as an advantage. Weaving through the pines, they finally made it to the edge of the meadow and stopped in shock.

"By Juwa!" Quail whispered.

A giant wooden box lay in the center of the clearing, harnessed to muscular Datsoes. An army of creatures stood around it, quietly waiting. Several were dead, victims of the traps Ranger had set earlier. Looking toward the top of the bizarre structure, they saw Bardune standing next to the Queen. Tied by his wrists, Isle swayed from a pole above them.

Squeezing the hilt of his sword, Ranger took a step forward, furious.

Quail grabbed his arm, trying to pull him back. "Ranger, wait! We need a plan."

Wrenching from her grip, Ranger pointed to the small figure. "That's Isle up there, I must get him down."

"Aye, but that is exactly what that ugly bastard is waiting for," Marco replied. "Let's think this through. Quail and I can lead the men in a frontal attack, while you sneak around and get the boy."

A soldier from the back of the group boldly stepped forward. "I will help you sir, there are no stairs I can see to climb up there. With your leg in a brace, you'll need a boost."

Ranger looked down at the brave youth. "What's your name, son?"

"Jenson, sir."

"You're the one that sounded the alarm?" Quail looked at him with surprise. He didn't look a day over 15.

Thickly lashed blue eyes returned her gaze. "Yes Ma'am. I'm ready to do my part to take them down. I heard what Ranger said about their leader, how he used to be a man. I'm sure I am not the only one who would like to have a discussion with him."

The way Jenson said *discussion* made Marco grin appreciatively.

"Here's the thing, Jenson. I'm going up there to save a Datsoe. One who used to be a boy. You have a problem with that?" Ranger's gray eyes were piercing, but Jenson remained calm.

"If he is a friend of yours, Sir, he is a friend of mine."

"That's good enough for me. Ready men?" Marco lifted his ax, preparing for battle.

Clasping Quail's shoulder, Ranger said, "Keep safe, don't get dead."

"Tell Isle hello for me," she replied.

"You can tell him yourself when we get back. Ready Jenson?"

"Ready sir," Jenson replied.

"Just call me Ranger." Looking at the rest of the men he continued. "Gather into groups, don't let them single you out! Together you can take one down faster than if you try to do it alone."

Marco's war cry rang over the meadow, followed by a rush of men.

Raising his eyebrow, Bardune stood above his small army, watching men pour from the tree line. "Why are they all yelling like that? It's rather annoying." From a distance it was hard to tell, but he didn't see the face he was searching for. Flicking a scale from his jacket, he looked over at the Queen. "Kill them."

Turning her head, the Queen let out a mighty roar, sending the Datsoes into action.

Man and beast clashed in the center of the field.

Embedding his ax into the skull of the nearest Datsoe, Marco yelled instructions to the men. Blades flashed in the sunlight, taking down one opponent after another.

Watching a dark-haired woman leap over the snapping jaws of a particularly nasty goat Datsoe, Bardune almost applauded when she beheaded it. "To be fair, that one deserved it. I've been tempted to kill it myself. Always eating my stuff…" Shaking his head, Bardune continued. "Who knew they would be so bold as to come out here and attack us? I thought we would have to drag our friend all the way to the gate. No matter." he shrugged. "I have a feeling I know who is behind this crafty attack. But where is he?" Wincing, he watched one of the muscular Datsoes harnessed to the odd carriage fall under a group of sharp swords.

The object of Bardune's obsession was fighting his way around the platform, followed closely by Jenson. Much to Ranger's dismay, there wasn't a single access point to the top. They had briefly considered having Jenson boost him up onto one of the enormous wooden wheels, but there wasn't a place Ranger could grab onto to pull himself up. Frustrated, he slashed through another Datsoe, stepping aside when the body fell.

"Maybe you can keep killing them until they form a large enough pile to climb," Jenson suggested. He was in awe of Ranger's skill and tenacity. Even with a broken leg, the Guardian was cutting through these creatures of death like blades of grass.

Panting, Ranger almost laughed. "Interesting suggestion, but it does give me an idea." Looking above them, he focused on a Datsoe circling overhead. "Let's get its attention." Pulling out one of his smaller daggers, Ranger threw it. He grunted with satisfaction when it plunged into one of the wings, gaining the creature's angry scrutiny. Diving toward them, it let out a squawk.

Ramming his sword into its gut at an angle, Ranger held on tight, allowing the Datsoe to pull him off of his feet. He wasn't sure who was more surprised, Jenson or the Datsoe. Trying to avoid the stream of blood pouring out of his victim's wound, he yanked the blade toward him the moment it got him high enough to step onto the wood. Without a backward glance, he limped toward Isle's swinging body.

A large wooden pillar rose from the center of the structure, obscuring Ranger's view of the front of the carriage. Thick ropes had been tossed over a wooden cross, suspending Isle's unconscious body. Climbing a small set of stairs, he grabbed Isle's limp arms. Suddenly, blue sparks shot from Isle, freezing Ranger into place. Once again, he felt his energy ebb, just as it had in the mushroom cave.

Lifting his head, Isle opened his eyes. With horror, he realized Ranger stood before him, and he was draining him without even trying. Frantically wiggling, he managed to break free from Ranger's grip and swing away.

Momentarily paralyzed, Ranger's heart sank when he realized how injured Isle was. Patches of skin were missing from large parts of his body, leaving dark scabs. Bruises marked his face, proving that Bardune had not been a gracious jailer. Flooded with guilt, Ranger fought the numbness and spoke.

"I'm so sorry, I never should have let you leave."

"Ranger! No! You need to get away! Bardune was waiting for this!"

Reaching out once more, Ranger gripped Isle. "It will be ok. Let's get you down, then figure out a way…"

One of Bardune's daggers pierced the back of his hand, pinning it to Isle's shoulder. Hearing his friend's gasp of pain, Ranger tried to pull the blade out with his other hand. When it refused to budge, he realized barbs lining the weapon were preventing him from extracting it without ripping a larger hole in his hand.

"Something wrong?" Bardune asked.

244

Turning his head, Ranger saw the King of Datsoes standing beside his Queen. Her scales shimmered in the sunlight off of her sinuous body. Her tail coiled around Bardune, maintaining constant contact. Ranger found himself wondering who was controlling the relationship in this odd pairing.

"Do you like it?" Bardune asked, holding up the dagger's twin. "I won these in a game of chance when I was still human. They look like normal weapons, but they are wonderfully lethal. You can't extract them without knowing the secret of releasing the barbs, unless you want to hurt your little pal there. I suggest you drop your sword, unless you want this embedded in his skull. I have excellent aim, and I assure you it will kill him."

The sound of metal clattering to the wood could barely be heard over the battle below as Ranger's sword fell, but it brought a surprising grimace to Bardune's face.

"Well boy. I guess you proved me wrong. He really does care." Focusing on Ranger, Bardune tilted his head questioningly. "You know you are going to die, yet you accept your fate for the sake of what, friendship?" Sneering, Bardune continued. "Is he worth it Ranger? Giving up your power, status, the privileges those sniveling followers rain on you because of who you are? You are willing to sacrifice all of that for one of us?"

"He's not one of you, and ten times the man you ever were," Ranger spat.

Bardune jerked back as if struck. "Strong words for someone in your precarious position," he growled. "You should be licking my boots, pleading for your pathetic lives. I will roll over these men and into that gate with ease. Nothing can stop me now, especially you." Shifting his gaze

245

to Isle, he said, "Do you remember what I told you would happen if it turned out I was wrong?" Walking toward what appeared to be a branch jutting out from the base of the platform, he pushed it forward.

The sound of clinking chains rattled under Ranger's feet, making him look down. Wooden planks started to slide back, revealing an inner chamber. An unparalleled stench wafted up, making him scrunch his nose.

A loud roar came from the blackness, making man and Datsoe alike turn toward the huge structure. The Queen's eyes pulsed, looking over the edge of the platform herself with what could only be described as a grin splitting her grotesque features.

"Were you curious why I built this contraption? It certainly wasn't for show." Bardune rested his hand on the Queen's neck, "You see, I knew we'd run into some obstacles along the way. I created a backup plan, a sure way of striking fear into all those who try to resist." His voice carried across the silent battlefield, and Bardune reveled in the attention he was receiving. Pushing the lever down even further, a massive door lowered toward the grass. "For years I have been grooming this beauty. When I created it, I knew it had potential. I took it deep into the caverns, where I have been feeding it, bonding with it."

The entire structure swayed left, then right, bowing under the movement of the inner sanctum's occupant as it moved toward the light. Gray scaled nostrils tipped a giant snout, followed by row after row of man-sized teeth. Slowly, the beast lumbered onto the field, making even the Datsoes take a step back in fear. What could only be described as a crocodile raised its oblong head and bellowed again, spraying geysers of thick drool across the meadow.

"Oh my Juwa," Quail gasped. "How can we even begin to fight that?"

"Well, it has tiny little legs, so it can't move that well," Marco replied. "That must be why Bardune had to cart the thing all the way here."

Jenson had made his way back to the soldiers and stood behind Quail with his jaw hanging open. Looking toward the top of the giant carriage, he could see Ranger next to a smaller figure, but couldn't quite make out what was happening.

"The biggest Datsoe you'll ever see." Bardune grinned, "It will do anything I tell it to."

Ranger could feel Isle shaking. Peeling his eyes away from the spectacle below, he tried to pull his hand free.

Swallowing a yelp of pain, Isle tried to remain still, hoping Ranger would be able to get the dagger out of his shoulder.

Turning toward the sound of Isle's voice, Bardune's eyes narrowed. He could see what Ranger was trying to do. "Well gents, I would say it's been nice knowing you, but it hasn't. Have fun getting to know my pet personally." With a final twist of the lever, he made the wooden cross come crashing down, making Ranger grab onto the same rope that held Isle suspended. Laughing, Bardune watched the Guardian try to hang with one hand. Swaying wildly, the pair were suspended over the giant Datsoe below. With a whistle, Bardune got the creature to look up, then open its massive jaws. Catching Ranger's eye, he bowed, took aim, and threw the second dagger. It sang through the air, slicing the rope that held them.

"You lose."

Watching the drama unfold, Quail watched Ranger

247

flail above the Datsoe's waiting mouth. Without a moment of hesitation, she ran toward the carriage.

"To the beast!" Marco yelled, following her lead.

With a battle cry, Jenson and the others raced toward the monstrosity.

The Datsoes that had been engaged in battle earlier remained silent, refusing to attack any of the soldiers that passed them. Without the Queen's sway, they were reluctant to fight on. Many were wounded, and terrified of being eaten themselves.

Ranger tried to protect Isle with his body, but he knew it was no use. They were falling directly toward the massive tongue. His only regret was that Isle was going to die with him. "I'm sorry Bud," he whispered, embracing the shivering boy.

Unbeknownst to Ranger, Isle wasn't shaking out of fear, but sheer rage. He finally had a friend, and Bardune wasn't going to let him even enjoy that. Hearing Ranger's whispered apology tipped him over the edge, and he began to transform.

Skidding to a stop, Quail and Marco watched in horror as Ranger and Isle fell into the giant's mouth, and its teeth snapped shut.

"Well, that was exciting wasn't it!" Bardune called down. "Join me, or you're next!"

Hurling the dagger Ranger had given her as a gift, Quail narrowly missed Bardune's head.

"Oh my, someone has spunk." Narrowing his eyes, Bardune assessed the angry woman below him. A snarl of pain behind him made him turn toward the Queen. Looking down, he realized that the blade had embedded itself into her side. "That was rather rude. Here now, let me…" Pulling out

248

the offending weapon, Bardune tossed it over the side of the platform. "Perhaps a bit of light will help what ails you my dear." Tipping his head back, his jaws extended, allowing an orb to pass through. Greedily absorbing it, the Queen let out a relieved sigh. Meeting her eyes, he bowed. "Your wish is my command." Snapping his fingers at the Datsoe below him, he said, "Kill them all."

Leveling its massive head, it looked toward the crowd of men with a hiss. Taking a small step, it let out another booming call.

Raising her sword, Quail cried out, "For Ranger!" Plunging the blade into the thick hide of the monster, she realized it had little effect. The Datsoe didn't even turn.

"Now what?" Marco asked.

"We keep stabbing until we find a weakness." Moving to a new spot, she tried again. Other soldiers had engaged the creature from the other side, narrowly avoiding its thrashing tail.

Suddenly, the monster threw its head up, and they could see something pushing against its neck from the inside. Bellowing and squirming, it was clear the Datsoe was in pain. Shuffling back, it tried to make its way back into the wooden carriage.

"What are you doing? Get out there and kill them!" Bardune yelled.

Weaving her way toward the edge of the wood, the Queen groaned.

"What do you mean something is wrong? He is invincible! Nothing can pierce that thick hide of his, especially a few puny swords!"

Black blood erupted from the Datsoe's neck, spraying in every direction. Ripping and clawing, Isle crawled out with Ranger on his back.

"Yes! Go Isle!" Quail cheered.

"Why are you cheering for a Datsoe?" Jenson asked.

"That's no Datsoe lad, that is Isle!" Marco laughed.

Making his way to the ground, Isle shook Ranger off, then climbed right back up the creature into the hole again.

No one could mistake the fact that Isle was destroying the giant Datsoe from the inside out. Coughing up blood, it fell to the grass, dead. Climbing to the top of the corpse, Isle raised his head, and let out a war cry, sending the other Datsoes fleeing into the woods.

Ranger studied the dagger still protruding from both sides of his hand. Pushing on different parts of the hilt, he finally figured out the mechanism that pulled the barbs back in, allowing him to slide the blade out of his flesh. Pulling a strip of bandage from one of his many pockets, he wrapped his hand the best he could.

"Ranger!" Throwing herself into his arms, Quail didn't care that he was covered in drool and blood "You're alive. I can't believe it!"

Returning her embrace, Ranger closed his eyes, filled with joy.

Taking in the scene, Bardune couldn't believe his eyes. His prize creature lay in a grotesque heap across the meadow. Men cheered, and his army was running away. Worst yet, Ranger stood, hugging the same woman that had thrown a knife at his head moments before. Thunder rumbled overhead, matching his rage.

With a commanding screech, the Datsoe Queen stopped several of the retreating creatures. Circling back, they engaged the soldiers once again.

Leaping down from his victorious perch, Isle attacked the closest one, saving Jenson from the jaws of death.

"So, that's Isle?" he asked Marco, panting from exertion. The Datsoe he battled was three times his size, and he knew he wouldn't have been able to take it down alone, despite his excellent swordsmanship. The creature that had saved Ranger sprang out of nowhere, knocking him aside. Marco offered him a hand, pulling him up.

Watching the two beasts tumble across a patch of wildflowers. Marco nodded. "Aye, you would never know by looking at him now that he was the tiny lad hanging from the rope up yonder." Gesturing toward the top of the platform, his eyes fell on Bardune and the Queen. She slithered her way off of the platform, carrying Bardune with her tail.

"Who is that?"

"I'm guessing that is the infamous Bardune, leader of the Datsoe army. Let's go chat with him." Swinging his ax at a nearby Datsoe, Marco leapt into battle with Jenson close behind.

Marco and Jenson weren't the only ones that noticed Bardune's retreat. Pulling away from Quail, Ranger watched them descend from the platform. Momentarily distracted, he was delighted when she handed him his sword.

"This is the second time I have retrieved this, thinking you were dead," she said sternly. "Knock it off, will you?"

"I will do my best," he replied, sliding it into his sheath. A thick fog started to roll in, making it difficult to see. Catching sight of a black scaled Datsoe sliding toward the tree line, Ranger could faintly make out Bardune beside it. The surrounding soldiers were making short work of the few Datsoes that had answered the Queens summons. Isle was fighting valiantly beside them. "We better make sure no one mistakes him for the enemy."

"You're right, I will spread the word. You should take a moment, gather your strength." Taking Ranger's nod as agreement, she engaged in a skirmish behind them. Quail didn't notice when Ranger slipped away, following Bardune into the mist.

Stepping into the trees, Ranger absently rubbed his arms, chasing away the sudden chill. Lousy time for this kind of weather, he thought absently. An eerie silence surrounded him, making Ranger draw his sword. His hand throbbed, his leg ached, but he couldn't let Bardune collect more Datsoes. This needed to end now. Concentrating on the forest floor, he searched for tracks.

Leaping from above, Bardune knocked Ranger to the ground. Kicking the Datsoe King aside, Ranger flipped up, clutching his sword. Slashing with his talons, Bardune met each blow from the sword with one of his own.

"You're so *different,*" Bardune said, finally breaking the silence. "Never have I met a human who simply refused to *die.*"

"You first," Ranger growled, slashing Bardune's arm open.

Bardune pulled away, looking at the wound on his arm with surprise. "I have to say, it has been a while since I have seen my own blood. Not red anymore, is it? Things change I suppose." He flashed a charming smile at Ranger. "Together, we could change the world. I offered a chance for power to your little friend, but he foolishly refused. I know you hold a high position in the Palace, together we could revolutionize things, bring peace to the land. Imagine the power you could have, ruling by my side. Why, the human Queen herself could be yours if you so desire."

"I'm not interested in anything you have to offer, you pompous, ignorant simpleton. Her majesty is beyond your reach, and I will die defending her and my people."

"As you wish. You have proven to be an admirable adversary, but our time together must come to an end."

"I would have to agree," Ranger said sharply. "The sooner I kill you and the monstrous thing you call a Queen, the better."

"Insolent mortal! I will take pleasure in ripping out your throat."

"You haven't had much luck killing me so far, I don't see how this will be any different."

Bardune lost all sense of humanity. Slashing wildly, he became the beast Ranger knew how to deal with best. Parrying every mindless attack, he drove Bardune back until finally, with a mighty shove, he knocked the Datsoe lord into the trunk of a tree. Lifting his sword, he pierced his shoulder, pinning him.

"You lose."

Bardune lifted his head, gaping at Ranger. Then his eyes shifted, and he smiled.

"Not quite."

Dozens of teeth sank onto Ranger's torso from behind, lifting him off of the ground. The Datsoe Queen's hot breath washed over him as her venom pumped into his body. A feeling of calm filled him as he reached for his last dagger and drove it into one of her nostrils.

Shaking her head from side to side, her unique crimson blood poured over Ranger, mixing with his own.

Squealing with pain, she opened her mouth when he stabbed her again, then again. Flinging him away, Ranger hit a tree, breaking multiple bones.

Laying on a bed of pine needles, Ranger felt nothing. It was blissful really; he couldn't feel the ache in his leg or the pain in his hand anymore. Faintly, he thought he heard Isle roaring in the distance, making his lips curve into a smile. Maybe he should get up, he thought, but not right now.

He didn't hear Bardune yell in triumph as he pulled Rangers' sword from his shoulder, or the Datsoe Queen's squeals of outrage and pain.

A small stream of blood trickled out from the corner of his mouth, and down the side of his chin.

The last thing he saw was a swirl of flakes falling from the sky, softly landing all around him as his heart stopped beating, and his life slipped away.

WinterNox the 1st of 222

D.P

Following Ranger's scent, Isle made his way across the meadow and into the forest. He couldn't think very clearly in his beast form, but it was better than before. Perhaps the time he had spent with Ranger and the other Guardians contributed to his clarity, but he was able to put together semi-rational thoughts.

The moment he opened his eyes and saw Ranger looking down at him with such concern on the wooden platform, his heart flipped. Bardune had been lying after all, and all of his insecurities melted away. He knew that with Ranger there, everything would be alright. They would defeat Bardune, and he could start a new life. No more hiding, scrounging for food, living in fear!

Even when they were falling into the mouth of the Croc-Datsoe, and he started to turn into his monstrous form, he felt at peace. He was a hero, Ranger said so the moment they emerged, covered in gore. It took him a minute to process, but he was filled with pride. Imagine, being on the team of the good guys. Something sparked in the back of his mind, a faint memory of a story he loved long ago, but it faded as quickly as it came when a soldier cried out in distress. Defeating the offending Datsoe, he looked around for his friend to celebrate. Not seeing Ranger, he followed his nose into the forest.

Snow started to drift around him, but for once he

didn't mind. His blood cooled, and he felt like he might turn back, until he caught the scent of blood. Ranger's blood. It mixed with Bardune and the Datsoe Queen, drawing a low growl from him. Rounding a set of pine trees, he saw a figure laying face up, stained with crimson.

Disbelief flooded him. Surely this was a mistake. Giant puncture wounds marked where the Queen had bitten Ranger. His body lay in such a way that Isle could tell it was broken. Looking at the tree above Ranger, he saw an impact point in the bark. Whining, he nudged his friend with his nose, trying to get a response. The once sparkling gray eyes were open, but flat and faded. Keening, Isle laid next to Ranger, and placing his head on the cold ground, wept. Fluffy flakes started to cover Ranger's face, and Isle brushed them off gently.

The Datsoe Queen's venom dripped onto the ground with a sizzle, seeping from the gaping wounds. Sniffling, Isle stood, backing away from Ranger's body. He let out a long and mournful roar, sending a plum of steam into the air. Rage consumed him, giving him a new purpose.

Revenge.

Circling the area, Isle traced the fight between Ranger and Bardune, piecing together what happened. Zeroing in on the Queen's trail, he realized Bardune was no longer traveling with her. Through a red haze he followed her trail with deadly intent.

It didn't take him long to catch up to her.

Slithering back toward the hive, she called to the remaining Datsoes. Still bleeding from the wounds Ranger gave her, she was impatient for Bardune to join her so he could heal her with his light. Such a unique gift was rare, she had come to depend on him. Where had he gone?

Hearing footsteps behind her, she turned. Shocked, she saw Isle charging toward her. Using every ounce of power she possessed, she called to him. Her eyes danced; her song floated through his mind like the most beautiful thing he had ever heard.

It made him sick.

Opening his jaws as wide as possible, he lunged, ripping a chunk of her tail off and spitting it onto the forest floor.

Outraged, she bellowed. She hadn't fought in decades, always having others do her dirty work for her. She was used to being adored, cared for. This was unacceptable. Twirling around, she slithered around Isle, striking wherever she could. This insolent upstart would learn his place! His armor prevented her teeth from piercing his flesh, so she tried another tactic. Winding around his body like a snake, she squeezed.

Gasping for breath, Isle whipped his tail around, stabbing her with his stinger. Arching, she tried to dislodge it, giving him enough freedom to grab her with all four arms. Pulling with all his might, he ripped her in half.

Stunned, her eyes met his, then went limp.

Reaching into her mouth, he snapped off one of the fangs that had started the plague so long ago. Clutching it, he made Ranger a silent vow. He wouldn't stop until every last Datsoe was dead.

*   *   *

As WinterNox arrived early, and the soldiers made their way back toward the gate, an eerie silence settled over the forest. Snow fell with a vengeance, covering all of the deceased Datsoe bodies in the meadow and path.

Deep in the woods, a hand shot up through the icy blanket, fingers curling in agony.

Sitting up, Ranger wiped his face with a wet sleeve. All he could hear was a loud ringing, his vision dotted with multicolored lights. Swaying, he didn't feel each gash start to congeal, turning into an intricate web of black flesh. Pushing up, he was overcome with nausea, making him lean over the cold ground and vomit. Hunched on all fours, he heaved until he couldn't anymore, falling onto his side.

Shivering, he was able to finally focus on the trees around him. Disjointed memories started to float into his mind, but it was difficult to focus. His whole body burned. Gritting his teeth, he gasped in pain. Writhing, he tried to rise, to get away from the all-consuming agony.

Finally able to kneel, his vision cleared. Looking down, he saw the holes in his clothing. Running his hands across the material, he noticed the dark skin stretching across his torso. Realization hit him. He had been bitten. He was turning into the very thing he had been hunting and killing for decades.

The irony wasn't lost on him, even in his condition.

What on earth was he going to do? He knew he couldn't fight off the infection, it would only be a matter of time before his Asalairi blood failed under the exposure and strength of the venom.

Hate filled him. Dark thoughts and bloodlust then gave way to a deep, overwhelming hunger. Saliva flooded his mouth, his stomach rumbled.

Squaring his shoulders, he struggled for control.

"Well well, looks like I guessed correctly. You are turning."

Looking up, Ranger saw Bardune step from the shadows. His curved horns were dusted white, his mocking smile exposed gleaming fangs.

"Having a rough go of it, huh?" Bardune asked. "I don't remember my transformation, but I've seen it happen many times since. I'm trying to decide if I am enjoying your pain, or curious why it is taking so long. What makes you different? Never in my 222 years as a Datsoe have I seen a human go through the process so slowly. The transformation should be instantaneous." Tossing a sword into the snow, it landed by Ranger's feet.

Looking down, Ranger recognized it as his own, but he couldn't seem to find the will to pick it up. Fumbling back, he tried to shuffle away.

"I wonder what you will become?" Bardune kicked Ranger hard in the ribs, sending him sailing through the air.

Tumbling, Ranger caught himself just before he fell into one of the pits the men had dug earlier to set a Datsoe trap. At the bottom lay rows of pointed spears, ready to skewer their victim.

"I find myself torn, watch you turn into my minion, or kill you? Decisions, decisions! But this is getting boring. Maybe I can speed the process up."

Pulling Ranger up by his hair, Bardune bit him on the base of his neck.

Ranger's fist flew up instinctively, breaking Bardune's nose with a satisfying crunch.

Reeling back, Bardune grabbed his face. "You ingrate! You should be thanking me; I'm only trying to help." he hissed. "Now, you've made me mad. Our Queen will do whatever I tell her, and I will make sure you kill each of your Guardian friends." Leaning down, he whispered in

Ranger's ear. "Slowly."

Rows of incisors tore through the roof of Ranger's mouth. "_NO_!" Thrusting his head back, he crunched into Bardune's nose again. Standing tall, Ranger planted his feet, then slammed Bardune in the chest with the palm of his hand, sending the Datsoe King back several feet. Extending his arms, he looked at his hands with horror. Fingers extended and twisted, while thick claws emerged from each tip. With a grunt, Ranger leapt forward, tackling his opponent, sending them both sliding through the raging blizzard.

Biting, kicking, snarling, they rolled, each trying to gain an advantage. Eluding Ranger's grip, Bardune jumped behind a tree, then popped out the other side with a flying kick. Ranger stumbled for a moment, holding his head, then answered with a right cross.

Their fingers locked, claws digging into the other's skin. Brute strength had their arms shaking as they pressed against one another, ignoring the blood that began to leak down their wrists. Ranger released the tension, quickly dropping down onto one knee and swinging his leg around to knock Bardune over. Bardune landed, sending snow flying from the impact. Pulling his leg back, he kicked Ranger's knee, making him tumble down. Straddling Rangers torso, he rained blows repeatedly anywhere he could land them. Knocking Bardune's hand aside, Ranger jabbed his claw into Bardune's left eye. Bardune yelled, grabbing Ranger's wrist. Latching on to one of Bardune's curved, twisted horns, Ranger ripped it off with a loud CRACK!

Blood poured down Bardune's face, his empty eye socket reflecting the darkness in his soul. Lunging forward, he found himself slammed into a tree, held aloft by one of Ranger's arms.

Gulping for air, Bardune tried to chuckle. "What are you going to do, kill me? Go ahead, embrace the Datsoe within!" Ranger squeezed his throat, cutting off his speech.

It would be so easy, Ranger thought. Just a little more pressure and it would be over. Then he could find the Datsoe Queen and end the entire problem. He had the power now! He had the ability to do whatever he wanted, strength, skill, he could control everyone and everything… wait, what was he thinking about? He was so hungry, and angry. Trying to focus on Bardune, his thoughts circled like angry bees.

"If only Isle could see you now, what would he think? So much for his hero." Bardune laughed.

Isle? Who was Isle? What was this moron talking about? Lifting Bardune even higher, he tossed him, then followed the flying body to attack again. Pain is what was deserved, death is what was owed. Then he could feast. The forest was his for the taking.

A face appeared in his mind. Huge, burgundy eyes beamed above a shy smile. Who was it? Grabbing the side of his head, Ranger stumbled, trying to remember. Isle? Was that a name, place? Think, think!

"Isle!" Ranger gasped. Memories flooded him, Quail, Cliff, Marco… his friends. Holding up his blood-stained hands, he stared in horror. What was he doing?

Bardune watched with disbelief as Ranger took a deep breath, relaxed, and his eyes faded from red to maroon. Was he still fighting the venom, even though he had been infected twice?! He couldn't risk it. Ranger was too much of a wild card, the Queen would never be able to control him. Ranger had to die. No more games, no more fun. Pulling out his trusty daggers, Bardune attacked.

Stepping aside, Ranger watched Bardune swing and miss. The combination of venom had made Ranger impossibly fast, and Bardune never had a chance. Again and again, he swung, never coming close to making contact.

Impossible! Bardune panted with pain and frustration. Even with limited vision, he was still the best fighter who ever lived. He would skewer Ranger and be done, if he would just hold still! Slogging through the ever-deepening snow, he slid the blades together, trying to intimidate his foe.

Lunging again, Bardune's eyes widened when Ranger stepped aside, revealing the pit of spikes behind him. Flailing, he twisted, trying to regain his balance, but it was too late. Wooden stakes pierced his body, including his black heart. Staring up at Ranger's looming face with disbelief, Bardune found himself wondering what had happened to his parents. They had been the only people in his life he was sure really loved him. Did they lose the farm? Did they miss him? His last thought was of his mother, crying on his father's shoulder the day he walked away from them and joined the army.

Watching the light fade from Bardune's eye, Ranger sighed with relief. The monster was dead.

Unfortunately, a new one had been born, and he needed to die as well. Regret tugged at Ranger's mind. This was almost like a second chance, but he couldn't risk going back to the gate. What if he lost control and hurt someone? He wanted to say goodbye to his friends, make sure Isle was going to be alright, but he knew his transformation wasn't complete. No, it was best if he just ended it all here and now. Looking down into the pit, he took a step forward.

WinterNox the 1st of 222

D.P - *Late Afternoon*

Quail paced like a caged Datsoe. "Where are they?" she asked again, making Kion's eyes roll. "It's been too long since we've seen him."

"Quail, for the fifth time, I am sure they are fine. Ranger knows how to take care of himself."

"He went after Bardune, I just know it. Isle disappeared not long after, who knows what they are getting into?"

Taking her shoulders in his hands, he stopped her restless motion. "Quail, you have survived a difficult battle. Marco and Leeon left for the Capitol long ago. They are riding my swiftest horses. Once the Queen hears of all that has happened here, she will no doubt prepare a hero's welcome for you all. This isn't the first time Ranger has been in battle."

Staring into his golden gaze, she whispered, "Something is wrong, I can feel it."

Tilting his head, Kion hesitated. Quail had known Ranger since she was a child. Even if there was nothing amiss, she would feel better knowing everything was ok. Removing his hands, he turned. "Berk!"

Answering the loud summons, Berk stepped into the room.

"Yes sir?"

"Tell the stable hand to saddle my stallion and a sturdy mare. Quail and I will be departing shortly."

"I wouldn't mind going along myself," Cliff said from a nearby chair.

"Make that two mares, Berk."

"Right away, sir." With a bow, Berk immediately left.

Kion looked at his friends. "Gather whatever you need and meet me at the stables in ten minutes. I have something to attend to." Following Berk out the door, he went to find Jenson.

*   *   *

Standing at the edge of the deep pit, Ranger tried to gather the courage to take the final step. He knew this was for the best.

Heavy footfalls behind him had him spin and crouch defensively.

Isle pushed his way through the thick foliage, tracking the scent of another Datsoe. Growling, he set his sights on the lanky figure squatting by a giant hole in the ground and charged.

Recognizing Isle, Ranger stood and held his hands up. "Isle, wait! It's me."

Stopping inches away from Ranger's face, Isle snarled. All he could smell was Datsoe, but there was something about the voice… deep, but somehow familiar.

Resting his palm on the side of Isle's snout, Ranger tried to calm his agitated friend. "Shh, shh, it's alright."

Snorting, Isle's tail whipped in circles. Focusing on Ranger's face, he inhaled deeply, then lowered his head to

266

study the growing black patches of skin.

"It's me Bud, really. "

Isle knew there was something very wrong. Whining, he bumped Ranger's torso questioningly.

"I don't even know if you can understand me." Ranger sighed. "I can't wait for this poison to take me. I could hurt you. I'm sorry, Isle. I wish I could be like you, strong enough to resist the urges I already feel. The hunger, Juwa, it is all consuming." Pressing his head against Isle's neck, he took small comfort in the heat and contact. Pushing away, he looked back toward the pit. "I have to go now, Isle. I hope you know how much our friendship has meant to me, even in this short amount of time. I have to trust that Quail and the others will care for you, I know Leeon at least will find a way."

The sound of horses approaching had them both turning with surprise.

"Ranger!" Quail's voice called joyfully. "Thank Juwa you are alright!" Sliding from the horse, she ran toward him.

"Stop where you are!" Ranger snarled.

Kion dismounted and pulled his sword, catching Quail around the waist. "Wait Quail, there's something wrong."

Through the drifting snowflakes, Cliff saw what the others hadn't noticed yet. Ranger was covered in blood, and his skin was turning black. Long fangs stretched under glowing eyes that matched Isle's burgundy. "Quail, he's infected. Stay back!"

"That's ridiculous," Quail snapped.

"Cliff is right," Ranger said. "You need to keep your distance."

Isle's low growl filled the forest. His eyes lay on Kion's sword, and even now, he defended Ranger.

"It's ok Bud, they should be scared. I don't know what I am capable of, and neither do you."

"I assume this is Isle?" Kion turned to Cliff. "I thought you said he was a human once, could speak? This is not what I imagined."

"He can change back and forth," Cliff said. Keeping his eyes on Ranger, he rested his hand on the hilt of his weapon. If Ranger turned, there was no telling what Isle would do. Swallowing, he realized they were all in real danger.

"Is it true? You're... you've been bitten?" Quail asked.

"Yes Birdie. The Datsoe Queen and Bardune both infected me." Ranger drew his sword. "I am actually glad you are here; I would like you to keep this." Kneeling, he slid the sword through the snow toward her. "This time you can't give it back."

"Are you out of your mind? This can't be happening!" She struggled to free herself from Kion's grip. "Release me before I run you through!" Holding her own blade, she waved it threateningly at the muscular guardian.

Loosening his hold, he gave her a warning look, then leaned down to retrieve Ranger's sword.

Taking advantage of his distraction, Quail ran to Ranger, who caught her trembling form with an "Oof!"

Clinging tightly to him, she whispered "You are still you. You'll just be like Isle, right? We can continue the hunt, things won't change..."

"No Birdie." Taking her arms, Ranger slid his hands down to clasp hers. "I can't stop this. I have no idea if I will

268

be able to refrain from attacking you much longer, and I want to. Just the smell of you makes me hungry. Everything inside my head is telling me to kill you all. You have no idea how hard this is."

"But what about your Asalairi blood?" she demanded. "That should give you an advantage. You don't have to turn, don't give in!"

"It's not that simple," he snarled. Immediately regretting the fear on her face, he released her hands and took a step back. "My apologies, Quail. Since I have been bitten by two Datsoes, the venom is spreading in a way I couldn't have anticipated," he paused, then tried to smile, "Not that I have any experience in this area."

A sob escaped Quail, taking them all by surprise. Even Isle winced.

Taking a deep breath, Ranger leaned forward and lifted her chin with two clawed fingers. "Don't cry Birdie," he said softly. "We all knew this could be a possibility, and I have had more than my share of near misses."

"But what about the cure? I've heard that the Capitol's best doctors have created a serum that counters the effects of being bitten. They have tested it on dead Datsoes and…"

Ranger cut her off. "Quail, we both know there isn't enough time. The Palace is a day's journey from the gate. I don't think I can make it that long."

"Kion's stallion could carry you! We could get there faster than you think. Please Ranger, you can't leave me!" Tears fell unchecked down Quail's face as she pleaded with him.

Stepping behind her, Kion met Ranger's eyes. "No Quail, it is too late. He knows it, you must accept it."

Turning into Kion's chest, Quail cried quietly. Wrapping his arms around her, Kion gave her what comfort he could. He understood her pain, Ranger had been more than her mentor and friend, but her father.

"I do have a favor to ask." Ranger rested a hand on Isle's armor. "Please look after Isle, he's been alone for a long time. Now that Bardune is dead..."

"Bardune is dead?" Cliff exclaimed.

Gesturing toward the pit, Ranger nodded. Curious, they all looked down and saw Bardune's body impaled at the bottom.

"Good riddance," Quail uttered. "That was better than he deserved."

Isle started vocalizing urgently, waving his four arms around.

"The Datsoe Queen is dead too?" Ranger patted Isle, understanding every word. "You did what to her?"

Mimicking his earlier motion, the other Guardians understood well enough how she had died.

"Victory is ours!" Cliff exclaimed.

"A hollow one at best," Kion murmured, still holding Quail with one arm. Looking between Isle and Ranger, he saw that even now, their special bond remained strong. He had always admired Ranger's courage, but this was beyond even that. Making a sudden decision, he gave Ranger the promise he was hoping to hear. "I will take care of your friend. He will always be welcome in my town. He will have a place to live, food on his table, and a friend in me."

"Isle is coming with me," Quail argued. "You don't even know him. He can live in my town, not yours."

Raising his voice, Kion said, "That is ridiculous. Why would he make a long journey just to get to your town, when he can simply stay here?"

Pushing his arm off of her shoulder, Quail furiously wiped the tears from her face. "Ridiculous, is it? I have fought by his side; he saved my life! I owe it to him!"

Isle's head swiveled back and forth, watching the two argue.

Despite his pain, Ranger couldn't help but laugh, until his knees buckled. Grabbing his torso, he was overcome.

Raising his sword, Kion stepped in front of Quail, who could only watch Ranger quiver with horror.

Loud popping sounds came from his body as his bones began to reshape themselves. His silver hair started to grow, thickening and curling down his neck and over his shoulders. Helplessly, they listened to his cries of fear and pain.

"Quail... we have to... you know he doesn't want this," Cliff drew his sword and took a step toward Ranger.

"Wait! There might still be time," she pleaded.

Shoving Cliff back with his tail, Isle stepped between them and Ranger.

"Isle," Ranger panted, "No, let them..."

Spinning, Isle grabbed Ranger up into his arms, and fled.

Quail's jaw dropped. "Where the Juwa does he think he is going?"

"Is it possible he understood us?" Cliff stuttered. "Isle is very young; he may have hope that the cure can save Ranger."

"Does he even know where the Palace is? Once he is on the other side of the wall, he will be attacked, killed!" Quail said.

271

"How fast is he? We may be able to catch up, convince him to stop," Kion suggested, making his way to his stallion.

"I can't even see him anymore. He is long gone. I have no idea how fast he is, or what he is capable of." Cliff picked up Ranger's sword and handed it to Quail. "I am at a loss here, what do we do?"

Kion's horse reared, almost unseating him. "Whoa whoa!" Fighting for control, Kion noticed the other horses crying out in distress.

"There must be a Datsoe nearby! Scan the trees," Cliff said.

"There!" Quail pointed to the sky. A long Datsoe dove, snapping at the horses. Narrowing her eyes, Quail raced after it. "Help me catch it!" she called.

"Looking at Kion, Cliff scratched his head. "Did she say catch it, or kill it?"

"Surely she meant kill it," Kion replied.

But that was not what Quail had in mind at all.

WinterNox the 1st of 222

D.P - Dusk

Cliff was trying not to vomit. Looking at the landscape below, his head spun, and he had to close his eyes again. Instead, he tried to focus on hanging on to the Datsoe as they rode through the clouds. He had to admit, when Quail put her mind to something, nothing was impossible. She caught the flying creature and bullied it into letting her on its back. Every time it snapped at her, she gave it a solid kick. She pulled the reins off of her mare and created an ingenious way to guide it.

Kion stayed behind with the horses, declaring he had no intention of gallivanting across the sky like a crazy person. It had been difficult to convince Cliff to climb onto the thrashing Datsoe, but in the end he gave in. Watching from the ground, Kion watched them soar above the trees with Quail tugging on the Datsoe to get it to obey. What a woman!

Worried that too much time had passed since Isle disappeared with Ranger, Quail guided the Datsoe toward the gate, hoping to catch sight of him. The carnage below was a sobering sight. It would take Kion months to clean up all of the dead Datsoes. She wondered if he would bury them.

"There!" Cliff called, pointing.

Sure enough, she could see Isle pushing through the

rose wall, well away from the archers. How was he doing it? The roses were supposed to keep every Datsoe out. Quail made a mental note to ask Isle later. Her first priority was to see where he was going, but she had a feeling she already knew.

*　　*　　*

In fact, there was no secret what Isle was doing. After Isle grabbed Ranger, he ran through the forest and across the meadow faster than he had ever gone before. He knew he had to avoid the gate, or he would be shot by archers. That left him with a problem, how to get through the wall so he could travel to the Capitol? He had been able to follow Quail's words enough to understand the word 'cure.' He sensed Cliff was getting ready to kill Ranger, so his instinct was to escape.

Standing before the roses, his eyes watered. What was he going to do?

"I suppose it might be possible to cross if one could move fast enough… or had the skin to survive all the thorns." The words floated through his mind.

"Isle." Ranger shrank from the roses, his body rejecting being near them. "Don't do this, let me go…"

Taking a deep breath, Isle pulled Ranger closer. Lowering his head, he leapt. Thorns pierced his shell, drawing blood, but he pressed on. His muscles bunched under each powerful stride, and he used his claws to cut through the thick vines. Weaving, ducking, slicing, he pushed on, making sure Ranger was never harmed. Struggling to breathe, covered in pollen, he stubbornly refused to quit. Painful pustules formed all over his face. No matter how much it hurt to touch the vines, or get hit by the poisonous petals, Isle was determined.

"Look at him go!" Cliff exclaimed. Hovering above the roses, they watched Isle force his way bit by bit through the foliage.

Quail bit her lip. This opened up a whole new set of concerns. If Isle could make his way into the city through what they once thought was an impenetrable barrier, other Datsoes could. She needed to talk to Ranger and get his opinion on this. Then realization hit her. She would never get the chance to ask him anything again. Swallowing the lump in her throat, she tried to get the flying Datsoe to dive, but it refused. The pollen was too thick, and it was unwilling to go down any further.

Isle cut through the last vine and stepped into a wheat field. Gently laying Ranger down, he rolled onto his back, vigorously wiggling, trying to dislodge some of the foliage. Standing, he shook like a dog, then scooped Ranger up once more. She couldn't tell for sure, but it looked like Ranger was unconscious. That was something at least, she thought. She didn't want him to have to experience the pain of transformation.

"What is he doing?" Cliff asked, watching Isle lift his head and sniff the air.

"I think he is trying to figure out which way to go," she replied.

Suddenly, Isle took off, running faster than Quail thought possible.

"By Juwa he is quick," Cliff exclaimed.

Kicking the Datsoe, Quail guided it, trying to follow Isle. Soon, they fell behind. The flying creature they rode couldn't keep up.

"We are losing him, what do we do?" Cliff cried out.

"I know where he is going. In the meantime..." Circling down, Quail forced the Datsoe to land, directly in front of two men on horseback.

"You are lucky I didn't shoot you down," Leeon exclaimed, holding his bow.

Marco stared at the Datsoe and for once, was silent.

"Speaking of luck, I can't believe we saw you from above," Quail said.

"How in the world did you get this thing to obey you?" Leeon asked, staring at the disgruntled creature.

Finally finding his tongue, Marco said, "What are you doing here? We are on our way to the Palace to inform the Queen..."

"That no longer matters." Quail took a deep breath. "Ranger has been infected. Even as we speak, Isle is carrying him to the Palace, hoping they can cure him."

"What? Ranger? Impossible!" Marco shook his head.

"We are trying to get there as quickly as we can, I am hoping we can prevent the Queen's guard from slaying Isle on sight. Do you want a ride?" Quail stared at them challengingly.

"Daft woman! I wouldn't be caught dead riding one of those things!" Marco declared.

"I will, yes." Dismounting, Leeon made his way to the Datsoe and clasped Cliff's outstretched hand.

"If all goes well, we will be there to greet you when you arrive, Marco. Pray to the Juduiverians that Isle can get Ranger to the doctors in time." Kicking her heels into the Datsoe's side, Quail pulled the reins up, then guided it in the direction of the Palace. She had her doubts. Isle was miles ahead of them, and with Leeon's added weight, they would lose valuable time. But she was glad he was there. Briefly closing her eyes, she said a prayer of her own.

*   *   *

Following his nose, Isle ran on. His mile eating gait brought him closer to the Palace, and the doctors that could save Ranger. He avoided populated areas as much as possible, not wanting to stop for any reason, especially to fight. He had been to the Capitol years ago and remembered it well. That had been the first time he had cake. He found some discarded in an alleyway, left over from a fair. He had been attracted by the bright torch lights and scents and kept to the shadows while he watched everyone laugh and play. After the noise faded, he wandered around in the darkness, making the horses in a nearby pen neigh with fear. Not wanting to attract attention, he quickly left, but not before he stepped on something spongy. Reaching down, he scraped frosting from his foot. The sweet scent seemed familiar somehow, and he put his finger in his mouth. The burst of flavor had him gobble up the rest, not caring that it had been on the ground.

He spent days after that wandering around, marveling at the architecture and gardens, all under the protection of darkness. Someday, he thought, he would see the Palace gleaming in the sun, see what the blooms looked like at noon, maybe meet the Queen! Reluctantly he finally left, knowing every moment he spent there was dangerous. If he got caught, he would have found himself tied to the sacrificial altar for FallHeart.

These memories drove Isle in his beast form,

knowing exactly where he needed to go. Every now and then Ranger would shift and cry out as the venom crept further through his body. This pushed Isle past his exhaustion, pain, and fear of being killed. Nothing mattered but Ranger.

Finally, The Palace came into view, laying at the center of the Capitol. Standing tall, a mighty wall wound around the perimeter of the town. A lone drawbridge built from ancient wood was the only way in and was heavily protected.

Isle scaled the wall in seconds, unaware that Quail, Cliff, and Leeon were winging their way toward the Capitol themselves, capturing a lot of attention from the residents below. People began pouring out into the streets to watch the flying Datsoe. Seeing people ride on the back of such a beast was unheard of, let alone what some suspected were the Guardians themselves!

Hopping from roof to roof, Isle shocked the residents even further, making many cry out in fear. But the Datsoe paid them no heed, leaving only spots of silver blood in its wake.

Knowing they were still behind Isle, but unsure of where he was, Quail decided to land the Datsoe at the entrance of the Palace, leaping off at a run and climbing the steps two at a time. Cliff and Leeon slid off, both a bit stiff from clutching the Datsoe so tightly with their knees. Taking the reins, Cliff wound them tightly around the Datsoes jaws, but he didn't have to worry. The creature was exhausted, and grateful for once to be on the ground. Leeon followed Quail into the Palace, hearing her demand to speak to the Queen immediately.

Isle had managed to pull himself up to the roof of the Palace, crouching against one of the brightly colored windows. Shifting Ranger, he was unsure of what to do next.

Opening his eyes, Ranger looked around him. Confused, he could swear Isle was standing in front of one of the stained-glass windows that stretched across the top of the Queen's courtroom. Isle was out of breath and reeked of fear. Reaching out a trembling, gnarled hand, he touched the side of Isle's jaw, gaining his attention. "Hey there." Speech was difficult with a mouth full of fangs, he grumbled to himself. Floating in and out of consciousness, he wasn't sure what was happening. All he knew was pain. Horrible, all-consuming agony. Looking over Isle's armor-plated head, he saw the sun setting over a familiar skyline. "No, this can't be!" Feebly struggling, Ranger tried to tell Isle to leave immediately, this was wrong, all wrong! But all he could do was moan incoherently.

Watching Ranger, Isle sniffled. What should he do? Panicked, he backed into the window, shattering the glass with the tip of his tail. Turning, he decided the doctors must be inside, so he ducked through the opening. A large wooden beam ran along the ceiling of a room that seemed to go on forever. Clinging to it, Isle made his way over a golden and silver corkscrew patterned floor.

A young girl's scream had him scurry toward a balcony that wound around the room. Flinging the papers she carried, she stumbled backwards toward an older woman who sat on a large white and red velvet throne. With a gasp, the woman stood, gripping her maya blue gown. Watching a large Datsoe make its way down one of the balconies supporting beams, she trembled. How had this creature made its way into her very chamber? It looked like it was carrying something, but she couldn't see inside the thick armor very well. Silver blood dripped from multiple wounds, and the creature was making odd little whining noises. Turning, she clapped a hand over the screaming girl's mouth, and pulled her behind the plush chair she had just vacated.

Isle was grateful when the shrieking stopped. Tilting his head, he saw a fancy lady pulling a girl behind a big red and white thing. She seemed familiar somehow. Her lime green eyes were wide with fright, and he realized with dismay that she was afraid of him. Perhaps if he showed her Ranger, she would understand. Ranger was known to all, wasn't he? Holding out a hand to show he wasn't going to attack, he hoped the lady covered in sparkling gems would help him.

Movement from the balcony alerted Isle just in time. Looking up, he saw archers take aim, and fire. Curling inward to protect Ranger, he fanned his tail out and pulled it up over himself. Isle's armor and shielded tail served him well, blocking most of the arrows… most. Struck on his extra arm, he roared, reaching over to pull the arrow out. Another found its way into his leg, spilling more silver blood onto the floor.

Pushing back her silver tipped tresses, the Queen couldn't help but wonder why the Datsoe wasn't attacking. Again, she got the feeling it was holding something, keeping it from harm. Her fingers flew nervously to a metal chain, clutching a silver dove with zircon eyes. Squeezing it tightly, she left an imprint on her thumb of a tiny rose held within the dove's beak. Her guard had leapt quickly into action, Karter's doing no doubt. She could hear his voice even now, telling the archers to shoot another round of arrows at the Datsoe. Still, it didn't move.

The second round of arrows found more vulnerable patches in Isle's armor. Collapsing on the ground, he continued to cover Ranger. He should have anticipated this, but his only thought had been to save his friend. Looking at Ranger's face, he realized he was awake. Their eyes met. Taking one of Isle's hands, he tried to speak, but nothing came out.

"Ready!"

Isle drew in a breath.

"Aim!"

His arms pressed closer to Ranger.

"F..."

Wide doors to the Queen's left burst open.

"Hold! Hold your fire!"

"Crazy Datsoe killing idiots–" Cliff muttered.

Rushing to stand between Isle and the archers, Quail, Leeon, and Cliff drew their weapons.

"You dare challenge the Queen's guard?" The tall commanding officer demanded angrily.

"Your majesty, please wait. There is much more going on here than meets the eye." Leeon exclaimed.

The Queen stood rooted to the spot for a moment. Finally, she spoke. "I trust three of the gates' Guardians have a good reason for putting themselves between my men and a Datsoe?"

Trusting Leeon and Cliff to handle the situation, Quail placed her hand on Isle's tail, trying to get him to lower it. "Isle, can you hear me? It's Quail."

Leeon took a bold step forward. "We do your majesty. This Datsoe is our friend."

Leeon's statement made everyone in the room gasp.

Knowing Leeon to be a wise man, the Queen hesitated. "Your friend?" Watching Quail speak softly to the creature, she considered her options. Then she overheard

Quail say 'Isle'. "Isle, is that what you called it?"

"Yes, your majesty, his name is Isle," Cliff replied, confused by her sudden question.

"Karter, have your men lower their weapons, and go get a medic." Studying Isle's size and wounds, she added, "Perhaps a team of medics. We don't know exactly what we are dealing with here."

The man she addressed, Karter, hesitantly lowered his bow and started to move toward the stairs. His yellow eyes jumped between the Datsoe and the Queen. Then to the Guardians.

"Listen to me, Isle." Quail sheathed her sword and pulled out an arrow protruding from his shell. A moan of pain filled the room, making the Queen take a step forward in distress.

"Your majesty, I insist you keep your distance from the creature," Karter exclaimed.

"I appreciate your concern, but I have nothing to fear from this." She gestured to the doors. "The medics Karter, now if you please!"

"I know, I know." Trying to comfort Isle, Quail patted his head. "Is he still with you? Do you have him?"

Shifting, Isle managed to push Ranger forward, spilling him onto the marble floor.

Kneeling, Quail gathered Ranger into her lap, pushing the long, snarled hair out of his face. He looked up at her with glazed eyes.

With a cry, the Queen rushed forward. "Ranger! What has happened? I should have known." Pressing her fingers to her quivering lips, she tentatively reached out her other hand. "When was he infected?"

"We aren't sure. We found him this way, but it seems

that the infection is spreading," Quail whispered. Studying Ranger, she saw that his face was changing, the distorted skin now a dark gray. One eye was red, the other burgundy.

Ranger could make out their shapes, but he couldn't see their faces anymore. He could only tell them apart by their scent. He knew the Queen was beside him, blindly he reached for her hand.

"Francine."

His speech was garbled, but she understood him. Gripping his hand within her own, the Queen murmured, "His Asalairi blood is prolonging the infection."

"Wait a minute, you knew he was Asalairi?" Cliff exclaimed.

"Your highness, do the doctors really have an antidote, or is that a rumor?" Quail interrupted Cliff.

"There is an experimental serum in the works, but I have no idea if it will work."

A medical team arrived, stopping short in the doorway when they saw Isle laying in the middle of the room. "There is your patient," the Queen snapped. "Do what you can for him. Cliff, Leeon, please assist them, Isle may gather comfort from your presence. The rest of you, gather up Ranger and follow me." Releasing Ranger's hand, the Queen stood.

Hesitantly, two men stepped forward and placed Ranger on a gurney and lifted him up.

"Wait!" Ranger struggled, almost tumbling back to the ground.

"Ranger, you have to go with them," Quail pleaded.

"Promise me," he whispered hoarsely. "If this doesn't work, I die."

His disjointed plea made her swallow back tears. She

realized he understood what they were going to try to do, and if it failed, he wanted her to kill him before he hurt anyone. Shaking her head in denial, her lip quivered.

"Birdie... promise..." His hand gripped his throat, and they all heard a loud pop. Wincing, Ranger recalled the same sound when Bardune rearranged Isle's larynx. Opening his mouth, all he could utter was unintelligible gargles. He had lost the ability to speak.

"I promise." Looking up at the Queen, Quail's tear-streaked face was filled with panic.

"What are you waiting for? To the hospital wing, immediately!" Queen Francine's voice washed over the frightened men, and they rushed to do her bidding.

"Cliff, Leeon, you good? I am going with Ranger."

"We will be fine, Quail," Leeon reassured her. "Go."

"I will join you shortly," Queen Francine patted Quail reassuringly, then watched them take Ranger from the room. Turning to Isle, she pointed to a young man standing awkwardly beside the Datsoe. "You there, why do you hesitate? Help him."

Swallowing, the doctor nodded. "As you wish, your majesty."

Groaning, Isle moved, making the young doctor leap back. Much to everyone's astonishment, he began to shrink. Karter put himself between Isle and the Queen, his arrow notched and ready to fly.

Peaking around his broad shoulders, Francine watched the transformation with interest. She didn't display the same surprise as everyone else when finally, the figure of a teenage boy lay before them.

Pushing himself up, Isle caught the eye of the fancy lady. She didn't look afraid anymore, in fact, she smiled at him. Leeon reached down, and pulled Isle onto his feet, supporting his lean frame.

Cliff stepped forward, clearly distressed by Isle's condition. He swayed, bleeding profusely from multiple wounds. "What can I do?"

"I'm sorry." Isle whispered. Blood spurted from his mouth.

"Isle you have nothing to be sorry for! You saved Ranger, you are a hero!"

"No... for this." Isle's eyes turned black. His fingers latched onto Cliff's forearm, and a blue light arced between them.

Cliff froze, feeling his energy drain.

Karter took aim, but Leeon leapt in front of him. "No! He's not hurting him!" Remembering the conversation he overheard, he realized that Isle must be using Cliff as an energy source to heal himself. Sure enough, his wounds began to heal. Completely spent, Cliff fell to the ground. Turning to Leeon, Isle latched on. Leeon would describe the sensation later to his wife, but no one else. If it was possible, his respect for Ranger increased. He knew Isle had drained him, and Ranger was willing to go through it again. Leeon was not.

Finally letting Leeon go, Isle turned to the fancy lady, and started to cry. "I'm sorry," he whispered, "I just wasn't ready to *die*."

Stepping around Karter, Queen Francine did the unthinkable. She wrapped Isle in her arms and held him while he wept.

Karter blinked, then lowered his weapon. The young doctor caught Leeon before he fell, led him to the plush throne, and helped him sit.

Spent, Isle looked up and noticed a crown resting on the fancy lady's head. She smelled like flowers and sunshine, and he decided he liked her very much. "Thank you," he said, pulling away from her embrace.

"You are most welcome, Isle." Looking down at the Datsoe kindly, Francine pushed a lock of black hair out of his face.

"You know my name?"

"I do indeed. Ranger told me all about you in a letter he sent. He told me you were brave, but I had no idea what he meant until now."

"Ranger! Where is he?! I can't remember...!"

"They took him to the medical wing. I am going there now; would you care to join me?" Holding out her arm invitingly, Francine waited patiently.

"Your Majesty!" Karter protested. "You can't just walk through the Palace with that, that, thing!"

Green eyes blazing, Francine turned to her captain of the guard. "Do you question me, Karter?"

A brief battle of wills raged silently, until he took a step back. "No, your majesty, of course not."

"Your Majesty?" Isle said. The fancy lady was the Queen?

Looking away from Karter's yellow eyes, Francine looked down. "Yes Isle?"

"Can we please go see Ranger?"

Assuring herself that Leeon and Cliff were being cared for, she nodded. "Yes." Offering her arm once more, she wasn't nervous at all when Isle slid his through hers, she swept him from the room.

Shaking his head, Karter followed. She had always been impetuous, he thought, but this was new, even for her.

A Datsoe allowed to roam freely throughout the Palace! He would be keeping a close eye on this situation, and the Queen.

Entering the first room in the medical wing, Francine hesitated in the doorway. Ranger was strapped to a table while doctors rushed about the room. One was barking orders.

"We need another injection immediately. The virus is fighting us! Get me another vial of the P-D1!"

Quail stood in the corner, but when she saw the Queen standing next to Isle, she immediately went to them. She knew how Isle felt about Ranger, and if he thought the doctors were hurting him, he might be upset. She placed herself in front of him, just in case.

The lead doctor inserted another needle into the base of Ranger's neck where Bardune had bitten him.

Ranger let out a roar as the serum attacked the Datsoe venom. He strained against his restraints, and the doctor had to wait to inject him again.

Isle let out a sound of distress, and Quail laid her hand on his shoulder. "They had to tie him down Isle, otherwise he could hurt himself, or others."

The head doctor reached for another vial. "Your majesty, this will be a lengthy process, and forgive me, but I want no distractions. This is delicate work. I ask that you clear the room."

"Of course doctor. Karter, please take Quail and Isle to the guest wing. Ask the servants to prepare several rooms for our guests, including Isle."

"But, your majesty, I want to stay with Ranger!" Quail protested.

"I understand, Quail, but I need you to look after Isle

288

and the others. I will remain here until we know the outcome. I promise to come to you once there is any change."

The Queen's tone brooked no argument. Reluctantly, Quail took Isle's hand, and they followed Karter. Gripping her tightly, Isle looked up at her somber face.

"Will he be ok?" he asked quietly.

"I pray to the Juduiverian's he will, Isle."

Falling silent, they let Karter guide them toward their rooms.

*   *   *

Realizing the Queen had no intention of leaving Ranger's side, the doctors worked on. For hours they injected serum, then stitched and bandaged each bite mark. They had to move around Francine, who held Ranger's good hand through it all. The lead doctor did the best he could to repair the deep wound Bardune's dagger had inflicted on Ranger's other hand but had to admit to the Queen that it would never be the same again. If Ranger lived, he thought. Replacing the cast on his broken leg, wrapping his ribs tightly, it seemed he was more bandage and brace than man.

Finally, exhausted, the medical staff left her to watch over Ranger and found their own beds.

Pulling up a wooden chair, she sat inches from the bed. Closing her eyes, Francine drifted in and out of sleep, praying for a miracle.

WinterNox the 36th of

222 D.P

Opening his eyes, Ranger squinted against the rays of the setting sun. He was propped up in a large bed next to a crackling fire. Trying to shift to his side, he realized he couldn't move. Alarmed, he tried again, then winced. It seemed to take all of his effort to raise his hand and raise the soft sheet he lay under. He was wrapped in bandages. Letting the fabric drop, he noticed a wooden pole suspending a glass jar above him. The jar was filled with clear liquid and had a thin bamboo tube that led straight into his bandaged arm.

Puzzled, he tried to remember what had happened. Bits and pieces came back to him, Kion's gate, falling into the mouth of a giant Datsoe, Quail crying in the woods. Wait, why had Quail been crying? She wasn't there when he confronted Bardune. Gritting his teeth, he tried to move again, only succeeding in sliding further down into the pillow. With a sigh of frustration, he looked out the window. Snow began to fall, building up on the rims of the glass. So, his suspicions were right, WinterNox arrived early.

The door opened, admitting a young, slim woman wearing a white medic's dress. Her ginger hair was pulled back into a messy bun, complementing her fair skin. Walking over to the pole holding the glass above Ranger, she didn't notice that he was awake. She measured the level of whatever liquid was in the glass, then turned to a bedside table that he hadn't noticed. There was a variety of needles, liquids, and other things that made Ranger raise an eyebrow. Was all of that for him?

Picking up his wrist, she checked his pulse, then, finally, her eyes rested on his. Startled by his calm gray gaze, she gasped.

"Sorry," he rasped. His voice sounded strange, but he continued. "I didn't mean to frighten you."

"Oh my Lords! You're awake, and it seems, alert." With a beaming smile, she set his arm down. "The Queen will be thrilled to hear this news. How are you feeling?" Staring at him, it was almost as if she was looking for something.

"I can't seem to move," he grumbled.

"Are you in any pain?"

"Some, but it isn't horrible."

"Good. I am going to let her Majesty know you are alert. Don't go anywhere!" Shutting the door behind her, the room was silent once more.

"Don't go anywhere, isn't she the funny one?" Ranger mumbled.

His eyes returned to the window, watching the snow again. What happened on the battlefield that placed him here? And what did she mean by "you're alert" like it was something substantial? How long had he been here?

His eyes started to droop, but the door opened, jolting him awake.

The Queen came into the room, joined by a tall, stern looking man. He immediately made his way over to Ranger and took his vitals.

"Hello Mr. Ranger, I am Dr. Stewart. How are we feeling today?"

"I'm not sure how you are feeling, Dr. Stewart, but I am just fine. And the name is just Ranger."

Catching the doctor's confused look, the Queen grinned. "You asked how 'we' are doing."

Rolling his eyes, the doctor cleared his throat. "Yes, very amusing. Well Mr. uh, I mean, Ranger, you gave us all quite a scare. Tell me, do you have any cravings for raw meat, or say, a desire to rip out my throat?"

Horrified, Ranger could only stare at Dr. Stewart.

"That will be quite enough! Of all the foolish things to ask. You are dismissed." Pointing a shaking finger at the door, the Queen sent the relieved doctor on his way. Scowling at the closed door, she had every intention of giving him a piece of her mind later. What kind of bedside manner was that?

"Hi Francine."

Turning to the bed, her expression softened. "Hello, *Mr.* Ranger."

"Don't make me laugh, it hurts."

"How are you really feeling?" she asked quietly.

"Stiff, sore, disoriented. It will probably take me a few hours to get on my feet again."

"Hours? Ranger, my dear, you have a long recovery ahead of you. Why, it has already been five weeks since you arrived…"

"Five what?!"

"You don't remember anything? This isn't the first time you've been awake, although you haven't spoken before today."

"Surely you must be confused Francine. I would remember five weeks of laying here." Frowning, Ranger thought back. "We were fighting, the first snow was coming,

I pinned Bardune to a tree with my sword. I told him he lost, then…"

A shudder ran through his body. "The Nest Queen!" he exclaimed. "I had no idea she was there, then she bit me. How am I not dead? Or worse! Why haven't I turned?"

"I thank the Juduiverian's every night, Ranger. I know you aren't a man of faith, but the chain of events that led up to you lying before me is nothing short of a miracle."

"Tell me what happened, please."

"Isle arrived in my courtroom, he was quite a sight, let me assure you."

"Isle! Where is he? How is he?"

"Calm yourself Ranger, he is fine. In fact, he is still a guest here. Much To Karter's dismay, I have him in a room next to mine. I felt it would make things easier for the staff if I tended to him myself."

Staring at Francine, Ranger began to chuckle. "Only you would do something like that. Imagine, the Queen herself bringing meals to a Datsoe."

"I'm glad I amuse you. The truth is, we have spent a great deal of time together. You were right, he is very special."

"He really is."

"He comes to see you every day. He talks to you, fills you in on all of the new things he has learned. The day I asked him to wear pants, he had quite a lot to say to you."

"You convinced Isle to wear pants?"

The Queen let out a bright laugh. "He is fully clothed now, but it took me some time to convince him why."

"It seems that I have slept through a lot." Patting the edge of his bed, Ranger encouraged Francine to sit next to him. "What happened after he burst into the Palace unannounced. I'm surprised Karter didn't kill him on the spot."

Gingerly sitting on the edge of the bed, Francine adjusted her dress. "Oh, he tried. It was a wise move on your part to send me that letter about Isle, or I may have let him. Isle's beast form is quite intimidating."

"He hasn't turned since then, has he?" Once again, Ranger tried to push himself up.

Placing a hand on his chest, she reassured him. "No, of course not. The only odd thing that he has done is refuse to eat chocolate. I can't quite figure out why. I brought him some, thinking it would be a treat, and he reacted rather poorly. Has he expressed his distaste for it to you?"

Shaking his head, Ranger was as puzzled as Francine.

"Hmm. Well, maybe Datsoes have some strange aversion to it. A shame really, it is handcrafted by one of the most gifted chocolatiers in the land. He does show a particular fondness for cake though, so the boy isn't completely crazy."

"Stuffing him full of sweets and giving him clothing. You've been busy. I am sorry for the trouble."

"He hasn't been any trouble at all! In fact, I am enjoying the time with him. He is a very clever person. If not for him, we couldn't have saved you. Quail, Cliff, and Leeon were on his heels, word of the cure had spread I suppose." Trailing off, Francine thought back to the moment Ranger lay on her marble floor, fighting for his life. Looking up, her pale green eyes were filled with emotion. "I thought I had lost you. There are still so many things I need to say to you. We've spent years avoiding certain topics. I've had quite enough of that. Asailari blood or not, we aren't going to live forever."

Studying her face, Ranger recognized the stubborn set of her chin. Even when she was 15 and made him a guardian, she had been strong willed. He supposed she was right, they did need to have a frank conversation, and it was his fault things had dragged on the way they had. Well, no time like the present. Taking a deep breath, he tried to think of where to begin. "Francine, I..."

The door burst open, hitting the wall behind it, making a hole in the golden wallpaper. Isle's hand clapped over his mouth. "I am so sorry your Majesty!"

"No problem, Isle, I will add it to the list of repairs that need to be done. Please, come in." Francine stood and stepped away from the bed, but she gave Ranger a long look.

"Thank you!" Rushing into the room, he gave Ranger a wide, toothy smile. "Are you really you today? Usually when I come you mumble and groan and I can't understand much of what you're saying."

"Mumble and groan?" Ranger lifted his eyebrow.

"To be fair, you have been really sick. I told M'Lady that you might have been complaining about the soup they have been giving you. It smells really bad. But now that you are making that serious face, you can have cake!" Turning toward Francine, his big burgundy eyes were filled with hope. "Is he well enough to have cake?"

"I believe we all deserve something to celebrate. I will go ask the cook to put something together for us." With one last meaningful look at Ranger, Francine left the room, closing the door behind her.

"Hey Bud. You look good."

Isle tugged on his shirt self-consciously. "M'lady seems to think it is better if I wear this stuff. It took some getting used to, but she went to a lot of trouble to have clothes made for me." Turning, Isle showed Ranger his pants, custom tailored to allow his tail to swing freely. "She asks so little of me, it was the least I could do to make her happy. She is really nice Ranger. And she loves you an awful lot."

Clearing his throat, Ranger smoothed the spot where Francine had been sitting. "Yes, I suppose she does Isle. Would you like to sit down?"

"I would very much like to give you a hug, but I was warned that you are very fragile right now."

"Isle, come here and give me a hug."

Bounding onto the bed, Isle wrapped his arms around Ranger, but tried to be very careful. With his free arm, Ranger held Isle tight. A moment passed, then another.

"I thought they were going to kill you. It was really scary."

Isle's muffled words had Ranger loosening his grip. "Why don't you tell me about it?"

Pulling away, Isle sat cross legged on the edge of the bed. "Well, I didn't see it happen, but you kicked Bardune's butt."

"Oh?"

"Yea, then you killed him. But by then the Datsoe Queen had bitten you, and you started to turn. That's when I found you. I don't remember much; I was in my other form. I do recall the other Guardians arguing, and Quail crying and then I grabbed you."

Ah, Ranger thought, that explained his memory of Quail in the woods. "Then what?"

"Well, I was shot a bunch of times with arrows. That wasn't very fun. I had to use Cliff and Leeon to heal myself."

Isle's ears drooped.

"Are they still here?"

"No, they left weeks ago. No one could give them a clear answer when you might wake up, so they decided to go. Leeon really wanted to get back to his wife. She's pregnant, you know, he told me."

"He mentioned that to me."

"Anyway, he began the journey back to his gate. Quail was really put out that she had to go, but after receiving a message from Kion's hawk, she got really mad and yelled a lot. I'm not sure what it said, but she left shortly after. "

"I see. And Cliff?"

"He went with Quail back to Kion's gate. They all came in and visited you a lot, but all you did was mumble."

"And groan?"

Isle grinned. "Maybe."

"Well, now that I am speaking clearly, I would like to say something to you. Thank you for saving my life. If not for you, I wouldn't be sitting here, thinking about my future. I haven't really done that in a while, and I've needed to."

"I didn't do it all by myself! There were lots of doctors and nurses and the other Guardians too. I didn't get to see that part, but I heard there were lots of needles and stuff. I tried asking Dr. Stewart questions, but every time I got near him, he acted really strange, like I was going to hurt him. He kept holding his hand over his throat."

Francine's voice carried through the door, and Isle could smell cake. Leaning forward, he whispered, "Ranger?"

"Yes Isle?"

"Would M'lady have anything to do with your future? I think that would be a good idea, for both of us."

Stuttering, Ranger was saved by the door swinging

298

open, allowing Francine and a young lady pushing a serving cart to enter.

"I thought you might like something more than soup, Ranger. You have had quite a bit these past weeks." Pouring a cup of tea for herself, the Queen settled into a chair in the corner of the room.

"Thank you. Isle, would you mind helping me sit up a bit further?"

Jumping from the bed, Isle helped Ranger get situated, then happily grabbed a piece of cake. Sitting on the floor next to Francine, they waited for the servant to hand Ranger a plate and leave the room.

They passed the time listening to Isle talk. He told Ranger about the books found in his room, (although he couldn't read, he enjoyed the pictures), and all the new exotic foods he had tried.

Ranger laughed at most of it, teasing Isle. "Ah! Royal life! I can see you getting used to it. When I go back out on patrol, you won't want to come with me."

Putting down his plate, Isle shook his head. "This has all been amazing, but wherever you go, I want to go. You are my home, Ranger. I hope that's ok."

Fighting back tears, Ranger swallowed. "That is just fine with me."

Looking at Ranger, Isle jumped up in distress. "Are you in pain? Should I get that scared doctor?"

"No Isle, I am fine. You've made me very happy."

Finally, he started to doze in the middle of their conversation, so the Queen suggested they let him rest. Reluctantly, Isle rose with a promise to be back soon.

Watching Francine wrap her arm around Isle's shoulder, Ranger smiled, then drifted off to sleep.

WinterNox the 39th of

222 D.P

Ranger accidentally woke himself up. He had been snoring, quite loudly he suspected, and was grateful no one was in the room to witness it. Staring absentmindedly at the ceiling, he wondered what time it was. It was light outside his window, but the cloud cover gave him no clues. His body still felt stiff, but he could move easier than before. Three days had passed, and despite his exhaustion, he enjoyed the time spent with Francine and Isle.

Isle had started bringing books in with him requesting that Ranger read to him. This opened a whole range of conversations, as Isle had a curious mind and keen intellect. They talked about art, philosophy, religion (a concept they surprisingly didn't agree on. Francine had gotten to Isle first and filled his head with Juduiverian lore) and more. Soon, Isle was sneaking into the Palace library and bringing Ranger books about math, astronomy, and history.

Francine's visits often overlapped Isle's, and she would listen while she worked on a tapestry. Carefully watching, she often had to shoo Isle from the room to let Ranger rest, only to find him there once again upon her return.

The sound of the door handle moving drew his

attention. Francine walked into the room carrying a tray.

"Good morning!" Looking around the room for Isle, she was surprised he wasn't there. "No Isle this morning?"

"I haven't seen him yet."

"I'm sure he will be along. In the meantime, I brought you breakfast."

"Why are you always trying to feed me?"

"You've lost a lot of weight; don't think I haven't noticed. You need to regain your strength." Swiveling a hinged table over Ranger's lap, she helped him sit up. "The chef made you poached eggs and bacon. And, since you've been asking for it, coffee."

"It smells fantastic, thank you."

"You are welcome. Ranger, I have something I need to tell you."

"Oh?" he asked through a mouthful of bacon.

"Well, I may have sent out a letter. I felt it was necessary."

"You didn't send one out to WolfCreek did you?" he asked her, gripping the handle of his fork tightly.

She stared at him with confusion "What? Oh! No, of course not, if you want to communicate with the people from your hometown that's your business, not mine."

Ranger let out a relieved sigh.

"Then whatever it is, it can't be bad."

Francine let out a chuckle. "Well, you may change your mind."

"Francine? What did you do?"

A loud crash echoed outside the door, making them both turn toward the door.

"Can't you watch where you're going?" Cliff's voice sounded aggravated.

"It wasn't my fault! It just fell!" Marco replied.

"Oh, will you two knock it off! At this point he'll be more concerned for his mental health than anything else," Quail snapped.

Banging on the door with his fist, Marco hollered, "Ranger, you awake in there?"

"For Juwa's sake, Marco, what if he is resting?" Quail whispered loudly.

"He's been resting for six bloody weeks! Hello, Ranger?"

Laughing, Ranger called, "It's open, come in."

The door flew open, denting the wallpaper once again.

"I'm going to have to put something there to save my wall," Francine said, sitting heavily into her chair.

Flooding into the room, Cliff, Quail and Marco surrounded the bed.

Looking up at them, Francine thought they looked larger than life. Lean and muscular, they had a dangerous air about them, and she was very glad they were on her side.

Leaning down, Quail embraced Ranger. Pulling back, he noticed her hair was pulled back. "Hello Quail, I like your hair."

"Well, I don't care much for yours. It is past your shoulders Ranger! But it is good to see your face, beard and all." Tweaking the tip of his beard, Quail smiled.

"She has started to wear it back to annoy Kion. He sends his regards by the way. I believe his words were; 'One of us has to stay here to make sure things don't fall apart.'" They all shared a laugh, knowing Kion wasn't exactly a sentimental person.

"Why does her hair annoy Kion?" Ranger asked.

"Who knows lad, they are back to poking each other about nothing. But, enough about romance, how are you feeling?" Marco leaned against the hearth.

Francine sincerely hoped he didn't catch his trousers on fire.

"Romance?" Quail's outraged comment was drowned out by Cliff.

"Good day, your Majesty!" He said loudly. "Our apologies, we didn't see you standing there."

"Good day to all of you. Thank you for answering my summons."

"We were all too happy to come," Quail replied, trying to regain some dignity. She was mortified by her own behavior. Yelling in front of the Queen didn't make a good impression.

"Tell me Ranger, how are you feeling?" Cliff asked.

"Well, I won't be needing sleep ever again," Ranger said, making them laugh. "Honestly, I feel fine. Body is sore, but rightfully so after a bite like that…"

"Hey guys!" Isle bounded into the room, tail swishing excitedly. "You got M'ladies letter!"

"We did, hello Isle! It is great to see you!" Clapping Isle on the back, Marco ignored his muttered "oof."

"Hello, Little Monster." Opening her arms invitingly, Quail waited for Isle to give her a hug.

Stepping forward, Isle wrapped his arms around her. Pulling away, Isle's lip trembled a bit. Not only had he found one friend, but a room full of them. He was the luckiest Datsoe ever!

Shaking Cliff's hand, Isle asked about Leeon. The last they had heard, he was still making his way home. Cliff explained that Kion had sent a hawk to the nearest town they guessed he was near, to fill him in on Ranger's recovery.

"So, Ranger, now that Bardune and the Datsoe Queen are dead, are you going to retire?" Marco stepped away from the fireplace, realizing his pants were hot.

"Retire? No way. As soon as Dr. Scaredy Pants, uh, that's what Isle calls him, says I am recovered, I am getting back out there."

"Dr. Stewart says the bite marks are a bit tricky. He's been checking them periodically, and they're still a dark gray." Francine answered the question they all wanted to ask. "He fears that they might not fully heal for that matter… but as for your hand and leg, I'm afraid those will also take some time. You will have to remain here throughout the rest of WinterNox."

"Ranger sighed, "Terrific."

"That's ok! Think of all the great food and books we can read. And don't forget the cake!"

"I'm going to have the cook teach you to bake your own cake Isle," Francine laughed. "She hasn't made this many in years."

"Could she do that? Teach me I mean. That would be great!" Isle clapped his hands with excitement.

Trying to push away visions of the kitchen burning down, Francine said, "I will see what I can do."

Stepping forward, Quail pulled Ranger's sword from her sheath. "I've been holding onto this for you. I believe it is time to give it back."

Offering him the hilt, she waited until he accepted it.

"Thank you, Quail."

305

"Quit dying, will you?"

"I will do my best to accommodate your request," he replied gravely.

The day passed faster than any of them thought possible. The Guardians could only stay for one day, they had decided it was time to follow Leeon's example and head to their own gates. Kion, Quail declared, could finish up cleaning the Datsoe mess. The Queen excused herself after a while to speak to the cooks about dinner. As soon as the door closed behind her, Marco whisked out a flask of whiskey, and passed it around. Laughing, he encouraged Isle to try a sip.

Sitting on the floor around Ranger's bed, they shared a fine meal, discussing plans for the future. Just because the Datsoe Queen was dead, didn't mean they could let their guard down. The people needed to be protected.

Knowing they would be leaving at first light, Quail, Cliff and Marco said goodbye to Ranger and Isle. Saying goodnight, they made their way to their rooms, and found their own rest.

Taking Isle's hand, Francine bid Ranger a good night.

"See you tomorrow," Isle called over his shoulder.

After the door closed, Ranger sighed. It had been a good day, and the scent of roast chicken still floated in the air. Despite this, he chafed at his situation. He wouldn't be able to see his friends again for quite some time, they had responsibilities to uphold. Who knew how long it would be before he was able to leave the Palace. He would have to wait patiently to see all of them again, but he was already making plans. With a yawn, he settled back into his downy pillow. There were worse places to be, he decided. He couldn't remember a time that he had ever been more cared for. Francine's doing, naturally. With a smile, he drifted to sleep.

Bardune's mocking laughter had Ranger jolt awake. Pushing up, Ranger wiped the sweat from his brow. The nightmares had begun a couple nights earlier, and he couldn't tell if they were memories or his twisted imagination. With a trembling hand, he grabbed the glass beside his bed and drank deeply.

Swinging his legs over the edge of his bed, he stood. He had been practicing with Isle's help, but knowing Francine wouldn't approve, swore his friend to secrecy.

Stretching, he thought about Isle. Earlier in the week he had spoken to Francine about drawing up official documents to officially adopt him. Tomorrow, he planned on presenting them, and wondered how he would react to being known as 'Isle Swordsman'. Sitting back down, he thought about their future. Would the Datsoe attacks lessen now that Bardune was gone? Even without the Queen spreading the plague, his services were still needed. He found himself looking forward to traveling with Isle. There would be the inevitable prejudice against him, but Ranger hoped with time people would accept Isle as he had.

The door opened, surprising him.

"I had a feeling you might be awake." She was in a simple white robe, and her hair spilled over her shoulders down her back.

"Couldn't sleep either huh?" he asked, patting a spot next to him. She smiled, walking around the bed to sit next to him.

"I'm almost surprised Isle isn't here," she chuckled.

"He doesn't have to sleep. It's very odd. He can choose to, but a Datsoe has different needs than humans."

"Well, Datsoe or human, he still eats like a horse." After a moment she continued. "It's been a while since we've been together like this."

"A long while," he agreed.

"You always slipped away before morning light."

"You know I had my duties to uphold. Besides, we weren't married. It would have ruined your reputation."

"I wanted to marry you. You said no."

"Things worked out the way they should have. Daniel was a good man, and he gave you George. Speaking of George, how is he?"

Francine sighed. "He and his family are doing well. It is a good thing he is on vacation, or he would have seen to it that neither you or Isle lived. He is a rule follower, just like his father." Sliding her fingers into Ranger's, she looked into his eyes. "Daniel was a good man, but I never got over you. You are a tough act to follow."

Brushing a lock of hair back from her face, Ranger said softly, "Francine…"

Cutting him off, she pushed on. "I know I could never fill Raja's shoes, that she was your first love, but I–"

Pressing his finger against her lips, Ranger stopped her. "From the day I saw you standing by your father's side, I knew you were special. You were so young, so strong. Every year I returned to the kingdom I watched you blossom into a kind and generous ruler. The people loved you, how could I not? Raja was very important to me, but so are you, Francine. I have always loved you deeply, that will never fade."

"If only you told me this years ago." With a watery laugh, Francine dropped her head onto Ranger's shoulder. "Do you think we could pick up where we left off so long ago?"

"I'd like that." Pressing his lips to hers, he poured his heart into the kiss.

Pulling away, she took a deep breath, "It's a good thing you've never kissed me like that before. Daniel never would have had a chance."

Tipping her chin up, Ranger smiled, then brushed his thumb across her lower lip.

Leaning against his pillow, she settled herself. "You know, you still owe me the story of how you and Isle met."

"I do indeed." Pushing himself back, he joined her.

"When did you realize he was different? Did he speak to you? I bet Quail wasn't keen on the whole situation."

"Well, I think we didn't actually start communicating properly with each other until…" he stopped, remembering the words Bardune had spoken when he learned Isle's name in the Datsoe nest.

"Until?" Francine pressed.

With a private smile, he whispered, "Until we both were waiting down in the isle of the dark."

The End.